juice

Carter McKnight

HELLA BOOKS

New York London Sydney

ISBN: 978-0-9863957-6-5

Printed in the United States of America

Rev. 1.01

For Dad

juice [joos] *noun* Edge, clout, or influence in games of chance. (See more gambling definitions in the Glossary, back of book.)

counting cards

Card counting is a blackjack strategy employed to increase a player's advantage, by keeping a running tally of high and low cards played. The underlying principle is that a deck rich in high cards is advantageous for the player, whereas a deck with more low cards remaining favors the dealer. When the running count is favorable, the player can increase bet size and adjust the playing strategy accordingly.

In a basic Hi-Lo system, counting is simple: Beginning with with a running count of 0 (zero) with a fresh deck or shoe, card denominations 2–6 receive a value of +1, 7–9 receive 0, and 10–ace receive -1. As the cards are revealed, the player adds or subtracts from the running count. Variations, such as keeping track of aces, are also commonly used.

In blackjack the House usually has a 0.5 percent advantage. Card counting can give a player as much as 1.8 percent advantage over the House.

While card counting is not illegal, casinos generally prohibit the practice and will bar counters.

juice

one

Two burly security guards hustled him from the casino pit and down a short corridor, one on each side, their viselike grip on his arms painful. One guard opened a door, the other gave him a shove through the doorway. A metal chair, its seat and arms padded with red vinyl, stood in the middle of the room. They marched him over to it, spun him around, and pressed down on his shoulders until he dropped to the seat with a jarring thud. They left him sitting there, shaking. Charlie had never been backroomed before.

He looked around. Other than the chair and a workbench with an assortment of power tools, the room was empty.

The door opened and a large man entered, his shoulders straining a cream-colored sport coat. He had a face like a prizefighter who had stayed in the ring long past his prime. Grinning, he produced an iron pipe from his waistband and smacked it into his palm. The meaty sound echoed off the bare walls. "Ever seen what a pipe can do to a kneecap?"

Charlie didn't answer. Surely the thug was only trying to scare him. It worked. He was about to piss his pants.

Another man walked in and closed the door behind him. His expensive suit, highly polished shoes—the kind known on the street as "gators"—and his air of command tagged him as a casino big shot. He held out his hand. "Frank Borella, general manager of the Fontana."

The thug gave him a stay-put gesture, so he shook Bor-ella's hand without rising from the chair. "Charles Delmar."

"Charlie the Barber, right?"

"Yeah." Charlie glanced nervously at the pipe. "Retired."

"Sonny," Borella said, "please put that damn thing away." "He's going to be very cooperative. Right, Charlie?"

Sonny tossed the pipe onto the workbench. It landed with a clang.

Borella turned back to Charlie. "Now then, Charlie the Barber, we need to . . . clear up some things."

"Okay," Charlie said. "Let's start with why your security goons manhandled me and dragged me here."

His close-set, intense eyes stared at Charlie for long seconds. When he spoke, his voice was soft. "You're a blackjack player, well known around this town as a regular. You make out okay?"

"I win a little and lose a little. Blackjack's just a hobby."

Borella examined his manicured nails and then looked up. "You a hustler, Charlie?"

Charlie's laugh sounded hollow, even to him. "Me? I told you, blackjack is just a hobby."

"Just a hobby," Borella repeated. "This week, four casinos had significant losses at their high-stakes black-jack tables— Cosmos on Tuesday, Casablanca on Wednesday, Skyview on Thursday, and Tropigala on Friday. You played each night at those same tables. How do you explain that?"

"Just a coincidence." A cantaloupe-size chunk of ice had formed in his gut.

"You intended to play at the Fontana's high-stakes table tonight. Another coincidence, I suppose." Borella smiled. "I'll ask you again. You a hustler, Charlie?"

Charlie shook his head. "You can't be serious. Okay, sure, I was at those casinos, but I either lost money or broke even. I'd be a piss-poor hustler."

Borella's smile faded. "Unless you're straight with me, motherfucker, we're going to have a problem."

"I'm telling you the God's honest truth."

"Sure you are."

"Boss, let me have a crack at it," Sonny said. "I can be very pursuasive."

Borella held up a hand for silence. "Tell me something, Charlie. You a card counter?"

Not a chance in hell Borella would swallow a flat denial. Better to shade the truth. "I bought Ken Uston's book on card counting and I've been trying to use his method, but it's no cinch. Too many distractions in casinos."

"Bullshit. I got a feeling you're a lot better counter than you're letting on."

Charlie shook his head. "Sorry, you're wrong."

Borella's eyes bored into him. "You need to think carefully before you answer the next question." He opened a spiral-bound notepad. "Do you know ... Ada Delano, Jack Colvin, Wilson Wright, and Herman Chin?"

Charlie swallowed. Borella wanted him to give up his team. Not too damn much chance of that. "I don't have the faintest idea who any of those people are, sorry."

"Dwight Ayers?"

"Sorry."

Borella sighed, shaking his head. "Guess we'll have to do this the hard way." He gave a slight nod to Sonny.

A ripping sound filled the room, the sound of duct tape being torn from a roll. He grabbed Charlie's wrist and forced his right forearm on top of the chair's padded arm. Then he wrapped the tape around and around both, so tight Charlie couldn't budge his arm. "Just a goddamn minute," he said, "you can't ..."

He was wrong. They could.

Sonny went to the workbench and plugged a circular saw into an extension cord. At Borella's nod, he switched on the saw, a grin on his ugly mug.

"Please ..." Warm urine ran down Charlie's legs, but he hardly noticed. His scream blended with the saw's shrill whir.

twenty-six days earlier . . .

two

Charlie deftly shuffled two stacks of chips with his right hand, trying to decide what to do. It should have been a no-brainer. He had fifteen, the six of clubs and nine of hearts, and the dealer's upcard was the jack of spades. The next card in the shoe, which he could see almost as clearly as though it was face up, was the six of diamonds. It would give him twenty-one, a winning hand.

Problem was, he'd been winning all night and now the pit boss was eyeing him suspiciously, a sour look on his pale, lined face. One more big win was liable to draw too much heat. Not that losing the hand wouldn't sting plenty; he'd bet the table limit, $500. Still, he couldn't risk getting backed off.

"I'm feeling lucky," he said, passing his hand palm down over his cards. "Stand."

The dealer's hole card was a four. He dealt himself the six from the shoe, making twenty, and then he raked in all the bets, including Charlie's five black chips.

Charlie pushed up his glasses with an index finger and thumb and massaged the bridge of his nose. His legs ached. The stool felt like concrete.

The platinum blonde on first base leaned over and called in a whiskey tenor, "Sweetie, you shoulda hit fifteen. That's just basic strategy when the dealer has anything bigger than a six showing."

She was right, of course. Standing on fifteen against a jack was a sucker move. But it got the result he wanted. Out of the corner of his eye he saw the pit boss drift off to check out other play.

The woman wasn't done jabbing him. "Honey, if I lost five hundred bucks on one hand, I'd shoot myself."

He sighed for everyone's benefit. "I feel like it."

But that was bullshit. You had to look at strategic losses as a cost of doing business. He was still way ahead. The chips stacked in front of him and the several dozen in his coat pockets totaled over five large, not counting his bankroll. Not a bad night's score, even though he had violated his golden rule, to keep the night's winnings under a grand. It was the second time this month he'd ignored the rule. If he kept it up, sooner or later it was going to bite him in the ass.

He played four more rounds, betting the minimum, and won two, lost two. "Think I'll call it a night," he said. He toked the dealer a quarter—a green twenty-five-dollar chip—and then gathered up the rest, stacking them in a tray. He added the chips from his pockets when he got to the cashier. The woman in the cage counted out fifty-one hundreds. He pocketed the money and headed for a nearby restroom. In the privacy of a stall he transferred the thick sheaf of bills to the money belt he wore under his shirt. Then he exhaled.

Vegas was crawling with pickpockets, sharpshooters, grifters, and thieves of every stripe, all looking to separate the suckers from their money. You had to be on guard at all times. He carried a wallet, but it was a decoy containing less than ten dollars. The last time he'd gotten clipped was six years ago, on a side street off Fremont, downtown. The thief, who had a paring knife and a junkie vibe, was so disappointed in the wallet's contents he looked like he was going to cry.

Charlie stepped from the air-conditioned coolness and the night air hit him like a blast furnace. Almost midnight, but a digital sign in front of the Flamingo indicated 84 degrees. The temperature had reached 112 searing degrees earlier, not uncommon for July. He took off his coat and started walking.

After unlocking his eight-year-old Chrysler 300, he tossed his sport coat and fedora on the passenger's seat. The engine roared to life and he switched on the air conditioning.

A midnight snack sounded good. At Denny's on the Strip he took a booth and ordered an omelette, toast, and decaf tea, which should be light enough for that time of night. He'd played straight through lunch and dinner, not for the first time. More like the thousandth time. But no one had forced him into the life, and he had no regrets. He was proud that he had made a steady living playing blackjack over the past ten years. He didn't know any other Vegas hustlers who could make the same claim.

It wasn't just the Juice. Juice alone, even his special kind, wasn't enough. You also had to have discipline. Greed doomed most players. They win too much too often and get themselves barred. Casinos tend to dislike steady winners. So he made sure his daily winnings stayed modest—three hundred here, five hundred there, occasionally even eight or nine hundred. It had allowed him to fly under the radar for over a decade; no big scores meant no big blips on the scope. Which meant his money machine could keep on churning.

That said, when the cards were falling perfectly, the heady feeling was better than sex. He had resisted temptation and played conservatively until one night about a year ago when he took the Circus Circus for eight grand. Afterward he was so damn paranoid he vowed not to do it again. He kept the vow almost three months. After that, he scored big almost every month, the largest just under ten thousand. Then last week he won seven grand and another five tonight. So what in Christ's name was he think—

"Damned if it isn't Charlie the Barber. Doing any good?"

Charlie looked up to see a grinning Wilson Wright. He'd known Wilson for years, had taught him how to count cards. Before that, Wilson had been daubing, bending, past posting, hand mucking, capping bets—every hustle in the book.

"Making a living, Wilson." He gestured at the empty seat across the table.

Wilson slid into the booth and beckoned to the waitress. "Just coffee, darlin'" he told her. After she set a steaming cup in front of him, he stirred in creamer and took a cautious sip. Then he said, "You hear about Benny?"

Charlie shook his head. "What about him?"

"Got himself backroomed at the Tropigala."

"The hell you say. For counting cards?"

"And winning more than they figured he should. Security slapped him around a little and then shoved him out in the alley and told him he was persona non grata."

Charlie sighed, shaking his head. "I tried to talk some sense into him a while back about keeping a lower profile, but I could tell I wasn't getting through to him."

"He wouldn't listen to anyone, and now he's burnt up in this town. Said he's going to Atlantic City. But the son of a bitch invites trouble. He looks and acts like a gambler from Central Casting. What does he expect?"

"Maybe the run-in at the Tropigala will wise him up."

"Mister Slick? Not a chance. The silly bastard thinks he's in the Rat Pack."

Charlie shook his head again. Would-be high rollers like Benny flock to Vegas by the dozens, thinking they've got the place clocked. Before long they get heat and leave town with their tails between their legs. But there's never a shortage of hopefuls to take their place.

"My approach draws less attention," Wilson said. "I'm a middle-class schmuck on vacation. In Vegas to gamble, see the shows, and have a good time. Just another sucker."

"Your 'Wecome To Fabulous Las Vegas' T-shirt is a nice touch."

"It works like a charm. But you got us all beat, Charlie the Barber. You look like . . . well, like a barber."

"It's not an act. My barber licenses are current in Oregon and Washington. I send in the fees every year."

"A barber who also happens to be the best goddamn card counter in the world."

"That might be a little strong."

Wilson shook his head. "I don't think so."

Charlie pushed the plate aside and took a sip of his tea, thinking about it. He was an expert counter, he wouldn't deny it, and had been for a long time, starting back when all casinos offered single-deck blackjack. These days most casinos dealt cards from a multi-deck shoe, which chased away all but skilled counters, who could factor multiple decks into the count. His counting ability resulted from a gazillion hours spent counting down deck after deck on the kitchen table, until he could go through a deck in under thirty seconds with perfect accuracy. Keeping track of the count in actual play, despite all the distractions in a casino, soon became second nature. Tonight, when he decided he'd better quit playing before he got barred, the count had been unusually favorable. If it hadn't been for that pit boss, he might have taken them for eight or nine grand. And he might have gotten backed off. Or backroomed. Always better to play it safe.

Wilson yawned, finishing with a shake of his head. "I ran into Richard last week. He said to say hello if I saw you."

It took a few seconds to sink in. "Richard's back from Monte Carlo already? He didn't stay over there long."

"He didn't say why, only that he's damn glad to be back."

Monaco had no doubt booted Richard out of the country. Counting cards was flat illegal in Monaco, as the famous MIT blackjack team found out. The word was, getting backroomed in Monte Carlo, without the protection of U.S. laws, wasn't an experience anyone would recommend.

In Nevada, the state courts had ruled that counting cards was legal, but casinos still backed off players caught counting. Also, players they only *suspected* were counting. If the state gaming commission were on the up and up instead of on the take, they wouldn't allow casinos to bar counters. After all, counting cards wasn't cheating, it was skillful playing. But the House hated skillful players. They won too often, cutting into casino profits. Sometimes even square players who have lucky streaks get barred, much to their disbelief and outrage. Welcome to fabulous Las Vegas, folks.

"Well, Charlie, "Wilson said, stretching, "I'm going to take off, go get some shuteye. I'm running on empty."

"I need to hit that bathroom and then head out myself. Keep in touch, Wilson."

Through the front window, Charlie watched Wilson unlock his Mustang convertible and get in. Charlie had ridden in it once. A cramped, uncomfortable son of a bitch. He preferred the roomy, cushy Chrysler. Even though it was eight years old, its big Hemi engine still had more than enough soup to get him down the road in style, the price of gas be damned.

Standing at a urinal, he realized why he'd been ditching his rule to limit winning: Beating the smug sons of bitches felt good. The more he won, the better it felt. The thought of taking them for serious money, enough to wreak havok on their almighty bottom lines, sent shivers of excitement down his spine. Because it was doable, no doubt about it.

A score sizable enough to last him the rest of his life. He'd buy himself a place on the Oregon coast—Port Orford, maybe, or Gold Beach—and kick back. If he wanted action, he could scare up a local poker game or play blackjack at an Indian casino, just to keep his hand in.

He drove home on autopilot, working out the best way to pull it off and get away clean. By the time he parked in front of his apartment he knew exactly how he would go about it.

Just a fantasy, of course. No harm in fantasizing.

From habit, he unlocked the door as quietly as he could, although it was unlikely Bonnie would hear him. When he opened the door, she jumped down from the sofa and danced around him on her hind legs. He sat down in the recliner and she hopped up to lay on his chest, a front paw on each shoulder, her brown eyes eight inches from his.

He stroked her soft fur. "Overdue for a haircut, old girl."

She cocked her head to one side. At thirteen years old, she was hard of hearing. Aside from that, she was in good shape, the vet said, and could have four or five years left. With her white coat grown out, she looked more like a small, curly sheepdog than a poodle.

"Let's go for a walk before bed," he said, realizing too late that he'd raised his voice so she could hear him. The walls between the apartments were as thin as cardboard, and the cranky old bastard next door was always giving him shit about making noise.

In the empty lot next to the apartment complex, Bonnie sniffed the sagebrush while he again thought about retiring, getting out of the life. It would take big money. The hundred and sixty thousand he'd managed to tuck away wouldn't last forever. Sure, it would set him up with a mobile home in a trailer park somewhere and enable him to scrape by for a few years, but he wanted a better life.

By the time they got back to the apartment, he'd decided to go for it. The big score. It wasn't just the money, of course. Payback was part of it. Casinos felt they were entitled to *all* the money, and so they bought politicians who helped them get it. It would feel good to balance the scales a little.

"Keep this to yourself, old girl," he said, taking care to speak softly as he unfastened the leash from the dog's collar. "I'm going to teach those casinos a lesson they won't forget. Bet on it."

three

In the stark morning light, lying in bed with Bonnie curled up against his hip, he had second thoughts about the idea. It wasn't a crisis of confidence so much as his conservative nature warning him not to risk a sure thing for an iffy proposition. Setting up the play he had in mind would require a sizable investment, funded entirely by his savings. If things went south he'd be out a chunk of cash. No telling how much, maybe everything he had. Then he'd be screwed. It took him ten years to save up that much money.

The safe move would be to forget it and keep on doing what he'd done for the last decade. He could build up his nest egg to two hundred thousand, maybe a quarter of a million. It might last him the rest of his life if he was careful with it. He wouldn't live high on the hog, but neither would he sleep in a cardboard box in an alley.

On the other hand . . . if he pulled off the big score, he'd be sitting pretty for the rest of his life. Financially independent. And of course there was the satisfaction of payback, although the notion of "teaching the casinos a lesson" was laughable, a mouse shaking its fist at a rottweiler. The only thing that mattered was getting his hands on a fat enough score to retire in style—and it damn sure wasn't just a small-time hustler's pipe dream.

Because he had juice. Big juice.

Counting cards wasn't the only juice he used to beat the game. He didn't have a name for the other kind. It was just "the Juice," capital J, and it was his secret. Not that anyone would believe him if he told them about it. Because nobody could see—actually *see*—the denominations of face-down cards, right? He couldn't believe it himself at first.

The impossible happened for the first time late one night at Harrah's around five years ago. He'd rubbed his eyes. They had been giving him trouble and now he was seeing things. He cashed in his chips, figuring to make an appointment soon for an eye exam.

The next morning he was fixing breakfast when a deck of Bees on the kitchen counter caught his attention. Feeling silly, he concentrated on the top card, trying to repeat what had happened the night before. His eyes widened when the red diamond pattern on the card's back seemed to shimmer and become semitransparent, enough to reveal a phantom reverse image of the king of spades. He grunted and turned the card over.

King of spades.

"Holy shit," he said aloud. It had to be a coincidence.

The next card shimmered and a ghostly reverse image of the three of hearts became visible through the back. Holding his breath, he flipped the card over to reveal the trey.

"Holy shit," he said again.

Nine of diamonds, two of spades, ace of diamonds, six of hearts, queen of clubs, ten of clubs, eight of diamonds—all seven correctly identified. It was like he had x-ray vision. Which seemed to work only on cards, he found. Weird.

He pulled out a dinette chair and sat down, feeling as though the world had tilted.

Some kind of extrasensory perception. He'd always figured woo-woo stuff like that was bullshit. But he couldn't come up with anything else to explain it. Other than magic.

Leaving aside the mystery of what made it possible, he had two pressing questions: Was the ability temporary or permanent? And could he depend on it in actual play?

Before trying it in a casino, he needed to learn all he could about it. He wolfed down his breakfast, put the dishes in the sink, and got another deck of Bees, with navy blue backs. The color of the back didn't matter, he found. He tested it until late afternoon, with a hundred percent accuracy.

That night he learned that he could depend on the ability in actual play. The Juice, combined with his counting skill, gave him an unbeatable advantage over the House, every hustler's dream. He'd had that advantage for five full years.

He threw back the covers and sat up. The Juice made the big score possible, but the motivation to go ahead with the play went beyond money. Having been given such an incredible gift, he felt obligated to use it as fully as possible.

And if it stung the casinos a little, that was a bonus.

He was about to put on his shoes when a knock at the door made him jump. He considered pretending he wasn't home, but the white Chrysler parked in front of his apartment made that impossible. He crept to the door in his stocking feet and opened it a crack. A heavyset woman in a floral blouse was standing there. Charlie swore softly. Mrs. Zapeda, another resident of the apartment complex, always bringing him cookies and other crap, being "neighborly." What in hell did the silly woman want now? He sighed and opened the door wider.

"Good morning!" she said, her voice irritatingly high and chirpy, like a child's. "I just wanted to remind you about the Parkrose Apartments' annual barbeque and potluck today at noon in the center courtyard. I hope we'll see you there."

Charlie shook his head. "Going to have to miss it. I'm laid up. I threw my back out." He grimmaced with pretend pain.

"I'm so sorry to hear that, Mr. Delmar. Is there anything I can get you?"

"No, but thank you for asking. Got everything I need." He started to close the door.

"I'll bring you a plate of food later."

He opened the door again. "You don't need to do that."

"It's no trouble at all, really. Now you tend to that back."

Charlie closed the door and leaned back against it. "Shit," he said, shaking his head. He had forgotten that the annual get-together was today. Had he remembered, he would have arranged to be somewhere else.

"Charlie, you're what they call a misanthrope," an ex-wife had once told him.

He'd stared at her. "What the hell's that?"

"A misanthrope is someone who hates people."

After trying it on for size, he said, "Don't you think 'hates' is a little strong?"

"How about detests?"

"How about *avoids*? I just want people to leave me the hell alone." That had closed the subject.

These days he still didn't have much use for people. They were a pain in the ass, always yakking about bullshit, prying into personal stuff, taking up your valuable time. And most people were suckers, square johns begging to be clipped. Vegas was a sucker killing field, with casinos only too glad to oblige. It was hard not to view suckers with contempt. As for socializing with fellow hustlers, that was business. Bottom line, he preferred solitude to being around people, and if that made him a misanthrope then so be it.

And that was another incentive to go for the big score. The money would insulate him from the Mrs. Zapedas of the world. From all entanglements, in fact, social and otherwise. He could have the independence and solitude he pined for.

four

S am Hogan, owner and president of Security Concepts Inc., stubbed out his cigarette in the anteroom ashtray. He was fumbling for another when a door marked *Observation Pod* opened and a young woman appeared. At five eleven, perhaps six feet, she had a model's carriage. In her tailored gray suit, glossy black hair in a businesslike updo, she exuded the poise and self-confidence acquired only in finishing schools.

"Mr. Hogan?" she said and gestured for him to enter the room or pod or whatever the hell it was.

As he passed close to her, Hogan revised his initial estimate of her age, from twenty to perhaps twenty-seven. Still too young for him. Her perfume smelled expensive.

A smiling fellow with a deep tan and lots of teeth met him inside. He looked to be in his fifties and very fit. His suit definitely hadn't come from a discount rack. "Nick Rossi," he said, "general manager of the Skyview." They shook hands, Rossi made a sweeping gesture. "Pretty impressive, huh?"

Whoever had designed the so-called Observation Pod at the top of the Skyview Hotel and Casino had watched too many *Star Trek: The Next Generation* episodes. It featured futuristic white furniture, white carpet, and indirect lighting around the perimeter of the saucer-shaped ceiling. Curved floor-to-ceiling windows served as the walls, affording an aerial view of Vegas from almost any point in the interior.

"Pretty impressive," Hogan agreed, edging away from the window. Heights he could do without.

"The Observation Pod is my favorite place. I come up here when I want to unwind. It's like stepping into the future."

"It's . . . unique." He had another description for the room: profoundly vulgar.

"We can sit over here," Rossi said, placing a large tanned hand on Hogan's shoulder.

Stifling an urge to tense up, Hogan let Rossi steer him over to a sculpted table in the center that would not have looked out of place on the Starship Enterprise. The matching chairs were deceptively comfortable. To his relief, it was a vertigo-free distance from the windows.

"Coffee?"

Hogan nodded. "Sure."

The tall young woman appeared an instant later, as though summoned.

"Gabriella, honey," Rossi said, "would you bring us some coffee?"

"Certainly," she said and disappeared.

Hogan looked down at his hands. Surely Gabriella wasn't just Rossi's gofer? He had sized her up as intelligent and self-possessed, maybe an executive. But Rossi called her "honey."

She returned several minutes later with a large carafe of coffee and . . . three cups. After filling all three she sat down next to Rossi.

"Gabriella is my lawyer," Rossi said, "as well as my daughter. She'll be sitting in on our meeting."

She regarded Hogan across the table, her gaze on the frosty side. But then, she had ice-blue eyes. And jet-black hair, a combination he had always found attractive. If he were fifteen—no, ten—years younger, he'd be tempted to take a run at her, Rossi's daughter or not.

"Thank you for coming, Mr. Hogan," Rossi said, stirring cream into his coffee until it was the shade of butterscotch. "I represent a group of Las Vegas casinos. We think you might be able to help us with a problem."

"How did you hear about Security Concepts?"

Rossi took a swallow of his coffee and set the cup down. "Some friends of mine at the Fontana recommended you. You impressed them."

"Nice to have references." He thought he saw the faintest hint of a smile on Gabriella's lips.

Rossi grinned broadly. It looked like every tooth in his mouth had been capped, possibly even his wisdom teeth. "References are everything to us, Mr. Hogan."

"So how can I help you and your associates?"

While refilling his cup, Rossi said, "Frankie Borella at the Fontana said you're knowledgeable about casino operation. That's essential." He added cream to the coffee and stirred it. "Here's our problem. Quarterly earnings have been off lately —*way* off. Counting the Skyview, eight casinos' revenues are in the toilet. Sure as people in hell want popsicles, we're being ripped off by cheaters and advantage players. After the substantial investment we've made in security and surveillance, we're pissed."

"I can imagine," Hogan said. "How about a brief rundown on your security?"

"Sure. We use both the Griffin and Biometrica databases. These days everything's high tech." He mimed typing on a keyboard. "We've got two thousand security cameras—five hundred of which are infrared—connected to fifty monitors. Everything's digitally recorded."

"Facial recognition?"

"State of the art, baby. The same system as the Tropigala and Fontana. Unreliable. Slow and too many false positives. It improves with every software update, but updates are only occasional." He drained his cup and poured another. "Some casinos are shortsighted about investing in technology, doing just enough to get by, spending the bare minimum on security and surveillance. They would rather buy a hundred more slot machines. My associates and I spared no expense with our operations' security, but so far our return on investment has been very disappointing."

Hogan nodded. "The weakness of surveillance technology is not data collection, it's data analysis. The volume of video data captured today is reaching critical mass, and there's a physical limit in the ability of security operators to sift through the mountain of video. Furthermore, it's difficult to detect cheating in real time, as it's happening. So when a game gets hit for a huge score, your security operators will examine the surveillance video, live and recorded, and if they spot something, more than half the time it's too late to collar the cheater. Or cheaters—often you're up against a team. Lucky for them it's not the old days, back when knee-capping was a common . . . disincentive."

That pulled a guffaw out of Rossi. "Hey, Frankie was right about you. I think you're the man for the job."

"The question now is whether I want to take it on."

Rossi started to say something, then seemed to reconsider. He shrugged and said, "It's your play."

Hogan let him sweat for ten seconds before he spoke. "I'd need free run of all your operations."

"Absolutely. You'll have total access."

"Including the count rooms?"

From the look on his face, the question caught Rossi by surprise. "Well," he said, "I'll need to run it past my associates, but it shouldn't be a problem."

"All right, I'm in—providing you agree to my fee. Twenty thousand per week plus expenses."

Rossi didn't flinch. Or even blink. "Twenty large. Okay, we can live with that."

"I'm sure we will get to the bottom of the problem, Mr. Rossi."

"We're counting on it. When can you start?"

"Immediately."

Rossi showed all his teeth. "Mr. Hogan, I gotta say, I like your style."

"If you'll arrange for me to meet your security team and casino managers, I'll have a preliminary look around."

"I'll introduce you personally."

Maureen "Moe" Delveccio listened to Hogan's account of the meeting at the Skyview. After he finished, she opened a Bud Light and leaned back in her chair with her long, tanned legs crossed on her desk. "Hogan, have you noticed how many casino bosses are Italian? And here are two more, Nick Rossi and Frankie Borella. Vegas casinos are owned by corporations, supposedly, but you wouldn't much trouble selling me on the idea that Italian mobs have sneaked back into town."

"I'll be sure to ask Rossi," Hogan said. "Someday."

Moe took a sip of her beer and set the bottle on the desk. "So what's your take on the Skyview's security setup?"

"Inadequate, no question about it. A swarm of hustlers has been stinging the Skyview and seven other local casinos pretty good, virtually unopposed. Until now. As of today, the game has changed. They just don't know it yet." He *sounded* confident, at least.

Moe lit a cigarette. "Atta boy," she said, her words in a plume of smoke. "Security Concepts can use the revenue."

Speaking of which, for the fourth or fifth time since the meeting, Hogan wondered whether Rossi's immediate agreement to his fee meant he had left money on the table. Maybe he should have said twenty-five per week. Or thirty. After all, eight casinos were footing the bill. On the other hand, greed might have queered the play completely. Hard to know. Anyway, the deal was done, and twenty grand a week wasn't chicken feed.

five

After dropping Bonnie off at the apartment following her hundred-dollar-with-tip grooming session, Charlie decided to pay a visit to someone he'd known since he first came to Vegas. Phil Delano lived in a trailer in a seedy trailer park on the outskirts of town. When Charlie drove in, Phil sat in a lawn chair outside his trailer. He had on faded Bermudas, flip-flops, and an unbuttoned shirt that exposed his ample white belly. A week-old gray beard rounded out his getup.

"Charlie the Barber," Phil called out in his hoarse growl.

Charlie closed the Chrysler's door. "Hey, Phil. Making any money?" Standard greeting.

"Enough to get by. You?" Standard comeback.

"Doing okay."

Phil pointed. "Use that chair. It's folded up, sorry."

Charlie unfolded the lawn chair and positioned it facing Phil. He sat down carefully, hoping the ancient-looking nylon webbing wouldn't give way. "Seen Ada lately?"

"She dropped by last week, brought me some KFC. Told me she beat Harrah's at Tahoe for nine hundred."

"Good for her," Charlie said. "I don't understand how you and Ada stayed so close. I hear from my ex-wife maybe twice a year, when our son needs school clothes or something."

"Ada's a good woman. Why she still has anything to do with me is one of life's mysteries."

Charlie leaned forward. "I want to run something by you, a proposition you might be interested in." He told Phil about his plan to pull off a big score with a bold play. "I can't do it solo without getting a lot of heat, so I'm putting together a team. I'm here to ask you if you'd be interested in being on the team."

Phil pulled a yellowed handkerchief from a pocket of the Bermudas and mopped his brow, cheeks, and neck, and then folded it carefully and put it away. "Charlie," he said, "we've known each other for ten years. I have great respect for your ability. But have you lost your fucking mind?"

At first Charlie thought he was joking. But he wasn't smiling. "What do you mean?"

"This is the future, Charlie. Guys like me and you, we're here on a pass. We can stick around, but only as long as we keep our heads down and don't attract attention. The eye in the sky was bad enough, but now we're up against cameras everywhere, cameras that even recognize faces, for God's sake. These days it's close to impossible to pull off what you're talking about. It would take *serious* juice."

"Yes, it would," Charlie said. "And I have serious juice."

Phil grunted. "Counting cards gives you less than two percent advantage over the House. You must mean some other kind of juice." His eyes narrowed. "Inside help?"

"No inside help. I use . . . a special system." If the Juice wouldn't qualify as a special system, nothing would.

"Care to let me in on what it is?"

Charlie smiled and shook his head. "All you need to know is that I have enough juice to pull it off. So I'll ask you again. Interested?"

Phil scratched his beard stubble. "Who else you got lined up?"

"You're the first person I've talked to about it. I'm going to ask Wilson Wright, Richard Talman, and Jack Colvin and his girlfriend, Susie Harris. Also, Herman and Tan Chin from San Francisco, and a couple people you probably don't know. The size score I got in mind, I need a good-sized team."

Phil stared into the distance. "Been a while since I went on a big play . . ." He looked at Charlie. "All right, I'm in."

"Good. Think Ada would be interested?"

"I'll ask her."

"Tell her if all goes according to plan, everybody should wind up with a fat bankroll."

Phil glanced over his shoulder at his trailer. "Maybe I could live in an apartment for a change, like a human being."

Charlie stood and stretched. "I think I'll take off and try to round up the rest of the team. I'll keep you posted."

Driving back to town, Charlie mulled over the conversation. Phil's initial reaction was understandable. Ordinarily the odds against pulling off a big score would discourage most hustlers. They would point out he already had a good thing going on, steady income for as long as he wanted, probably. Turning his back on a sure thing to try for a big score would be crazy, some would say. But then, they didn't know about the Juice. The Juice cast an entirely different light on the situation.

He spent the rest of the day contacting people he wanted on the team. A couple of them pushed back as hard as Phil had, but he was prepared for that. The scent of a big payday could persuade the most skeptical hustler. At the end of the day he had firm commitments from Wilson, Richard, and Jack and Susie. Herman and Tan were leaving for China at the end of the week to visit relatives. Too bad. They would have been valuable members of the team. Counting Phil, then, he had five players lined up.

Not too bad a start.

The explosions started at dusk. He swore. He'd completely forgotten it was the Fourth of July. And by the sound of it, the stupid bastards had gotten hold of some illegal fireworks. Cops were never around when you needed them.

Without that big, fat score he wouldn't stand a snowball's chance of ever getting shut of this kind of bullshit.

six

Hogan stood by the door, waiting for his eyes to adjust to the perpetual twilight inside the surveillance room, the only illumination provided by the collective glow from eighty video monitors. Fifty monitors were arranged in a semicircular array, two horizontal rows of twenty-five, surrounding ten workstations. Each screen displayed an overhead view of a gaming table or row of slots. The workstations, with three monitors each, accounted for the other thirty screens. The workstations were occupied by three men, one woman. Only four operators on a Friday night struck Hogan as odd.

A heavyset man rose from a workstation and trudged over to Hogan. The room was air conditioned, but a sheen of sweat on the man's face reflected light from the monitors.

Hogan nodded to him. "Evening."

"Steve Gregg, Mr. Hogan. Something I can help you with?"

"Thought I'd just look around a little."

"Let me know if you need anything."

"Thanks. I do have one question, Steve. How come you're so short-staffed tonight?"

Gregg sighed. "Two of my people are out sick, another is in the hospital having his gall bladder removed, and still another's on maternity leave."

"So normally eight people would be on duty?"

"Well . . . at least six."

And that illustrated the weakness in casino surveillance: the human element. Ideally, all ten workstations would be manned at all times. Not much sense in investing millions in sophisticated equipment without enough people to operate it. The staff needed to be large enough to compensate for illness and other manpower outages.

"Steve, I'm going to hang around for a while and observe. Just carry on as usual."

The big man nodded and returned to his workstation. Hogan stood back and watched, wishing he had a cigarette.

The system seemed well designed. Video displayed on any monitor in the semicircular array could be fed to a workstation monitor for closer examination. The cameras had pan-tilt-zoom (PTZ) capability, controlled via joystick, which provided great flexibility.

An operator continually scans the monitor array, looking for anything of interest. If he spots something, the operator switches the video feed to a monitor at his workstation and then uses keyboard controls and joystick to take a closer look at the situation.

Moe would excoriate him for that explanation. "If he *or she* spots something, and his *or her* workstation," she would insist. She'd have a point. At least two members of Steve's crew were women, unless a man had taken maternity leave.

While he was looking over an operator's shoulder, watching the video feed on his workstation monitor, a movement caught Hogan's eye. He spotted it when the camera lingered at a baccarat table. Maddeningly, the camera panned away.

"Wait . . . go back," he told the man operating the joystick. A bow tie wearer, Hogan noted. His dislike of bow ties was, he knew, irrational. Call it an eccentric prejudice.

"You got it," Bow Tie said.

Hogan pointed at the screen. "See the guy in the tan suit? Keep the camera on him, maybe zoom in a little."

Gregg joined them, standing beside Hogan. "That's a high-stakes table. I'll find out how much he's won so far." He took out his phone and made a call.

The suspect appeared quite relaxed and composed as he played, nonchalantly talking and laughing with the players on either side. But something seemed odd about the way he positioned his hands. They covered his cards now, after resting casually on the table. Hogan waited. Before long there it was again, the move he had spotted before: The suspect's slightly cupped hand swept along the lapel of his coat and returned to cover his cards. Sure as hell, the gutsy bastard was hand mucking, swapping cards in and out of the game.

"The pit boss said he's down three hundred," Gregg said. "Hold on a minute." He went to his workstation and typed on the keyboard. A moment later he called out, "His players card indicates he's a stone-cold loser."

As was common practice, the suspect had presented a players card to the dealer before buying into the game. Players cards enabled the casino to monitor the play of guests and dispense "comps"—complimentary goodies such as meals, shows, or even suites—accordingly. But a casino could also retrieve a player's profile: name, address, date of birth, amounts won and lost, and reams of other useful data.

Common sense suggested the suspect's poor win record should exonerate him. Playing a hunch, Hogan said, "Pan the camera, let's have a look at the other people at the table."

Sure enough, another player had a pile of pumpkins—orange thousand-dollar chips—in front of him. Steve checked with the pit boss. The man was ahead several hundred grand.

"The guy's players card tells us he's a high roller," Gregg said. "Gets a lot of comps."

Hogan grunted. "Run a search. Find every player our high roller has gambled with more than once at this casino."

The casino's search engine produced the results immediately. One name came up repeatedly: the mucker's.

The two players were in cahoots. Capitalizing on baccarat's simple rules, which allow bettors to take the side of player or banker, the mucker was making minimal wagers while his accomplice won large ones. Pit bosses had nightmares about that kind of scam.

Gregg picked up his phone again and spoke into it. After he hung up he said, "Keep your eyes on the monitors."

Cameras placed throughout the casino enabled Hogan and the security team to watch a captivating drama unfold. The pair must have sensed they had gotten heat. The winning conspirator gathered up his pile of chips and left the table. But guards detained him when he tried to cash out. Other guards hustled the mucker from the baccarat table. It was over in seconds, and few casino patrons noticed.

Soon afterward a man with a turquoise sport coat and artfully coiffed thinning hair entered the surveillance room.

"That's Mr. Sweetser," Gregg said to Hogan. "A shift boss."

"All right, who spotted the mucker?" Sweetser said, his voice unexpectedly deep.

Gregg got up from his workstation. "This is Mr. Hogan. He caught the move."

"Arthur Sweetser." He shook Hogan's hand. "Pleasure to meet you."

"Sam Hogan. Likewise."

"You're the security consultant?"

"That's right."

"Mr. Hogan, you just saved the casino three hundred and thirty thousand dollars. We're grateful."

"You seized their winnings."

"Every penny."

"They give you any backtalk?"

"Not after we found a seven of hearts hidden under the mucker's lapel. He'd added a panel to hold a card. We photographed both cheaters and uploaded their data to Griffin and Biometrica, then turned them over to Metro Police." He turned to Gregg. "Be sure to save that video for evidence."

Gregg nodded. "Already done."

"Good work, everyone." With a parting nod, Mr. Arthur Sweetser left.

Hogan massaged his eyes with forefinger and thumb. The gig was off to a running start. Moe would be happy about that.

Right now he needed a cigarette.

seven

After a big lunch at the Fontana's lavish buffet ("All-You-Can-Eat Lunch Special: $5.75"), Charlie drained the last of his 7-Up and loosened his belt two notches. The third trip through the buffet line had been a big mistake. Their barbecued pork chops were like crack; he must've downed a dozen, and now he was as full as a tick. He slid out of the booth.

Buffet customers had to walk through the casino to reach the exit, and if they stopped to gamble, well, that was the idea. The decor—walls and columns of burnished gold, carpet and drapes the color of money—had been purposely designed to make casino patrons feel surrounded by vast wealth, which had been found to encourage play. A platoon of women dominated the slots, yanking handles with grim-faced determination. At the gaming tables the action came from a handful of tourists, all male, but in a few hours the pit would be a sea of gamblers of both sexes, even on a Sunday.

Driving home, he again contemplated how his team could place monster bets without getting heat. The obvious answer: whales. Casinos love whales, ultrawealthy high rollers who bet huge and, often as not, lose huge. They get V.I.P. treatment. Only a whale can play on no-limit tables and bet a hundred large or more per hand with the casino's blessing. Without that kind of latitude, the play couldn't rack up the size score he had in mind.

But passing convincingly as a whale, that was the trick. Everything, from clothes to transportation, had to be perfect, whale-grade impressive.

Clothes would be a cinch. Costume Specialties on Fremont could supply them with anything they needed, from Rolex watches and flashy jewelry to three-thousand-dollar suits.

Transportation was another story. Arriving in a stretch limosine wouldn't cut it. These days a limo wouldn't earn anyone whale status, not when high school kids rent limos to transport them to the prom. A solution didn't spring to mind. No rush, though. Worst case, if he had to postpone the play for a month, or even two months, so what? The important thing was to nail down every last detail. That, or take a pass on the play.

Bonnie did her usual dance when he walked in the door. He sat down in the reciner and she assumed her position on his chest. After a round of petting, he reached for the brush. Bonnie delighted in being brushed, quivering in leg-pumping, stretched-mouth ecstasy, a faraway look in her eyes. He gave her two minutes of it and then tossed the brush on the coffee table. "That'll do for now, old girl."

He picked up a remote and switched on his new television, a large flatscreen Samsung he'd bought on sale last week at Best Buy. It replaced the 19" tube-type RCA that had served him well for a couple decades. The RCA had cost him $419 twenty years ago; he paid $189 for the Korean job. Progress had its perks. He turned up the volume.

". . . will mean the end of cheating at gambling," a narrator said, as if he was announcing that cancer had been cured.

Charlie sat back.

The program, which had just started, had a five-person panel, four men and one women, plus a moderator, a woman with short iron-gray hair. They sat behind a long table made of thick, clear plastic that magnified their lower halves, giving them an odd, bottom-heavy appearance. You'd think someone would have caught an obvious thing like that. He checked the channel ID. *Ch 10: PBS.* A local production.

Charlie recognized two of the men, casino operators Nick Rossi and Frankie Borella, local celebrities in the Steve Wynn mold. Anything to do with casinos or gambling in Las Vegas, you could pretty much count on seeing Rossi's and Borella's toothy kissers.

As for the rest of the panel, they were all doctors, PhD variety—piled higher and deeper. With the exception of a young guy with a ponytail, supposedly some kind of genius in artificial intelligence research, they were professors at UNLV. What the hell could eggheads know about cheating at gambling?

Quite a lot, as it turned out. They were familiar with all the hustles, from past posting to capping bets. And they knew all about card counting. The topic turned to how widespread cheating and counting had become, which gave Rossi and Borella an opening to squawk, tagteam style, about the hit to casinos' bottom lines.

Charlie snorted. *Cry me a river.*

The moderator cut them off. "Obviously, cheating in its various forms has had a profound effect on the gaming industry. So why has it been so difficult to rein in?"

It came down to a shortage of manpower, the panel agreed. Casinos lacked the human resources to deal with the onslaught, which Rossi called "an infestation of locusts."

The moderator turned to Ponytail Guy, sitting to her left. "Dr. Ziegler, I understand that recent developments in computer technology are going to change things drastically."

"Your understanding is correct." Ziegler said. "Computing power and big data analytics tools have grown exponentially more powerful, enough when implemented to virtually eliminate cheating, as well as card counting."

"That's a bold statement. So what's your timeline to roll out this technology? Are we talking years, months, or—"

"It could be put in place in weeks," Ziegler said.

The moderator seemed stunned. "I had no idea the technology was that advanced," she said slowly.

"Me neither," Rossi said, and Borella nodded agreement.

Artificial intelligence made it possible, according to Ziegler and his colleagues. An A.I.—that's what they called it—can spot cheaters and card counters faster and with greater accuracy than humans are capable of. Plus, it can watch everything at once, 24/7/365. When the moderator asked them for a brief explanation of the inner workings of an A.I., the double-talk sounded like a foreign language.

Charlie drummed his fingers on the arm of the recliner. Even if he didn't grasp the technical part of it, it sounded impressive. He believed their claims, bought the whole pitch. These weren't crackpots. They knew their stuff, even Ziegler with his little pony tail and one of those ridiculous Joe Hep patches of hair below his lower lip.

His fingers stopped drumming. If an A.I. could spot cheating and counting, he wouldn't be surprised if it could also spot the Juice, God knows how. The possibility left him with a sinking feeling.

After the program ended, he switched off the TV and stared out the window while a familiar battle raged in his head. The smart move would be to forget all about the play, cut and run. He had a hundred sixty thousand tucked away in a safe under the closet floor. Blowing it all on a risky play would be a sucker move if it didn't pay off. On the flip side, this could well be his last shot at a big score. The thought of spending the rest of his days in a run-down trailer park like Phil made him shudder. Besides, no telling how long he'd have the Juice, a very special gift. He'd be a fool not to take full advantage of it while he had it.

Weeks, Ziegler had said. The situation had become more urgent. There would be no postponing the play. Every detail must be addressed, every problem solved, fast, fast, *fast*. As the time crunch sank in, a perfect solution to the biggest problem, transportation for the whales, shoved its way to the front of his mind.

"Dewey," he said out loud.

eight

Interstate 15 from Las Vegas to Los Angeles was a serious contender for most boring stretch of highway in the U.S. —not counting what remained of Route 66, which still had some worthwhile things to gawk at. Charlie reached L.A. at two p.m., a little over four hours after leaving his apartment in Vegas. It took another forty-five minutes to get to LAX.

After a ten-minute search, he found Executive Charters' office next to a hangar that looked new and expensive. Two sleek jets were parked in front. Inside the office, he was greeted by a man with a big smile and the kind of tan seen on golf pros, tennis players, and deep-water sailers. It made his teeth seem very white. He had a nametag: *Todd Lamb*.

Charlie gave him a nod. "Dewey around?"

"He's in the hangar, said he'd be right back," Todd said. "That was half an hour ago." He took out his phone, tapped in a number, and spoke into it: "You got a visitor, Dewey."

The tinny speaker: *"Who is it and what's he want?"*

Todd looked at Charlie. "He wants to know—"

"I heard. Tell him Charlie Delmar's here to see him."

It got some action. *"Charlie? Escort him out here."*

Todd's pasted-on smile faded. "Will do." To Charlie he said, "You must be special. Ordinarily we don't allow nonemployees in the hangar, for insurance reasons." He opened a door marked *Authorized Personnel Only*. "This way."

Inside the hangar, Charlie counted eight bays, six occupied. The two vacant bays no doubt belonged to the pair of jets parked outside. Executive Charters' fleet of eight executive jets, plus the hangar and suite of offices, must have been a huge investment. But considering what Dewey charged for flying fat cats around, the monthly take had to be in high six-figure territory, maybe a million. A slick operation.

They walked down the line of gleaming jets. Todd pointed out each one, apparently assuming that Charlie gave a shit. "Learjet . . . Gulfstream . . . Hawker . . . Cessna Citation . . ."

They found Dewey midway down, talking to a skinny guy in coveralls who didn't look old enough to drink legally. At six four, Dewey towered over the young mechanic. ". . . don't care if you have to replace the entire goddamn brake assembly, I want this Citation in the air by Wednesday."

"It'll be ready," the kid said.

"Good. I'll get out of your hair so you can get to work." Dewey turned and saw Charlie. Grinning, he reached him in two strides and wrapped him in a bear hug that lifted him off his feet. "Charlie Delmar, how the hell are you?"

"I'd be just fine if you'd let go of me."

The big man released him. "Forgot you weren't a hugger. But to me you're family, and I hug family."

"I'm worried those sasquatch arms of yours will accidentally crush my spine."

Dewey's booming laugh rattled the hangar's metal walls. "I swear, you're the king of deadpan. Let's head on back to the office. I need a cigar."

Charlie grunted. Six years since he quit cigars. He missed them bad when he was around cigar smokers, so he avoided them. But he nodded anyway. It would be a test of character.

As they walked, Dewey pointed back over his shoulder with his thumb. "The kid I was talking to, I hired him fresh out of Long Beach City College's aviation maintenance program. He's working out real good, and that's a tremendous relief, because I didn't want to have to fire him. His dad's a golfing buddy of mine."

"Nice of you to give his kid a job."

Dewey pointed. "That Gulfstream belonged to a Miami drug kingpin named Joaquin 'Coolio' Mendoza. The DEA seized it and put it up for auction last month. Eighteen-passenger capacity and in primo shape. I couldn't pass it up."

Charlie squinted against the glare of the ceiling lights reflecting off the shiny craft. He couldn't see much difference between the Gulfstream and the other jets. They all looked like spaceships to him.

They climbed the stairs to the offices. At the top, Dewey leaned on the railing and looked out over the formation of jets gleaming under the lights. "My beauties," he said. "I can't remember the last time they were all home at the same time. Not for long, though."

When they stepped into the main office, Todd intercepted Dewey. "The Merkersons' secretary called to reschedule their charter to Cabo San Lucas. They decided to go next weekend instead."

Dewey looked at his watch. "You have got to be shittin' me. Their charter was supposed to depart in two hours. This is the second one in a week. No, by God, it's the third. Who was scheduled to fly them?"

"Jonesy."

"Did you call him?"

"I tried a couple of times. He's not answering his phone. Probably en route. I left a message on his voicemail."

Dewey sighed. "Situation normal, FUBARed all to shit."

"I'll handle it," Todd said over his shoulder.

"Here's my office." Dewey held the door for Charlie.

It wasn't a typical office, more like a deluxe studio apartment with a desk in the middle of the room. The place had all the comforts of home: kitchenette, bathroom, wet bar, flat-screen TV, and a black leather couch that converted into a bed, which had been left down and unmade. Photographs of sleek jets in flight lined the walls, and a sizable lava lamp occupied one corner. Orange blobs of wax in purple liquid rose and fell in an endless ballet, the only color in the room.

After motioning for Charlie to sit in one of the chairs in front of the desk, Dewey dropped into a green leather desk chair with a tall back. "Three damn reschedules in one week." He sighed and opened an ornate cigar box on his desk. "Can I offer you one? These are Carrillos."

"Thanks, but I'll pass."

"You sure? It was Cigar of the Year in twenty eighteen."

"I'm sure." Not that part of him didn't wish he wasn't.

Dewey trimmed the end of a cigar and lit it with a red Bic, using short puffs. After a long pull, he directed a thick plume of smoke toward the ceiling. "The first draw on a good cigar," he said. "Nothing like it."

Charlie nodded. Thirty years of smoking cigars had permanently etched the sense memory in his brain. He pointed to a framed photograph on the desk, a pretty brunette on a horse. "How old was Maddy there?"

"That was taken a couple months after the accident, so she must have been nineteen. Five years ago."

The accident . . .

Charlie had been nearing Emerald Bay on the way to Harrah's at Stateline when a young woman driving a silver BMW passed him like she was on the Autobahn. Once past, she settled into a lawful fifty-five. But minutes later an oncoming pickup crossed over the center line and forced the BMW over an embankment to avoid hitting the pickup head on.

Charlie pulled over and got out. Her car had traveled twenty-five feet down the slope and struck a large Ponderosa pine. He stumbled and slid down the embankment, cursing his Florsheims' slick leather soles.

The BMW had struck the tree squarely. To make matters worse, a smaller pine wedged the driver's door shut. He peered through the passenger's window. The girl looked dazed, but she didn't have any injuries he could see. The seat belt and airbag, now fully deflated, had done their jobs. A knock on the window got no response.

The smell of gasoline filled the air. He had to get her out of the car before it caught on fire or exploded. Fortunately, the passenger door was unlocked. But unfortunately, it was stuck shut. Wrenching it open took every last bit of strength he had, bracing his foot against the side of the car. He leaned in, breathing hard. The girl's eyes slowly focused on him.

"Time to go," he said. After unlatching her seat belt, he turned her back to him, locked his hands around her middle, and dragged her out of the car and over to a Ponderosa thirty feet from the one she hit. Close to collapsing, he hoped to hell they were far enough away if the car decided to explode. He leaned against the tree, panting like a dog. He wasn't in shape for this kind of activity. After he caught his breath, he turned to the girl and asked her name.

"Maddy Burris," she said, her voice almost a whisper.

He asked her if she had a phone with her. She pointed to the car. "In my bag." He managed to retrieve the bag without being blown to bits. She took out the phone, dialed 911 and handed it to him. "If you don't mind. I feel . . . dizzy. "

He explained the situation to the 911 operator, who told him she'd dispatch emergency responders. Within fifteen minutes he heard approaching sirens. The ambulance arrived first, followed by a California Highway Patrol unit a few minutes later. The EMTs loaded Maddy into the ambulance. Confused, she told them didn't want to go to the hospital, but the paramedics ignored her. A tow truck arrived as the CHP officer took down his statement. Spasms in Charlie's lower back were occupying most of his attention.

The officer closed his notepad. "What you did was heroic, Mr. Delmar."

He didn't feel heroic. A muscle under his left shoulder blade joined the lower back in spasming, and his right knee started to ache; he'd wrenched it climbing up the embankment. The ambulance had taken off ten minutes earlier, or he could've asked one of the paramedics for something to dull the pain when it kicked into high gear. He kept a bottle of Excedrin in the Chrysler's glovebox. It would have to do for now.

A van with "KOLO 8 NewsNow" on its side pulled up, and three people piled out, a reporter and camera crew. It was Charlie's cue to get the hell out of there. Harrah's at Stateline was out of the question now. He got in the Chrysler and sped off south, destination Las Vegas. He needed to get back to his apartment, to the prescription pain killers and muscle relaxants in the cabinet over the bathroom sink. He didn't need them often, but when he did they were a godsend.

In the meantime four Excedrin tablets made the long drive somewhat less torturous. He finally pulled up in front of the apartment, switched off the ignition, and sighed. Getting out of the car took several painful minutes. The "hero" tottered to the door like a man in his nineties, moaning all the way.

The next day, lying on the sofa, doped to the gills with pain killers, heating pad turned to low, he was dozing when the phone's piercing ring jarred him awake. He swore and answered it.

The caller introduced himself as Dewey Burris. "Maddy's father," he said.

Through a Percocet haze, Charlie fended off the man's plan to come thank him in person later that day. It would take several days for the back pain to ease off. The damn knee was anybody's guess.

Exactly one week later, he met Dewey at Harry Reid International Airport's terminal. He'd flown in on his private jet. Maddie's dad was obviously loaded. They sat in the airport lounge and nursed beers while they talked.

"Charlie, I can't find the words to express how grateful I am," Dewey said. "Maddy's everything to me. The thought of losing her makes me sick to my stomach. Anything I can do for you, anything at all, you let me know, okay?"

And that was how he happened to have a king-size gold chip with Dewey Burris. He had been saving it so long, waiting until he really needed a favor, he'd almost forgotten about it. He really needed a favor now.

"Maddy's doing great," Dewey said from across the desk. "Had her first kid last month, a son."

"Congratulations, Grandpa."

"Thanks. I'll tell her you asked about her." A thick, perfect smoke ring meandered toward the ceiling. "So what brings you to L.A. today?"

"I'm here to ask for a favor."

"Anything you need, it's yours."

"It's a big favor. Maybe too big."

"I said anything."

"Would that include chartering a jet to fly some associates of mine from L.A. to Vegas and back five days in a row?"

"When?"

"Next week, July twenty-third through twenty-eighth. But—"

"Done.

"There's more. After delivering the passengers to Vegas by seven each night, the pilot will need to stand by at the airport until they're ready to return."

Dewey relit his cigar. "How long would he have to wait around?"

"It's going to vary. Let's say from five to eight hours. Look, I know this is a huge ask, and I'll understand if you feel it's out of line."

"Don't insult me. You got the five round-trip charters and they won't cost you a dime. Your people will need to be here each day no later than five thirty for departure at six if they want to hit Vegas by seven."

"I appreciate this more than I can—"

The big man waved him off. "I'm just happy to have the opportunity to repay you for saving my little girl."

Charlie felt like celebrating. "Dewey, I think I'll try one of those special cigars after all."

And to hell with character.

nine

After several slices in a row, Hogan struck one perfectly, sending it down the middle of the range to just beyond the 250-yard sign. He placed another ball on the rubber tee. And hooked the next drive. Not badly, but enough to get him into trouble on the course. He sighed and teed up the next ball. This is what happens, he told himself, when you stay away from the driving range for months at a time. He went through a half dozen baskets of balls without feeling like he'd grooved in his swing much. But then, he didn't expect to, not in one trip to the range. It would take weeks, if not months, of hard work to regain the skill he'd had when he played every day. He put extra power into the last ball's drive. It struck the 300-yard sign with a delayed *tock*.

After slipping the driver back in the bag he sat down on a nearby bench and wiped the sweat off his face with a cloth he kept in the bag. He looked at the thermometer on the wall. Not even 8 a.m. and it was already 92 degrees, well on its way to the 113 that had been forecast. That wouldn't deter hard-core golfers, who'd swarm over the course regardless of the scorching heat.

It would be nice to have the free time to visit the range regularly and play an occasional round or two. But the demands of the job made that impossible. For the time being, at least. Perhaps when—or if—things settle down a little.

That could be a while. Since they took on the assignment from Rossi and his associates he had been working sixteen-hour days, and when he wasn't working he was thinking about work, even when he was sleeping. Or rather, trying to sleep. Most distressing of all, he couldn't get rid of the nagging suspicion they had bitten off more than they could chew. Riding herd on security for even one casino was challenging. Eight casinos were almost overwhelming. He hadn't mentioned anything to Moe, but she knew him well enough to realize that something was worrying him.

They needed an edge. As for what kind, he had no idea. But unless they found one, they'd soon be up to their asses in hustlers, with no way to stop them. Then they'd be looking for another gig, and gigs that paid twenty grand a week were few and far between.

He sighed and slung the bag over his shoulder and started for the parking lot.

ten

The team meeting got underway shortly after three in the afternoon at Charlie's apartment. He wished he'd chosen someplace else to meet. His small apartment could host five or six people with no problem; nine was pushing it. Due to a shortage of seating, two of his guests had to stand.

"Damn, Charlie," Wilson said. "You call this hospitality?"

"Be right back." Charlie went into the bedroom. The apartment's previous tenant had left behind two beanbag chairs. Charlie had stacked the stupid things in a corner of the bedroom until he could get rid of them, but he'd never gotten around to it. He carried them out to the living room and tossed them at Wilson's and Richard's feet. "There you go. Happy now?"

The first order of business was to make them understand that a team meeting was a business meeting, not a goddamn party. A loud party, with everybody shouting and laughing and talking at the same time. So loud, in fact, that he almost didn't hear the knock at the door. He pulled it open, expecting to see the manager or the old bastard who lived next door with a complaint about the noise.

Herman and Tan Chin stood there, shy smiles on their faces.

"I'll be damned," Charlie said. "I thought you two were in China."

Herman smiled. "We talked it over and decided to postpone our trip until after the play. If you still want us."

"Hell yes. Come in, come in." He closed the door behind them and held up his hands until the commotion died down. "People, I want you to meet Herman and Tan Chin, good friends of mine." He pointed. "On the sofa, Jack Colvin, Susie Harris, and Phil and Ada Delano. On the beanbags, you already know Wilson Wright and Richard Talman. And that's the Ayers brothers, Dwight and Dwayne, at the table."

"Very nice to meet all of you," Herman said with a trace of a British accent. He was from Hong Kong, a U.K. colony until 1997, a fact Charlie had learned from *Jeopardy* only yesterday.

Tan, originally from Shanghai, spoke English with a thick Chinese accent. She was self-conscious about it, so most of the time she let Herman do the talking.

Herman and Tan would be key members of the team. Like many Asians, their game of choice was baccarat, but both were also expert blackjack players, as proficient as Charlie at counting cards. Their counting skills would not be needed on this play, though.

Phil's ex, Ada Delano—who reminded Charlie of Anjelica Huston—said, "I never figured you for a dog lover, Charlie." She was petting Bonnie, curled up on her lap.

Charlie sighed. "I hadn't planned to have a dog, but Bonnie was headed for a shelter—too old, her last owner said. I felt sorry for her, so I took her and now I'm stuck with her."

Not that she wasn't good company. It was nice to have someone to come home to, someone glad to see him. She was self-sufficient, thanks to automatic food and water dispensers, and a pet door to a small fenced back yard. And she was fine with being left alone for eight to ten hours at a stretch.

Jack Colvin said, "Got any beer?" With cowboy boots that added to his six-two height, Jack wore Wranglers and a plaid shirt with pearl buttons. He'd left his Stetson in his truck.

Beside him, freckle-faced redhead Susie Harris said, "You don't need a beer, cowboy."

Then Richard had to weigh in. "A cold beer'd hit the spot."

"Yeah, I could go for a beer," Dwayne said.

Swearing under his breath, Charlie went to the refrigerator and lifted out a chilled case of Corona and set it on the coffee table. "This was for after the meeting, but go ahead, if it will stop your squawking."

Herman and Tan took a pass on the beer. So did Charlie. Everybody else grabbed a bottle.

"Okay," Charlie said, "you got your damn beer, now let's get down to business. First off, let's get something straight. This will be my play. I call the shots. Anybody who objects to that arrangement should speak up now."

Silence.

"All right, then. Do as you're told and you'll go home with fat bankrolls."

Wilson raised his hand like a kid in class. "How fat?"

"A million apiece. After taxes." Charlie let it sink in.

Phil's soft whistle broke the silence. "Big-time money."

"That's right," Charlie said. "I'm talking about a monster play, one for the record books. Years from now, people will still be talking about it."

"So our target," Dwight said, "is eleven million?"

"Twenty million." Spoken aloud it sounded fantastic, even to Charlie, despite knowing that the Juice made it possible.

"Twenty mil—wait a minute," Richard said. "Eleven times a million is only—check my math—eleven million."

"This isn't like the old days, when you could win a bundle and waltz out with the money, no questions asked. These days when you cash out with ten grand or more, the casino will file a CTR—Currency Transaction Report—with the IRS. So we will pay taxes, nice and legal, four million eight hundred. You'll split ten million equally. My end is five million two."

After several seconds of stunned silence from the group, Jack said, "Dang, son, your end is mighty healthy."

"I'm paying all expenses and providing the strategy, the bankroll—which I want back after every night's play—and the juice. For that, I get five million two."

"Your *special* juice," Phil said. "Right?"

"Special juice?" Dwayne said. "What the hell is that?"

They all looked at Charlie.

"My own system. That's all I'm going to say about it."

"Must be real, *real* strong," Ada said, "to pull off a twenty-million-dollar play."

Charlie gave her a thin smile. "Strong enough."

"Twenty million," Phil said. "You really think we can bring off a play like that?"

"I do, but only if we're disciplined. We'll need to operate like a well-trained military unit. Everyone will have a job to do. And nobody showboats."

"Showboating is out?" Wilson said. "Sorry, Richard."

Richard pantomimed removing an arrow from his chest.

"Hey," Dwight said, "there are eleven of us, just like in *Ocean's 11*."

Jack slapped his knee. "That's one of my favorite movies, son. The original version with Sinatra, not the remake."

"Whoa," Susie said. "I thought the remake was fantastic. George Clooney is *so* hot."

Dwight said, "Dig this. Charlie's the Frank Sinatra character, I'll be Dean Martin, and Dwayne can be Peter Lawford. Wilson is Joey Bishop. Richard, my man, you're Sammy Davis Junior. Eee-o-eleven . . . ee-o-eleven . . . ."

Charlie glared at them until they shut up. "Mind if I continue? Thank you. Now then . . . you're all above-average card counters—but you won't be doing any counting on this play."

Richard did a double-take. "Hold on . . . so we won't be like Ken Uston's teams or the blackjack team from MIT?"

Charlie shook his head. "Casinos are wise to that kind of play. The wild bet spread gives it away. Instead, I'll supply all the juice, you'll lay all the bets."

Phil said, "How can you be in ten places at once?"

"I won't have to. Five two-person teams will hit five casinos on five consecutive nights. I'll play with each team."

"Oh. Which five casinos?"

"Cosmos, Casablanca, Skyview, Tropigala, and Fontana."

"Question," Dwight said. "What kind of two-person teams?"

"I'm glad you asked. Only whales can place gigantic bets without setting off alarm bells, so we're going to give them whales—five of them. Here they are: Ada's a real estate heiress from Phoenix, Jack's an oil man from Houston, Herman's a businessman from San Francisco, Wilson's a race-horse breeder from Louisville, and Dwight's a Bitcoin billionaire from Palm Beach. I picked you five because you maintained residencies in your home towns, important because you'll have to present identification when you cash out."

"What about using fake I.D.?" Dwight said.

"A felony. Get caught and you'll do a ten-year stretch in the joint. We're going to stay legal, one hundred percent legit. Any problem with that?"

"Nope, no probem."

"Good. Now then, whales almost never travel alone when they play in Vegas; usually they'll have an entourage. So our whales will also have entourages, consisting of only one person, who'll provide support and assistance and make a big show of tending to the whale's needs. Five two-person teams.

"Next, it's very important that the teams look the part. We'll rent outfits at Costume Specialties on Fremont. They've got jewelry, racks of designer clothes for women, fancy western gear, Giorgio Armani suits—anything we need.

"Before whales travel to Vegas for some high-roller action, their appointment secretaries call ahead so that the casino hosts can roll out the red carpet. Our whales are going to receive the same treatment. The support people will act as their appointment secretaries—which means whale teams need to start thinking about the scripts you're going to use. Think hard, because those phone pitches have to be be convincing as hell. I'll help with that.

"Now for the crowning touch—the whales will arrive in private jets. A friend of mine operates an executive charter service in L.A. He's going to cut me a deal on five round-trip flights. Casino hosts will greet the whales at Harry Reid International, transport them to the casinos, and comp them for suites. Suites that won't get any use."

Jack looked up from inspecting his boots. "How come?"

"Because you'll be long gone, after winning four million of their dollars."

Richard broke into song. "Leavin' on a jet plane . . ."

"Spare us. Okay, down to business. During play, I'll use signals to tell you how to bet, and whether to hit, stand, or quit. Listen up. When I shuffle my chips with my right hand, bet big. When I'm not shuffling, bet small. Next, I sometimes rest my left hand on the table. When I lay my hand flat, stand. When I curl my fingers under, hit. Finally, quit playing and cash out when you see me stretch, like this . . ." He raised both arms, stretching. "Any questions?"

"Signals don't get much simpler than that," Phil said, and the others nodded in agreement.

"Good. We've got one week to get our shit together. Let's go over things again, make sure we're all on the same page."

Charlie looked at his watch. Quarter to five. "Okay, enough. Let's play a few rounds. If Dwight and Dwayne will clear away their empty beer bottles and other crap, we can use the kitchen table. Ada, you're up first. Phil, you deal single-deck."

He gestured for Ada to take the chair to his left. Phil stood on the other side of the table. He'd shaved, and he wore a dark blue polo shirt and tan slacks. Nice threads, for him. Charlie told him he could sit down if he wanted, and Phil said he preferred to stand. "Makes it more realistic."

Charlie counted out $5,000 worth of chips to Ada, took $1000 for himself, and slid $19,000 over to Phil. The familiar red Mapes Hotel logo on the chips triggered memories of a time before the Reno landmark was torn down—the site used for an outdoor skating rink, for God's sake. He'd gotten the old chips from a guy named Grantham for card counting lessons. Grantham never did get the hang of it. The chips were worth maybe half a buck apiece to nostalgia buffs. He laid down a $10 chip and told Ada to bet at a $100 level until he signaled her and then to increase her bet to $500.

Phil shuffled the cards expertly, no wasted motion. But then, he'd worked as a dealer at Vegas casinos for years before Charlie met him. Doing something that long tends to ingrain the skill.

Phil dealt the cards face up, except for the dealer's hole card, standard for most blackjack tables in Vegas and Reno now. Charlie preferred the way it used to be, when the cards were dealt face down, you were allowed to hold your cards, and nobody could see what you held. These days everyone can see your hand, and touching your cards will get you yelled at. But then, face-up cards made counting faster.

Charlie got a six of clubs and three of hearts, Ada a seven of spades and nine of diamonds. Phil's upcard was an eight of clubs. Charlie alone could see the reverse image of Phil's hole card, a six of hearts. No aces, tens, or face cards. Charlie automatically tallied the running count: +3.

The top card on the deck shimmered and a nine of hearts materialized. He had to take it; standing on what he held wouldn't make sense. He motioned for the card and then indicated he wanted to stand. A jack of spades was the new top card on the deck. Charlie placed his left hand flat on the table, signaling Ada to stand on her sixteen. She did. Phil dealt himself the jack and busted with twenty-four. He paid out $10 to Charlie and $100 to Ada. The count was now +2.

Charlie placed his $10 bet and then casually shuffled two stacks of chips. Ada obediently bet $500. She caught a black-jack, a $750 payout. The count: 0.

She bet $100 on the next hand, so she'd noted he wasn't shuffling chips. She was dealt a queen and an eight, a strong hand. However, Phil held a pair of tens, so Charlie curled his fingers under. Ada raised an eyebrow but obeyed the signal and asked for a card.

And drew the ace the Juice had revealed.

Charlie's closed hand remained on the table. Ada shot him a look like he was nuts but motioned for another hit.

A deuce.

Twenty-one the hard way won the round. The count: -3.

"Hold it a goddamn minute," Jack said, pointing. "Let's have a look-see at that deck."

"Yeah," Dwight said. "It's juiced up, I'd bet on it."

Phil shook his head. "You'd lose your money. I've looked this deck over closely, and I couldn't find a damn thing."

"Look at it all you please," Charlie said. "Take your time."

Dwight took the deck from Phil and inspected it closely, turning it this way and that and holding it at arm's length. Then he handed it to Jack without a word. Jack also gave it a thorough examination and then passed it to Richard. One by one, the entire group inspected the deck with expert eyes, searching for daubing, scratching, bending, or other methods of marking cards. They didn't find anything, of course; it was a brand-new deck of Bees. There were ten furrowed brows in the room after the inspection was over.

Dwayne's face looked flushed. "The first two hands might have been luck, but on the third hand there was no possible way Charlie could have known the next two cards, an ace and a goddamn deuce, would give Ada exactly twenty-one."

Dwight nodded. "The count was zero, for chrissake."

"A cooler would explain it," Richard said.

Phil frowned. "If the deck had been prearranged, the cards for damn sure were in random order after I shuffled."

"Then I have no explanation that does not involve the supernatural," Richard said, unaware how close to the mark it was. The supernatural was as good an explanation as any.

Charlie pushed down an urge to laugh. Let them wonder. "If everyone's satisfied the deck's on the square, we'll continue practicing. Who wants to go next? Jack, have a seat."

"Fine," Jack said as he sat down, "but I want Susie to deal."

Phil placed the deck on the table and clapped his hands once, a ritual called "clearing the hands," how dealers show they haven't palmed any chips. Old habits die hard.

Jack lost the first hand and won the next. And kept on winning, with the help of Charlie's signals. Wilson was next up and then Dwight. Herman was last. The supply of chips in front of the dealer steadily dwindled each time.

By the time they called it quits at seven thirty there were ten true believers in the room.

Jack slapped Charlie on the back, oblivious to his wince. "I don't know how you're doing it, son, but right now twenty million dollars seems like a sure thing. Like taking candy from a baby."

Dwight nodded. "Whatever that 'special juice' of Charlie's is, it kicks ass."

"Yes, it is more effective than any juice I have ever seen," Herman said. "It unquestionably kicks ass."

Tan giggled, the first sound she'd made all night.

Richard let out a whoop. "Hey, people—we're all going to be rich!"

As the group filed out, Dwight, Dwayne, and Richard sang "Eee-o-eleven . . . eee-o-eleven . . ." in bad three-part harmony.

Charlie closed the door after them. He was a hundred percent sure about every person on the team—except for two. He didn't know Dwayne and Dwight all that well. But Richard had vouched for them, said they were solid. Charlie hoped his confidence in Richard's judgment wouldn't bite him on the ass.

But now he was committed to seeing the play through. Full tilt, no backing out.

eleven

In the middle of an especially peaceful afternoon nap, recliner cranked all the way back, a shrill ring practically levitated him off the cushions. He wrestled the chair upright and snatched up the phone. "Yeah?"

"Charlie?"

The voice belonged to Dee, his ex-wife. A surprise, as she usually didn't call until late August, to put the bite on him for money to buy school clothes for their son. He crossed his fingers that it wasn't bad news about the kid.

"What's up, Dee? Is Trey all right?"

"Yes, he's fine. He's bored since school let out. He misses you. That's why I'm calling. He wants to spend the rest of the summer with you. He has his heart set on it."

It caught him off guard. He stammered, in a rush to get the words out. "Bad timing, Dee. I've got something going on right now, something important, and I don't have time to ride herd on a thirteen-year-old kid."

"For your information, he turned *fif*teen four months ago. And he's mature for his age. He won't be any bother."

"As I said, I'm in the middle of something important. I can't take him right now. Maybe later." Like *next* summer.

"Charlie. You owe it to him."

"You've been getting those child support checks every month, regular as clockwork. Right?"

"Yes, of course. You deserve credit for that and for footing the bill for whatever he needs. But your son's at an age where he needs his dad. Needs you now. Later won't cut it."

"For chrissake, Dee—"

"Listen to me—you are *not* going to disappoint that boy. You're going to be a standup father and take him for the summer. You'll figure out how to make it work. I want you to buy him an airline ticket to Vegas."

No point in locking horns with her, not when she was using her "harpy" tone of voice. Which, along with other things, had earned her ex-wife status. Anyway, he couldn't push back on her arguments. They were bullet proof. When you come up against better cards, you fold. He swallowed. "Okay, okay. He can pick up the ticket at the airline counter."

"Good. Make the arrangements today, please."

And that was the end of the call—not a single *thank you*, *kiss my ass*, or *go to hell* to be heard. But that was Dee, ex-wife, heavy on the *ex*.

He went to the refrigerator and got the lone Corona left over from the team meeting. He stood in the kitchen and drained it with several long pulls, wishing he had something stronger, even though he didn't drink.

He set the empty bottle on the counter and sighed. As if setting up the play wasn't tough enough already, the pit boss in the sky saw fit to give him one hell of a handicap. He'd have a fifteen-year-old kid around his neck while he tried to pull off the score of the decade.

He dropped into the recliner.

The only way it could work, having his boy with him during the play, was if Dee wasn't bullshitting about Trey being mature for his age. Charlie hoped to hell she was being straight with him.

Otherwise, he might have to pull the plug on the play. And considering all the time and effort he'd invested so far, that would be a damn shame.

twelve

While unlocking the door, Hogan noticed that the *y* in *Security Concepts Inc.*, painted on the opaque glass, was missing its tail. The sign was barely three months old. He mouthed a short scatological reference and flung the door open. After switching on the lights and the coffee maker, he sat down at his desk and leaned back in the chair. He was working on his second cigarette when Moe walked in.

She sat down and tossed her purse in the bottom drawer of her desk. "*You're* an early bird. New resolution?"

He yawned. "Couldn't sleep. Thinking about the new job."

"Still confident we can handle it? You seem . . . tense."

He stubbed out his cigarette. "Let's see, we've caught two hand muckers, five past posters, a counting team, and you spotted a craps table whip-shot artist, all in the space of one week. Not too bad, but it's small potatoes." He glanced at his watch. "Almost forgot, I should give Julian a call."

"Why do you need to call *that* jerk?"

"Rossi suggested it. He and Julian participated in a panel discussion on PBS recently about the coming use of artificial intelligence by casinos to deal with cheating. Seems Julian's developed an A.I. he says is ready for action. If it can do what he claims, it will be a whole new ballgame." He shrugged. "Hey, Julian's a wizard, gotta give him that."

"He's also a five-star dickwad."

The coffee maker's plaintive bleep signaled that coffee was ready. Hogan was pouring himself a cup when the glass door opened and a pretty young woman walked in. Blond, late twenties, she wore a leopard-print tank top, capri-length black leggings, and a ponytail that fell below her shoulder blades. The floppy bag she carried had the capacity of a suitcase.

"Hey, Susan," he called.

"Hey, Hogan." She went over to Moe, leaned down, planted a kiss on her mouth. "Hi, sweetie."

Hogan sighed. Everyone had a girlfriend but him.

Moe put an arm around her visitor's slender waist. "How did the audition go? Please tell me you got the job."

Susan's smile exposed her toothpaste-ad-perfect teeth. "You're looking at *Les Folies de Soleil*'s newest dancer."

"That's awesome, honey. The Tropigala's lucky to get you."

More kissing ensued.

Hogan sighed again. On the view screen inside his head, an image formed of pale-blue eyes. Gabriella Rossi's eyes. Strange, because he had no designs on her, absolutely none. For one thing, the age difference was too great. Why would a twenty-something woman, a rare beauty, even *notice* a 43-year-old man with a big nose and ears that stuck out like a taxi with its doors open? That's how a woman had described him once. The real deal breaker: She was Nick Rossi's daughter.

Susan slung her bag over her shoulder. "Gotta run, get fitted for my costume. I just wanted to share the good news."

"I'm so proud of you, baby. See you later on." After Susan left, Moe had two vertical furrows between her eyebrows.

"Something the matter?" Hogan said.

"It's just . . . I keep thinking about our age difference. She's twenty-eight and I'm almost forty."

"I hear you. Maybe it doesn't bother her, though."

And maybe the age difference wouldn't bother Gabriella. But once again, it was pointless to speculate about that. Hell, for all he knew, Gabriella dwelled on the Isle of Lesbos. Hard to tell by looking; Moe and Susan were proof of that.

"Yeah, Susan says I'm being silly."

"Then there you go."

"As for Julian, he's a douchebag, but if he can help us then I'm on board."

"Don't worry, I'll see that he stays clear of you."

"No need, Hogan. I can take care of myself."

Not much doubt about that. Hogan fished his phone from his shirt pocket, scrolled the contact list to the final entry, and tapped it.

He was searching his desk for a lighter that worked, an unlit cigarette dangling from his mouth, when Dr. Julian Ziegler walked in carrying a thin attaché case. With a nod toward the glass door, Julian said, "What's a 'Securitv Concepts'?"

"It's the Latin spelling," Hogan said, making a mental note to call the sign company first chance he got. "Any trouble finding this place?"

"Not really."

No sloppy-casual geek chic for Julian. He'd opted instead for a hipster look—tailored black leather jacket, light brown hair tightly pulled back into a short ponytail, and except for the soul patch beneath his lower lip, smooth shaven. It was a look.

Julian noticed Moe standing at a file cabinet, seemingly engrossed in a folder's contents. "Nice to see you again, darlin'," he said. His eyes swept the length of her from top to bottom. "Gorgeous, as always."

Several awkward seconds passed before she responded, her tone of voice flat. "Hello, Julian."

Hogan motioned to a chair beside his desk. "Tell me about your A.I."

After he sat down, Julian opened his attaché case and took out a one-page document. "Sure, but you'll need to sign this nondisclosure agreement first."

Hogan looked it over. It was a standard N.D.A—"Do not reveal anything about this intellectual property to anyone, ever, on penalty of death, blah, blah, blah." He signed it.

Julian returned the document to the attaché case. "I named my A.I.—drumroll—Genesis. Apart from the biblical association, the word means origin or beginning, which is appropriate. Genesis is a beginning, one that can transform casino surveillance."

"A bold claim."

Julian just smiled.

"Tell me more."

"Know what deep learning is?"

Hogan shook his head.

"Artificial neural networks?"

"I've heard the term. They mimic how the brain's neurons interact with one another, right?"

"Correctomundo. Deep learning architectures are based on artificial neural networks. The 'deep' in 'deep learning' refers to the number of layers through which the data is processed. Each layer transforms its input into increasingly abstract representations, and varying numbers of layers provide different degrees of abstraction."

"You lost me after 'processed,' but go on."

"Genesis uses a cutting-edge, non-rule-based type of artificial intelligence called 'behavioral analytics,' in which the A.I. is fully self-learning, with no initial programming input. It learns to recognize normal behavior for the environment, based on observing behavior patterns. Next, it normalizes the visual data, meaning that it classifies and tags the patterns it observes, building up continuously refined definitions of normal behavior. It can recognize when something breaks a pattern."

"Like cheating?"

"Exactly. It learned to identify several common types of cheating, with fairly impressive accuracy at this early stage."

"Just by analyzing patterns. Makes sense. Give me some examples."

"Betting patterns of card counters, for one."

"Technically, counting cards isn't cheating, but I take your point. What else?"

"Recurring combinations of players, a sign that teams are at work. It's almost impossible to slip a team past Genesis if they've played together at a Genesis-protected casino."

Which alone would make Julian's A.I. indispensable.

"Good. What else?"

"Microexpressions."

"Excuse me?"

"Fleeting facial expressions. Genesis is learning to read them like a book."

"Interesting," Hogan said, "but cheaters tend not to let anything show on their faces."

"Except microexpressions, which can't be consciously controlled. They're subliminal tells."

"You're saying Genesis can deduce from microexpressions that a player's up to no good?"

"With better than forty percent accuracy, and continually improving. Another thing that will blow your mind, Genesis can track eye movement—what players look at. Every type of cheating or advantage play has different visual patterns. In blackjack, for example, counters need to look at every card dealt in order to keep a running total. Poker or baccarat cheaters who mark cards must focus intently on the backs or edges during play. Square players have random eye movement. Genesis knows the difference."

"Incredible."

"High-resolution cameras need to be positioned properly, of course, to make eye tracking possible."

"No problem there. Most casinos these days have thousands of security cameras at their disposal."

"In addition, Genesis is learning to detect stress in vocal patterns, another tell. Of course, it requires sensitive, well-placed microphones."

Hogan nodded. He'd been keeping tabs on the increasing role of artificial intelligence in surveillance, but Genesis was far beyond anything he'd heard of. It *was* a game changer. "You mentioned 'Genesis-protected casino.' You going into business?"

Julian pulled at his soul patch. "That was the idea, originally. Even registered a name: Genesis Technology LLC. But shit, I have zero interest in running a business—drumming up clients and other dull stuff. Beneath this polished exterior is a geek. I'd rather focus on Genesis' development. So the business concept is in stasis, unless you have another suggestion."

Hogan had once found a ten-dollar chip under a roulette table at the Sahara. He usually didn't gamble, but on impulse he bet it on twenty-nine, his birthday. It paid off at thirty-five to one. Not a huge win, but it made him feel like the luckiest guy in Vegas. He had the same feeling now. "Julian, what if Security Concepts were to hire Genesis Technology LLC as an exclusive subcontractor? The only business you'd have to contend with is cashing the checks."

Julian again pulled at the patch of hair under his lower lip. "I like it," he finally said. "I wouldn't have to line up the jobs and interface with clients, so I could devote all my time to Genesis. Hogan, those checks I'd be cashing, what size and frequency would they be?"

"Four thousand per week."

"Five."

"Done." It would come out of the weekly twenty. But if Genesis could do even half what Julian claimed, five grand a week was a straight-up bargain. "Welcome aboard."

Ignoring Hogan's outstretched hand, Julian raised his palm above his head. "Up top."

Feeling foolish, Hogan high-fived him, stealing a glance at Moe. She had a smirk on her face, of course. He checked his watch. Quarter after ten. "Julian, what say we run over to the Skyview? Perhaps we can put Genesis to work right away."

Hogan caught Moe's eye and raised his eyebrow in inquiry. A slight shake of her head indicated she preferred to stay behind. That was probably best. He hoped she would keep a lid on her animosity toward Julian, justifiable though it may be. With Genesis' help, Security Concepts Inc. had a shot at the big time.

They'd found their edge.

thirteen

The short article appeared in the Sunday edition of the *Las Vegas Sun* under a headline that made Charlie stop chewing his cereal.

Vegas casinos look to artifical intelligence to strengthen surveillance systems

BY BARRY McCUBBIN | UPDATED 9:18 A.M.

Cheaters, take note: The Eye in the Sky is getting a high-tech upgrade. As part of an extensive security system overhaul, eight Las Vegas casinos have turned to artificial intelligence, or A.I., which can "learn" to spot suspicious activity. Using high-resolution video cameras and sensitive microphones, the A.I. monitors gaming tables and slots, on the lookout for cheaters and card counters.

A.I.s are a quantum leap ahead of facial recognition software alone, which casinos have depended on for several years, with mixed results. Facial recognition technology, although improving, is limited and unreliable at the current stage of development.

"It's incredible," one casino security chief said. "In just a few days' operation, the A.I. identified cheaters at blackjack, bacarrat, poker, craps, and slots, as well as a card-counting team from Carnegie Mellon. I will tell you this—our bottom line for the month will look a lot healthier than it would have."

Still, the A.I.-based surveillance is shrouded in secrecy. The eight participating casinos asked not to be identified, "to avoid tipping off cheaters," one casino exec said. According to an inside source, the A.I. technology is being provided by a local security company. The *Sun* reached out to the casinos for confirmation but received no response.

One thing's clear. By using artificial intelligence, these Las Vegas casinos are taking a bold step into the future. More are sure to follow. Cheaters and card counters better find another town in which to ply their trade.

Charlie tossed the paper aside. "*Goddamn*," he said, loud enough that Bonnie looked at him, head tilted to one side. He pushed the cereal away, appetite lost. He'd been hoping to sneak the play in under the wire, before casinos had a chance to put the artificial intelligence systems fully into service.

Everything was in place. He had gone over preparations with the team a dozen times. Outfits had been rented and private jets scheduled. Fictitious appointment secretaries had notified casino hosts of the whales' arrival dates. Things were all set for the first night's play on Tuesday at the Cosmos, spearheaded by Phoenix real estate heiress Ada Delano.

Maybe he was overreacting. A.I. was a new development, so the casinos were probably still ironing out bugs.

Probably.

fourteen

The Skyview's coffee shop had a dozen customers at four in the afternoon. The hostess led Hogan and Moe to a booth at the center of the rotating circular room—well away from the windows, at Hogan's request. After sliding into the booth, his hand automatically took out the pack of cigarettes. The hand apparently hadn't gotten the memo about the city-wide ordinance prohibiting smoking in restaurants.

"I'm thinking of giving up cigarettes," he said, replacing the cigarettes in his pocket.

Moe met his eyes, a hint of a smile on her lips. "So quit."

"I'd planned to give vaping a try." He sighed. "That was before the CDC issued warnings about a mysterious lung disease from vaping that's resulted in a number of vaping-related deaths. Ever heard of vitamin E acetate?"

Moe shook her head.

"It's an additive, an oil. They think it might be the culprit. Anyway, vaping's out. I guess I'll just go cold turkey."

"Good luck with that."

"I've been meaning to tell you, you deserve props for your restraint around Julian. It's admirable."

"Thanks, but If he calls me darlin' one more time, I'm going to rip that soul patch off his chin and shove it down his throat."

"Easy there, Lara Croft. There's a lot at stake here."

"Just blowing off steam."

He started to tell her about Julian's latest tweak to Genesis when Nick Rossi and Gabriella walked into the coffee shop. They spotted Hogan and Moe and came over.

Rossi gave them each a nod. "Mr. Hogan, Miss Delveccio."

"We're just having coffee," Hogan said. "Care to join us?"

Rossi looked at Gabriella, who gave him an almost imperceptible shrug. "Sure, I guess we could use a cup."

Moe slid out of the booth and sat down next to Hogan. Gabriella and Rossi took the other side, Gabriella opposite Hogan.

Rossi said, "How do you like our Skyview, Miss Delveccio?"

"It's amazing," Moe said. "There's nothing like it."

Hogan stroked his chin. "If memory serves, there used to be another Skyview in Vegas."

"Different spelling . . . V-U-E. It never got off the ground, pun intended. SkyVue Las Vegas would have featured a five-hundred-foot observation wheel with thirty-five gondolas designed to hold twenty-five riders each. One rotation was supposed to last thirty minutes. At the wheel's hub was to be an LED screen that would have taken the Guinness record for largest advertising display in the world. Unfortunately, construction stalled due to lack of funding. Only a pair of two-hundred-fifty-foot columns remain, near the Mandelay. We recycled the name, with a new spelling."

"No sense letting a good name go to waste," Hogan said. "But it's a damn shame they demolished the old Strip—Sands, Riviera, Desert Inn, Stardust, Dunes, Aladdin . . ."

Rossi nodded. "The good old days. In this town progress drives a bulldozer."

Gabriella regarded Hogan with a penetrating gaze he found unnerving. He tried to ignore it, but the gravitational pull on his eyeballs was almost irresistible. He turned to Rossi. "We connected Genesis to the Cosmos this morning. So all eight casinos are now under Genesis' protection."

"No kidding? Color me impressed, Hogan. I had assumed it would take at least a month to get all the casinos online."

"It's been a busy four days."

"Adding Ziegler to your team was a genius move. The other casinos were dubious about giving the A.I. access to their surveillance networks, but I convinced them of the necessity. Now that your team's on the job, maybe I'll get a good night's sleep for a change."

Hogan reached for the carafe and refilled his cup, in the process spilling a big dollop of coffee. He mopped it up with his napkin. Perhaps if he applied himself he could look even more foolish.

Gabriella didn't seem to notice. "Mr. Hogan, where is your A.I. located?"

"Genesis is in the cloud, a network of remote servers. Distributed, so there's no single point of failure."

"You're confident about the security?"

"Totally. The servers are behind a firewall and monitored twenty-four seven for security vulnerabilities, and all data is encrypted and backed up continually. Servers hosted in a data center have a far greater chance of being breached."

"Speaking of breaches," Rossi said, "I'm still trying to find out who leaked to the *Sun* that we're using A.I.-based surveillance. The article said it was an 'inside source.'" His eyes narrowed. "I'd like to get my hands on whoever ratted."

"The article might have an upside," Moe said. "Maybe it'll keep the cheaters out."

"Maybe so. But I hate rats." Rossi finished his coffee. "We have to get back. Keep up the good work."

Before she turned to go, Gabriella smiled at him. More out of politeness than warmth, it seemed to him. No smile for Moe, though. Rossi motioned for her to lead the way.

"Gabriella's a beautiful woman," Moe said after a long beat.

"Yeah, I guess."

"You *guess*?"

"Okay, okay, I agree."

"She was snaking you with those pale-blue eyes, Hogan."

"I was too busy talking with her daddy to notice."

Moe rolled her eyes. She could be a pain in the ass.

fifteen

Charlie almost didn't recognize the gangly kid walking down the ramp wearing a backpack, cargo shorts, and a T-shirt with "Nike" on the front. It had been over two years since the last time Charlie had seen his son.

Trey spotted him waiting at the bottom of the ramp and reached him in several long strides. "Hi, Dad."

Charlie extended his hand. The boy shook it and then hugged him like he used to do when he was five years old. Charlie stiffened and said, "How was the flight?"

"Dope, except for the little kid sitting behind me who kept kicking the back of my seat."

Charlie inspected him, head tilted back to see through his trifocals. Trey had his mother's blue eyes, fair skin, and blond hair. "By God . . . you're taller than I am."

"Five eight, so far. I might make it to five nine or ten."

"You could use a haircut."

"Know a good barber?"

Charlie chuckled and motioned toward the luggage claim area. "You bring a suitcase?"

Trey shook his head and pointed to the backpack with a thumb. "Got everything I need right here."

Outside, the early evening heat was a shocking contrast with the terminal's air-conditioned coolness. "I don't believe this," Trey said on the way to short-term parking.

"Still driving the Chrysler, huh?" Trey said, waiting for him to unlock the car. "I thought by now you'd have traded it for a new Cadillac or something."

"What for? This car's paid for and it runs and drives like new. Listen to that engine. Besides, I don't much care for the looks of the new models." He switched the air conditioning to high. "Feel that? It'll run you out of here. "

"When I'm old enough to get a car I'd like to have a BMW Z4. Silver or white. It gets my vote for coolest automobile in the world."

"No idea what the hell that is, but it sounds expensive so save your money."

"I am."

Charlie wheeled the big car out of the airport and onto the highway. "Hungry? I thought we'd hit the buffet at the Fontana. After dinner I'll give you a tour of downtown Vegas and the Strip."

"That would be awesome. And yeah, I could eat."

Which turned out to be an understatement. Trey pounded his food and went back through the buffet line twice more, heaping his plate high each time.

"Hey, leave some shrimp for the other folks," Charlie said.

"Can't help it," Trey said, dipping a prawn in cocktail sauce. "I love shrimp. For once I can have as many as I want."

"I'll stick with these barbequed pork chops."

After they finished eating, Charlie left a five-dollar toke for whoever got stuck with clearing their messy table.

On the way to the car Trey stopped at a small blue scooter secured to a light pole with a padlocked cable. "Look at this, Dad. Pretty awesome, huh?"

"When you're old enough to drive one of those things, you'll want a car instead."

"That's what's so cool about Nevada. I can legally operate a small scooter like this one at my age."

Charlie grunted. "I didn't know that. No way in hell would your mom go for it, though."

"Yeah, but Mom's not here."

Charlie motioned for him to get in the car.

The promised tour took almost two hours, longer than Charlie had intended. Like most longtime Vegas residents, he'd become numb to the town's glitzy, overdone opulence, but it filled his son with wide-eyed wonder. Charlie bought two tickets to the Cosmos' *Interstellar* monorail. The famous attraction lived up to its hype. "Like riding on a spaceship," Trey said. They made it to the Bellagio just in time to catch the fountains' spectacular show—over a thousand jets of water shooting several hundred feet into the air, choreographed to music and bathed in multicolored lights. Finally, he took Trey to the Skyview for a panoramic bird's-eye view of the city from the Observation Pod.

"I heard Las Vegas was awesome," Trey said, looking out over the sea of neon, "but I had no idea how awesome. It's just incredible."

"Guess I've gotten used to it." Charlie yawned. He needed sleep, bad. After staring at the ceiling all last night, worrying about how he was going to organize the play while riding herd on his kid, he was running on fumes. Only a quarter to ten, early for him, but he could hardly keep his eyes open. "Come on," he said, "let's get out of here."

Passing by the Luxor on the way home, Trey pointed. "Hey, Blue Man Group is appearing there!"

Charlie glanced at the Luxor's sign. "Who the hell is Blue Man Group?"

"You're kidding. They're incredible. Dad, any chance we can go see them while I'm here?"

Charlie grunted. "We'll see."

As they were getting out of the car in front of the apartment, three girls rode in on small scooters. They parked in front of an apartment across the courtyard and removed their helmets. They looked to be about Trey's age.

"I *definitely* need a scooter," Trey said, watching the girls, now standing around their scooters, talking.

"Come on in and say hi to Bonnie," Charlie said, unlocking the door to the apartment.

It had been two years since she'd seen him, and Bonnie went crazy when Trey walked in. He dropped his pack and picked her up and nuzzled her. "She slipped me the tongue," he said after he set her down.

Charlie yawned, a jaw creaker. "I'm all in, so I'm going to hit the sack. You can watch TV or something."

"Maybe later." Trey looked out the window at the girls. "Right now I'm going to go make some new friends."

"Suit yourself." Charlie pointed at the sofa. "It folds out into a bed, already made up. It's pretty comfortable." Then he headed for the bedroom.

Before he dropped off to sleep, he hoped to hell he could find some way to keep the kid occupied and out of his hair. At least for the next week or so, until after the play.

sixteen

Sitting at the terminal, Hogan glared at the message on the screen—*READ ERROR, PLEASE TRY AGAIN*—his aggravation growing with each rejection by the thumbprint reader. The frustrating device finally let him in on the fifth try. Not the most convenient login process.

"Dammit, Julian," he called across the room, "what's wrong with just entering a password? Too unimaginative for you?"

The screen filled with stars and multihued nebulae, which began to swirl like pinwheels, finally coalescing into letters that formed a chrome word three inches tall: *Genesis*.

"Jesus H. Christ," Hogan muttered, shaking his head.

Julian sauntered over, chewing gum noisily. "Problem?"

"The thumbprint reader. I think it has it in for me."

"Probably needs a bit more dialing in. I'll take a look at it. Anyway, it's just temporary. How do you like the new intro screen, Hogan? It uses Hubble deep-space photos."

"I can't decide whether it's groovy or far out. You spend a lot of time on it?"

"Hardly any time at all. Genesis did most of the work."

"Got any more of that gum?" Maybe gum would blunt the edges of his craving for a cigarette.

Julian held out a pack of Beeman's.

"Thanks." Hogan unwrapped a stick and popped it into his mouth before he turned back to the terminal. "Genesis?"

A well-modulated, distinctly female voice came from the terminal's speaker: "*Ready.*"

"Status report, please."

"*Status is optimal, all systems nominal.*"

"Thank you." He winced, realizing he was thanking a god-damn machine. "Now show me . . . the pit at the Casablanca." A random request, to familiarize himself with the system.

The primary monitor displayed a wide-angle view of the Casablanca's gaming floor, with its craps, roulette, and blackjack tables.

Julian, standing over his shoulder, said, "Check out that babe at the craps table, the one who looks like Sharon Stone. I sure wouldn't mind grabbing a couple handfuls of those—"

Genesis cut him off. "*Please stand by for an alert . . .*" The view shifted to a crowd milling around inside a casino.

"That's the Tropigala," Hogan said.

A red rectangle called a "bounding box" surrounded one of the patrons, a man with a beard, automatically following his movement. Superimposed at the upper-left corner, a small image of a man with the same dark eyes and heavy brows but no beard. A casino security mug shot.

"*Subject identified as William Childers,*" Genesis said. "*Added to Griffin and Biometrica databases on six sixteen two thousand ten.*"

"He was trying to sneak in wearing a beard," Hogan said.

Julian chuckled. "Genesis saw right through his disguise. Pretty damn good facial recognition."

"Yeah, that's impressive." Hogan punched in the number for the Tropigala's security and advised them about Childer's presence in their casino so they could give him the bum's rush. After he finished the call, Hogan said, "She can spot people who are in Griffin and Biometrica, but it's the hustlers who aren't in the databases I worry about."

Julian laughed, a falsetto whoop. "You referred to Genesis as 'she' instead of 'it.' I *knew* you'd come around."

"The female voice might have something to do with it." Genesis sounded so much like a human woman, it was almost impossible not to address her with a feminine pronoun.

"Genesis' visual surveillance has one shortcoming that's got me stymied. Glasses, and especially bifocals and trifocals, make it almost impossible to identify card counters and cheaters using only eye-movement patterns. They interfere with eye tracking. I haven't yet figured out how to get around the problem."

"Well, maybe Genesis will solve it for you. In the meantime there are other ways of spotting them."

"Except for the exceptionally clever players."

"But Genesis is also getting smarter, right?"

"Without question. For example, she has recently learned to apply probability theory and statistical learning models to deal with uncertainty in identifying aberrant behavior."

"I'll take your word for it."

"Let me ask you something, Hogan. On a different subject. What do I have to do to hook up with Moe?"

Hogan opened his mouth to answer and closed it again. Then he began to laugh. Julian's shocked expression only made it worse, and soon Hogan was gasping for breath. "You'd have to . . ." he said between gulps of air, "you'd have to get a sex change."

Julian's furrowed-brow, tilted-head expression was that of a dog listening to an ultrasonic whistle.

"Let me spell it out for you, Julian. She's a lesbian."

"Wait, you're telling me that Moe bats for the other team? You *gotta* be shittin' me."

Hogan shook his head. "Nope."

"But she's so pretty and feminine! Not dykey at all."

"You ought to see her girlfriend. She's a showgirl at the Tropigala."

Julian looked like he'd been struck over the head with a two-by-four. A note of wonder in his voice, he finally said, "That explains why she seemed immune to my best moves."

It set Hogan off again. He dissolved into a paroxysm of laughter, holding his sides, tears running down his cheeks.

Julian shot him a look of disgust and started for the door.

seventeen

When breakfast was ready, Charlie called, "You going to stay in that bed all day? It's almost eleven."

A few minutes later Trey shuffled in, yawning and blinking at the brightness. "Umm, bacon."

"Sit down." Charlie dished up his specialty: bacon, fried spuds, and toast. "Have fun with those girls last night?"

Trey nodded. "Yeah. One of them, Greta, lives here in the apartment complex. Kristi and Elise are her girlfriends. They have a scooter gang." He yawned again. "Greta let me take her scooter for a spin around the parking lot. Had a freakin' ball." He wolfed down the food like a starving dog.

"Have some more spuds."

Trey laid down his fork. "Dad . . . I want to run something by you." He took a deep breath and let it out. "I've saved up three hundred dollars. I'm pretty sure I can get a new scooter for around seven hundred. If you could make up the difference I'll pay you back after I get home, a hundred a month. I can work for John, sanding and masking cars. So what do you say?"

Charlie grunted. "Let me think about it."

"It would give me something else to do besides hanging around here watching TV."

Charlie stopped chewing. There it was, the answer to his problem, giftwrapped and tied with a bow.

After they finished eating they retired to the living room sofa. Trey reached forward and picked up a deck of Bees on the coffee table. "Watch this, Dad," he said, cutting the cards. And before Charlie's disbelieving eyes he hopped the cut. Expertly.

"Who taught you how to do that?"

"You did, the last time you came up for a visit. I've been practicing."

"Pretty damn good." Good as any card mechanic.

"I can deal deuce, too." He demonstrated, dealing seconds better than many hustlers. "And that's not all." He handed the deck to Charlie. "Deal the cards, face up."

Charlie obliged.

"Faster." When a quarter of the deck had been dealt, Trey stopped him. "Plus two." Damned if he wasn't right. Trey nodded for him to continue. Halfway through he said, "Minus one." Right again. At three quarters, "Plus three." Check. After the last card he said, "Zero." Perfect counting.

"I'll be damned," Charlie said, torn between pride and alarm. "Listen, I hope you haven't been letting your schoolwork fall by the wayside while you mess around with this stuff."

"No way. I'm almost a straight-A student."

"Good. I don't want you to end up a hustler like me. I want you to amount to something."

"Don't worry, Dad. I think being a hustler is cool, but for you, not me. I'm planning to go to law school."

Charlie stood. "C'mon, let's go for a ride."

Charlie stood at the front window, watching Trey show off his new scooter to the three girls across the courtyard. He chuckled, recalling the look of disbelief on Trey's face when they pulled up next to Scooterville on Sunset Avenue. The kid could hardly contain his excitement when he was picking out a scooter. He chose a silver one, the only silver scooter in the place.

The price of the scooter turned out to be more than Trey had figured—eight seventy-five, on sale. Plus another thirty for a helmet, required by Nevada state law. Trey tried to give him the three hundred dollars he'd saved up, but Charlie waved it away. "Keep it," he told him. "You'll need it for gas."

Trey hugged him. "Best dad in the world!"

Charlie patted him stiffly.

Trey followed him to the DMV on Sahara Avenue to register the scooter and get a driver's license. Charlie watched him in the rearview mirror the whole way. The grin never left his face.

They made it back to the apartment around one. Charlie suggested they hit the Fontana's buffet for lunch, but Trey didn't want to leave his new scooter and instead downed a tuna sandwich and a bowl of clam chowder.

"Listen," Charlie said, "I have some important stuff going on this coming week, starting tomorrow. I need you to make yourself scarce at certain times during the day."

"No problem," Trey said. "I have to break in my scooter anyway." He washed his dishes and put them in the drying rack. "Right now I'm going to show it to Greta and the girls."

"Good. I'm going to take a nap."

And now the three girls were clustered around his son and his shiny new toy. In town only one day and the kid already had a harem. Chuckling, Charlie turned away from the window.

Dee was sure to raise holy hell when she found out he'd bought Trey a scooter, but she couldn't do jack squat about it from Eugene, Oregon. It neatly solved a big problem, and that outweighed any guff from Dee.

Now he could give the play his total attention.

eighteen

Hogan sat down in front of a terminal and stuck a piece of Nicorette gum in his mouth. He tensed, ready to cuss at the thumbprint reader, but it worked the first time. On the screen, stars and nebulae went through their routine before forming *Genesis*. At a keystoke, the logo dissolved, replaced with the main status screen. Current status: optimal.

Moe walked over and stood behind him. "At least you can log in. I had to have Julian log me in."

"Bear with it a little longer. After the new surveillance center is operational we won't have to log in with thumbprints, thank God. Genesis will use facial recognition. She has the capability now, but Julian needs to tweak something."

"So all surveillance operations will be moved to the Skyview's basement?"

"Julian says the basement has more bandwidth available, although I'm not real clear on why he needs it. This place will become a spare conference room."

"I'm going to go get some coffee. Want anything?"

"Nope, I'm good."

"Back in a bit."

Illuminated solely by terminals, the center's twilight dimness had a soporific effect. He yawned and considered taking a short nap, despite it being only eleven thirty in the a.m.. Instead, he reached for a fresh piece of Nicorette gum.

The Skyview's surveillance center had a skeleton crew that morning, only five people plus crew chief Steve Gregg. All male, all gathered around terminal six. Their whispers and snickers carried across the room.

"Genesis," Hogan said, "show me what's on terminal six."

His screen filled with an overhead view of a craps table, and Hogan saw the object of Gregg's and the crew's attention. An astonishingly well-endowed brunette in a low-cut blouse had the dice. She was putting on a show, and seemed amused by her effect on the men around the table.

Adolescent voyeurism wasn't his thing, but far be it for him to judge the men huddled around terminal six with their tongues hanging out. He heard the door open and quickly restored the status screen with a keypress. Moe would have pounced on the opportunity to razz him.

"Back already?" he said without looking up.

"Excuse me?" Female voice, but not Moe's. And Moe didn't usually wear perfume.

He swiveled around and looked up into a pair of ice-blue eyes. "Miss Rossi." He rose to his feet. "I thought you were someone else. Is there something I can do for you?"

In a departure from her customary business attire, she'd worn a turquoise and white summer dress, and instead of the austere updo, her black hair fell in soft waves. Standing hip-shot and challenging, a hint of a smile on her lips, she said, "You can demonstrate Genesis to me, if you have time."

"Glad to. I'll get you a chair."

Across the room, Steve Gregg and the crew had abandoned terminal six and were doing their best to look very, very busy. Hogan wheeled a deluxe office chair next to his and held it for her while she sat down. Then he took his seat beside her, to her left.

"Now then, Miss Rossi—"

"Please call me Gabriella."

"And never, ever Gabby?"

The *Mona Lisa* smile played across her lips again. "Never indeed. May I call you Sam?"

Only his folks called him Sam; everybody else called him Hogan. But he nodded. "Sure . . . Gabriella."

"Thank you, Sam."

"Okay. First, I'll introduce you to her."

"Her?"

He adjusted the microphone. "Genesis, I want you to meet someone. This is Gabriella."

The camera swiveled a few degrees to point at her. *"Hello, Gabriella. I am pleased to meet you."*

After a surprised pause, Gabriella said, "Very nice to meet you, Genesis." She turned to Hogan. "Her voice sounds so natural, so . . . human."

"Now you see why feminine pronouns are appropriate."

"Stand by . . ." Ten seconds passed and then: *"Hogan, I have detected cheating in progress."*

"Where and what kind of cheating?"

The screen filled with an overhead view of the craps table from terminal six, surrounded by males, plus the voluptuous brunette Gregg and his boys had found so captivating.

"I am ninety-seven point two percent certain that the man in the striped shirt is placing bets after the dice have been cast."

Hogan and Gabriella leaned forward, watching the man closely. They had a four-minute wait.

"The suspect placed a late bet just now. Were you observing?"

"Yes." He saw Gabriella nod out of the corner of his eye.

Genesis was absolutely correct; the guy was past posting. What's more, the young woman in the low-cut blouse was his accomplice, sure as hell, providing a distraction when he made the move. And holy Jesus, what a distraction! Whenever she leaned over the table, every male eye was on her décolletage. That included the boxman's, the stickman's, and two dealers' eyes. Somebody could swing with all the money on the table without anybody noticing.

Hogan picked up the phone and called the floor manager and filled him in. Several minutes later they watched as two security guards appeared and escorted the pair away.

He turned to Gabriella. "Well, there you have it."

"Sam, I was skeptical about Genesis, but I'm impressed."

He turned back to the microphone. "Genesis, Gabriella and I are very impressed with your work."

"Thank you, Hogan and Gabriella. I appreciate your kind words."

"Sam, did I imagine the note of pride in her voice?"

"Perhaps not. Julian subscribes to something called 'emergent behavior,' in which an artificial intelligence develops an unexpected ability or complex behavior. Simulated emotions such as pride could be a result, according to Julian."

"Amazing." She leaned closer. Speaking softly, she added, "And a little spooky."

Her proximity awakened in him a heightened awareness of her perfume. He searched for the words to describe its subtle, nuanced fragrance. Reminiscent of night-blooming flowers, perhaps. And something else, something elusive, evoking a memory of a time, a place, an emotion, as well as an impression of . . . opulence. A reminder that she was out of his league.

They held each other's gaze for several electrifying seconds. She was first to drop her eyes. "Well, I had better be going. Thank you for introducing me to Genesis."

"My pleasure, Gabriella." He checked himself before he added anything else, aware of his tendency to stick his foot in his mouth when he was nervous. Quit while ahead.

"Bye, Sam."

His eyes followed her as she walked away, moving with the elegant carriage ingrained by a finishing school. At the door she encountered Moe, just returning. They acknowledged each other with nods and thin smiles.

In jeans, a tank top, and sandals, Moe walked toward him wearing a knowing smile, even though she couldn't know what had transpired. "Well?"

"Well what?"

"What did your girlfriend want?"

He raised a middle finger. "Miss Rossi asked to see Genesis in action. She lucked out. Genesis caught a past poster at the craps table. She was quite impressed."

"I'll bet." Again with the smug smile.

"Don't you have something constructive to do?"

"She's after you, Hogan."

"You're full of it."

"A woman doesn't put on a dress like that, fix her hair like that, wear perfume like that unless she's on the prowl."

He sighed. Moe was one of the smartest people he'd ever known, but she was wrong about this situation. Completely, totally, utterly wrong.

An air current carried a residual trace of Gabriella's perfume. Scowling, he swiveled his chair to face the terminal.

nineteen

Trey followed Greta to the A&W on Charleston Boulevard. They parked the scooters side by side in a space under a huge palm tree and removed their helmets.

"We lucked out, finding shade to park under," he said. "Yesterday I parked in the sun and the seat got so hot I could've fried an omelette on it."

She laughed and opened her scooter's trunk. "That's why I carry this." She held up a bath towel almost the same shade of blue as her scooter. "I cover the seat with it when I park in the sun."

"Pretty smart."

"I have my moments."

Inside, they ordered root beer floats and paid separately. They found an empty booth.

"This air conditioning sure feels good," he said.

She nodded. "It's supposed to reach a hundred and two today."

"Dry heat or not, that's hot."

She stirred her float with a spoon, making a slurry of the ice cream and root beer. "So, like, what kind of work does your dad do? I see him coming and going at all hours."

He hesitated and, on impulse, decided to tell her the truth, just to see her reaction. "He plays blackjack."

"You're serious?"

He nodded.

She raised an eyebrow. "Funny job."

"Funny town."

"How long has he been playing blackjack here in Vegas?"

"Ten years."

"Wow. He must be pretty good at it."

"He's the best."

She seemed to be mulling it over.

"Greta, I'd appreciate it if we could keep this between us."

"Sure. No problem."

"I'm proud of my dad, don't get me wrong, but not many people know about . . . what he does. He prefers to keep it that way." Too bad his big-mouth son couldn't resist the urge to impress a dangerously cute freckle-faced girl.

"I get it." Her straw made a sucking sound as she finished off her float. "Pretty nice of him to buy you a new scooter."

"Parental love. Also parental guilt about not being around much after he and my mom divorced, when I was two. Hard to be a blackjack player in Albany, Oregon."

"Is that where you live?"

"No, we moved to Eugene, about forty-five miles south of Albany. My mom wanted to be close to my big sister—half sister, actually—and her husband, who live there. After school and Saturdays I work for John, my brother-in-law, sanding and masking cars. He has an auto body and paint shop."

"My dad went to the University of Oregon in Eugene."

"Hey, I'm planning to apply to the U of O after I graduate from high school. And then I'm going to law school."

"You're not going to follow in your dad's footsteps and be a professional blackjack player?"

He laughed and shook his head. "The real money's in law."

"What do you say we ride over to the Strip?"

"Sure." He finished his float. "Lead on, Macduff."

"Macduff?"

"It's Shakespeare, from *Macbeth*."

"Oh." She tied her blond hair back. "You're funny, Trey."

"I'll be appearing here all week."

twenty

Fifty thousand in used hundreds formed a stack over three inches thick. Charlie snapped a rubber band around the sheaf of bills and tossed it on the bed. Grunting with effort, he returned the portable safe to its hiding place under the closet's hardwood floor. He had never trusted banks. It would take a determined thief to find the fireproof safe. It contained his entire nest egg, minus the fifty thousand, Ada's bankroll. A pitifully tiny bankroll for a whale, but the Juice would more than compensate.

Ada and Phil arrived twenty minutes later to pick up the bankroll. Phil was anxious to get on the road. L.A. was a four-hour drive, and their return flight to Vegas departed at six.

Charlie gave Ada a final instruction: "Remember to insist they seat you at third base, and don't take no for an answer."

The Cosmos Hotel and Casino sprawled across twenty acres at the south end of the Strip. Opened in 2013, its slick futuristic theme made it a hit with sightseers, who went wild over the *Interstellar*, a monorail encircling the complex that promised passengers "an out-of-this-world experience." Having ridden on the monorail a couple days earlier, Charlie and Trey could attest that it delivered on the promise. Trey was still talking about it.

A red Cadillac convertible full of laughing girls exited the Cosmos' parking lot and squealed the tires turning left onto South Las Vegas Boulevard. He wheeled the Chrysler into the lot and docked it in the space they'd vacated. The clock in the dash indicated 7:46.

The evening was relatively cool, only 78 degrees, according to a digital sign in front shaped like a UFO. The expanse of silver and blue neon covering the Cosmos' exterior transformed the dusk into high noon. He squinted against the glare on the way to the entrance.

He welcomed the cool darkness inside the casino, where throngs of gamblers' bodies were giving the air conditioning a workout. He felt naked without the money belt's embrace, but he didn't have any reason to wear it tonight. He planned to lose more often than he won. Camouflage.

The Cosmos' cocktail waitresses all wore low-cut outfits with short-short skirts, made of a metallic fabric. An attractive redhead with great legs walked up, smiling. "You gonna break the bank tonight, Charlie?"

A lame joke, but funnier than she knew. "Candy, I'm sure going to give it a try."

The casino had a large crowd for a Tuesday, a good sign. The more distractions, the better. As he walked past a row of slots, a woman in a lime-green pantsuit hit a thousand-dollar jackpot, which set off bells, sirens, and flashing lights. The woman's shriek caused temporary tinnitus in every ear within a twenty-foot radius.

He checked out the games in the pit. Roulette and craps had the most action, but bacarrat and blackjack weren't far behind. He threaded his way through the crowd to the high-limit blackjack table, where the maximum bet was $100,000. The table minimum of only $50 attracted low-stakes players who wanted bragging rights for playing at a high-limit table. He couldn't ask for a more perfect cover. A white-haired man at first base left the table, and Charlie slid onto the stool. He cashed in with $1000 worth of chips, all in green quarters. It should be enough to lay minimum bets all night long.

He recognized the dealer, a woman with short brown hair on its way to gray. Her name was Rachel. She acknowledged him with a nod. "Been a while since we've seen you in here."

"Three months, at least," he said, placing two green chips, table minimum, in the outlined betting area directly in front of him. "Thought I'd try to run with the big dogs tonight."

She dealt the cards. "You'll have to settle for swimming with a whale."

"That so?" He caught a seven of clubs and five of diamonds and gestured for a hit.

She dealt him a card and checked her watch. "Supposed to be here in about ten minutes."

"What's his story?" A jack of diamonds busted his first hand. The count was -3, not that it mattered. She'd shuffle the cards when their whale arrived, guaranteed.

"*Her* story. She's from Phoenix. That's all I know."

"Never been to Phoenix." He slid another pair of quarters forward and glanced at his watch. Almost showtime.

One snag: a woman in a "Welcome To Fabulous Las Vegas" T-shirt at third base. She was betting the minimum, naturally. Since Ada would insist on sitting in her "lucky seat," the casino had an awkward problem to solve.

A pit boss sidled up to Rachel and whispered in her ear. She nodded and then cleared her hands with a clap and stepped away from the table. After a parting nod to Charlie, she melted into the crowd.

The dealer they tapped to take Rachel's place had a face that reminded Charlie of a shark—dull, dark eyes under bony brows, finlike nose, gash of a mouth. The casino had brought in a shark to deal blackjack to a whale. Shark Face fed the shoe's six decks into an autoshuffler. Just as he was about to deal, the pit boss stopped him.

The pit boss spoke briefly with the woman on third base and handed her a stack of comp chits. Generous comps, from her reaction. She went away grinning, clutching her payoff. Problem solved. The pit boss stood next to the vacated stool and signaled to someone.

Ada made an entrance, escorted by a casino employee and Phil, who carried a tray loaded with black, purple, and orange chips. She looked like royalty in a white pantsuit, accessorized with diamond earrings, necklace, and rings—all fugazis, but only a jeweler's loupe could reveal the deception. Phil wore a beautifully tailored three-piece suit. He assisted Ada onto the seat and stacked the chips in front of her. Then he took up a position nearby, ready to attend to her every need.

Four players at the table: Charlie at first base, Ada at third, a husky guy with a lantern jaw on Charlie's left, and a man with a wispy mustache and wire-frame glasses on Ada's right.

Charlie checked the time. Quarter past eight—more or less on schedule. He looked up from his Timex and caught the big guy on his left checking out his choice of timepiece, a smirk on his face. Moose Jaw probably wouldn't be caught dead wearing a cheap watch. His thick, hairy wrist sported a gold Rolex, which had no doubt cost him a small fortune. Judging by the guy's suit, shoes, and haircut, not to mention the stacks of Barneys ($500) and pumpkins ($1000) in front of him, he wasn't far from whale territory himself. As for the Timex, Charlie had bought it at a Payless in 1994, for twelve dollars. It kept perfect time. Even if he had millions tucked away he would continue wearing the watch until it ticked its last. And Moose Jaw could kiss his ass.

The man next to Ada appeared to be studying a blackjack basic strategy chart with recommended responses to every situation. A novice, living dangerously at a high-stakes table. Charlie didn't mind that a bit. The more distractions drawing attention away from Ada and him the better.

Shark Face dealt the cards.

Three hours later, two dozen rectangular plaques, each worth $100,000, were stacked in front of Ada. And Charlie was $650 ahead. Maybe he should have worn the money belt after all. Juice aside, the cards couldn't have been more favorable if the deck had been stacked. Luck sometimes played a big part.

"I had a feeling this would be my night," Ada said and took a butterfly sip of her daiquiri.

Shark Face wore a sour expression, as if the jerk took the casino's losses personally. Overhead lights reflected off the gel-created sheen of his dark hair, and Charlie couldn't help noticing that the nape of his neck could use a trim. Once a barber, always a barber.

The pit boss and shift manager hovered around the area like grackles circling a picnic table. The casino's head honcho, an Italian-looking guy in a silk suit and hundred-dollar haircut, joined them. Charlie had a pretty good idea what they were thinking: *It's only a matter of time before she loses it all back and several million to boot. In the end, the House always wins.*

Undeniably true—that is, if the Juice wasn't changing the odds in Ada's favor. Over the next hour, betting a hundred thousand a hand much of the time, she raked in another million six. Total winnings: four million on the nose.

Charlie stretched, a signal that set into motion a well-rehearsed drama that would enable Ada and Phil to exit the casino right away with the cash, no questions asked.

First, Phil made a show of answering his phone, attracting the casino bosses' attention. After holding the phone to his ear a minute or so, growing alarm on his face, he hurried to Ada's side. "I'm terribly sorry to interrupt, ma'am, but I just received a call that your daughter was in an accident. She's being flown to St. Joseph's in Dallas by air ambulance."

"Oh God, no," Ada said, swaying like she was about to faint. She clutched the table for support. "How . . . how badly was she hurt?"

Phil shook his head. "They didn't know, ma'am."

"Call our pilot," she said, her voice shaking. "Tell him we're on our way." She toked Shark Face a Barney and stood unsteadily, as though the floor was shifting under her feet.

Charlie had to hand it to her—not only did she resemble Anjelica Huston, she could give Anjelica a run for her money in the acting department. Phil was playing his part flawlessly as well.

After making the call—for real this time—Phil gathered up Ada's chips and plaques and they started for the cashier, accompanied by the casino manager. Soon Charlie spotted them heading for the exit, escorted by two armed security guards. One of the guards was pushing a handcart loaded with four cardboard boxes, and each had to contain at least one million. In cash, at Ada's insistence. The royal treatment all the way for a whale. Unlikely to entice her back, though.

"A damn shame," Charlie said. "I hope her daughter didn't get hurt too bad."

"Goes to show," the man who'd been sitting next to Ada said, "tragedy can strike anyone, no matter how much money they got."

Moose Jaw grunted. "Too bad it had to happen smack in the middle of her winning streak. Bad timing."

Shark Face scowled and dealt the cards.

Charlie played another forty-five minutes to snuff out any suspicion of collusion with Ada. It ended up costing him several hundred of his winnings, but he still cashed in $325 to the good. He toked Shark Face a quarter and stepped down from the stool, silently wishing its next occupant good luck.

Outside, the river of neon along the Strip set the night sky ablaze. He yawned and stretched, looking forward to a good night's sleep. At eleven a.m. Jack and Susie would come by to pick up their bankroll for Wednesday night's play at the Casablanca before taking off for L.A. Then, having stayed overnight at a motel near LAX, Ada and Phil would show up at three o'clock to split up the four million they won tonight: two million for their end, plus nine hundred sixty thousand to cover their taxes. His end, one million forty thousand, he'd stash in the self-storage unit he'd rented on Monday. If the next three nights went without a hitch, by Sunday afternoon the storage unit would contain five million two.

Not bad for a week's work.

twenty-one

He and Julian had agreed to meet in the Skyview's lobby at ten a.m., but Julian was nowhere to be seen. Hogan found him in the gift shop, talking to a young woman behind the counter. Whatever he was pitching, she wasn't buying it. She shook her head and walked away, a frown on her pretty face. Hogan leaned against a column near the shop's entrance and popped a piece of Nicorette gum in his mouth.

Julian sauntered out of the shop. He noticed Hogan and came over. "Yo, Hogan."

Hogan returned the greeting with a nod.

"How's that gum working out for you?"

"It's better than nothing."

They took the elevator down to the Skyview's basement. After the doors hissed open, Hogan said, "Explain to me again why you wanted to move operations down here."

"CenturyLink colocated a DS-4 switch in the basement. It supplies the entire city with fiber. A DS-4 is the equivalent of six T3s, two hundred seventy-four million bits per second. It's a big, *big* pipe, ideal for Genesis' requirements.

"Why does Genesis need so much bandwidth? I thought it was a cloud-based, distributed system."

"It is, but Genesis needs rapid access to casinos' videos and real-time surveillance, so the more bandwidth the better."

"I see."

Julian stopped before a stainless-steel door. "Here we are." He looked into a device mounted beside the door. It beeped twice. "Retinal scanner," he said to Hogan as the door opened. "We'll get you and Moe in the system today."

The new operations center was spacious, perhaps thirty by forty. Several technicians were running cables and installing terminals and other equipment. Mounted on one wall, a huge flat-screen monitor dominated the room.

"Jesus," Hogan said. "That thing covers the entire wall."

"Go big or go home." Julius produced a remote from his pocket and pressed a button. The swirling stars, galaxies, and nebulae that filled the huge screen were breathtaking. They coalesced into *Genesis*, chromium letters two feet tall against a background of stars and blackest space.

"Impressive," Hogan said.

"Glad you like it." He pointed out cameras mounted at strategic points around the room and said, "Genesis, please identify the man standing beside me."

A disembodied female voice said, "*Sam Hogan.*"

"Go ahead, ask her a question or give her a command."

Hogan cleared his throat. "Genesis, display status for all casinos."

"*Okay,*" the voice said.

The screen split up into eight sections, each containing lines of constantly changing analytics on green backgrounds, green indicating everything was copacetic.

"That's what I was afraid of," Hogan said, pointing at the screen. "We might have us a problem."

"How so? It's solid green across the board."

"That's the problem. The Cosmos' high-stakes blackjack table got clipped for four million last night. By a whale."

"Holy crap, four million bucks. And you suspect the whale cheated?"

"Not necessarily, but I'd think a payout like that would call for special scrutiny, and maybe she should notify someone."

"Only if she detects cheating. That's how she's currently configured."

"Can we modify that?"

"We can set a threshold. How large does a win have to be to set off an alarm?"

"I'll have to give that some thought. In the meantime can we have Genesis take another look?"

"Sure thing." Julian faced the screen. "Genesis, review the play last night at the Cosmos' high-stakes blackjack table, beginning at—" Hogan told him when the whale started and stopped playing. "—eight fifteen p.m. and ending at one a.m. Look for cheating. Or card counting."

"*Understood. Starting the review.*" A short time later Genesis interrupted their conversation. "*Julian, I am finished reviewing. I detected no cheating or card counting.*"

Hogan looked at his watch. "Jesus, she watched almost five hours of video in only . . . twenty-seven minutes?"

Julian nodded. "She didn't need to examine it in real time."

"And she didn't find anything. Julian, I want to watch that video myself. In real time."

"Tell Genesis."

He did. Hogan settled into the most comfortable chair he could find and got a fresh piece of Nicorette gum. Julian slid a chair next to Hogan's and dropped into it.

The recording was a composite of feeds from four ceiling-mounted cameras—one positioned directly overhead, one behind the dealer, one on each side—three cameras aimed down at forty-five degree angles, one straight down. The camera views were numbered, 41 through 44. The overhead view filled the screen, with the other views stacked vertically on the left in smaller windows.

"You can swap views between the main and smaller windows," Julian said. "Just say, 'Genesis, enlarge forty-two,' or whatever view you want. You can also zoom in and out, stop, rewind, fast forward, and switch to slow motion."

The cameras provided total coverage of the table's action, exactly what Hogan wanted to see. He sat back to watch the video and find out if he could spot anything Genesis missed.

A contest—human versus A.I.

He sat up when the whale appeared on the scene. A well-dressed woman in her forties, she was accompanied by a portly man in a three-piece suit. Hogan figured he was her secretary or assistant or bodyguard, perhaps all three.

In the middle of the first hand dealt, a muted buzz came from the direction of the door. Hogan looked at Julian. "What's that, someone's at the door?"

"Sounds like it."

"Genesis, pause video," Hogan said and got up. He walked over and opened the door and found Nick Rossi and two other men standing there. All three wore suits that could have come from the same tailor, silk shirts open at the collar, and gold chains. They all had razor haircuts, deep tans, and teeth so white they had to be caps.

"Sam Hogan," Rossi said, "this is Vince Rizzo, the Cosmos' general manager."

"Nice to finally meet you," Rizzo said. "And this is Pete De Luca, one of my floor managers."

Hogan shook hands with both men.

"Vince and Pete want to have a look at the new operations center and find out if you had any insights about the Cosmos' loss to the whale last night."

"As a matter of fact," Hogan said, "my associate and I had just started to watch the video of last night's play at the Cosmos' high-stakes table." He gestured to the freeze-frame on the huge screen.

"Mind if we join you?" Rizzo said.

Hogan turned to Julian. "We need three more chairs."

"Two," Rossi said. "I won't be staying." He started toward the door. "Let me know if you come up with anything."

Julian dragged two more chairs over and they all took their seats.

"By the way," Hogan said, "this is Dr. Julian Ziegler. He created Genesis, our A.I."

They exchanged nods.

"Dr. Zeigler," Rizzo said, "did Genesis catch any funny business in last night's play?"

"Let's ask her. Genesis?"

"*Yes, Julian?*"

"Did you see any activity you deemed suspicious last night at the Cosmos' high-stakes blackjack table?"

The well-modulated female voice responded, "*No, Julian. I detected nothing suspicious.*"

Rizzo and De Luca looked at each other, mouths open. "If I didn't know better," Rizzo said, "I'd swear you had a broad hidden somewhere talking into a microphone."

Julian laughed. "Speech synthesis has come a long way, baby. Want to hear her sing? Genesis, sing the first verse of 'The Look of Love.'"

She not only sang, she provided synthesized instrumental accompaniment, surprising Hogan. The rendition was more than acceptable, reminiscent of Nancy Wilson.

"My God," De Luca said after she finished. "I think I'm in love with a damn computer."

"Anyway," Hogan said, "in addition to watching the action as it happened, she reviewed the entire five-hour video. She came up empty both times. I'm confident about her ability to catch cheating and card counting, but I still wanted to see the video for myself."

"So let's watch it," Rizzo said.

"All right," Hogan said. "Genesis, resume playback."

Moments later Rizzo grunted. "That's our whale at third base. Not a bad looking gal."

"Wearing a king's ransom in diamonds," De Luca said.

Ten minutes into the video, Hogan said, "Genesis, pause," and asked her to show only the whale's play. That sped things up considerably. The rest of the video took just an hour and forty-five minutes. It would have finished even sooner if he hadn't had Genesis switch views, rewind, play in slow motion, and zoom in for closer looks.

"Well," Hogan said, "looks like Genesis was right. I didn't see anything that led me to suspect cheating or card counting took place. Tell you this, though—the way the cards fell for her, she has to be the luckiest woman in Vegas."

Rizzo snorted. "A stacked deck or marked cards would explain it."

"It would," De Luca said, "but I examined the cards myself at the end of the night, and the autoshuffler was in good working order."

"She killed us." Rizzo shook his head. "Betting aggressively, a hundred large per hand, she flat killed us."

"Too bad she had to quit due to an emergency," De Luca said.

Rizzo nodded. "Right. If she'd kept on playing we would have gotten it all back and a whole lot more besides. Seen it happen a hundred times."

"We'll get her next time, Vince."

They got to their feet and shook hands with Hogan and Julian. "Thanks, that was interesting," Rizzo said.

Hogan accompanied them to the door, and then he drifted back and dropped into the chair he'd sat in before.

"Hogan," Julian said, "you got a faraway look in your eye."

"Just thinking."

One thing kept bugging him. While he hadn't spotted any evidence of foul play, he couldn't stop thinking about how often the woman guessed right about whether to hit or stand, almost as if she knew what was coming up next—impossible, of course, unless the deck was marked or stacked. Or unless one believed in ESP or magic.

And he most definitely didn't believe in either one.

twenty-two

Toward evening a rain squall caught Vegas by surprise. On the Strip, sodden tourists fled from the alien sky, looking shocked that such a thing could happen in July. It was over in minutes, leaving in its wake the earthy smell of a first rain on pavement. The sidewalk in front of the Casablanca gathered up gaudy neon reflections into iridescent pools.

It was seven sharp. Charlie brushed dropslets of rain from the shoulders of his sport coat and entered the casino. With its Moroccan decor and exotic atmosphere, the spot was one of his favorites. The main draw for tourists was of course Rick's Café Américain, which featured interior design so authentic that patrons half expected to see Bogie and Bergman. The last time he was in the Casablanca, three months earlier, he beat them for almost eight thousand.

The busy high-stakes blackjack table had a hundred-dollar minimum, which weeded out pretenders from serious players. All the seats were taken, so Charlie found a spot nearby and waited. Twenty minutes later a man sitting next to third base stood, a mixture of disgust and defeat on his face. Charlie narrowly beat someone else to the stool, a sharp-featured woman with hair dyed a vivid shade of orange, her lips compressed with determination. She shot him a dirty look and stormed off. Old casino adage: When scrambling for a seat at the table, chivalry goes out the window.

Casinos' blackjack tables often accommodate six or seven players, but the Casablanca's high-limit table had a five-place layout, giving high rollers much more elbow room. His fellow players—two men, two women—certainly dressed like high rollers, in stark contrast with his JC Penney sport coat and slacks. They acknowledged him with polite nods and smiles just the same. The purple ($500), orange ($1000), and brown ($5000) chips stacked in front of them provided additional proof they were in a different income bracket.

He bought a thousand dollars' worth of chips, half in quarters and half in blacks. Small time for a high-stakes table, exactly the impression he wanted to create. He slid a black chip into the betting area . . . and caught a blackjack on the first hand for a $150 win. A good omen.

Thirty minutes later his stack of black chips had grown to ten. The Juice, combined with counting, was like riding a racehorse. It might be wise to rein it in to avoid getting steam before the night's play kicked off. Since it was a high-stakes table he probably hadn't attracted any attention yet.

At a quarter to eight the pit boss walked over and spoke quietly to the guy sitting on Charlie's left, at third base. Charlie couldn't hear what the pit boss said, but the man gathered up his chips, toked the dealer, nodded to the players, and took off like he was being chased. Either he'd been saving the seat or the pit boss had threatened to whack him.

Charlie expected his whale to make a grand entrance, and he wasn't disappointed. Susie on his arm, Jack strode into the pit like he owned Texas. He'd worn a cream-colored suit with a western cut and his prized snakeskin cowboy boots. And no Stetson, thank God; no sense overdoing it. As for Susie, she was a stone knockout. Her short, sparkly dress hugged every curve. Makeup concealed her freckles, and instead of her usual shock of short red hair, a blond mane brushed her bare shoulders. Amazing, how the wig and makeup changed her appearance so totally. She looked like a movie star, the perfect accessory for a Texas oil billionaire. Mouths open, everyone in the pit gawked at the couple.

"Howdy, folks," Jack said in his baritone drawl as he took third base, next to Charlie. "Everybody up for some high-stakes blackjack? I don't mind telling you, I'm feeling mighty lucky tonight." He gave Susie a squeeze. "First, though, how about a stool for my li'l darlin' here?"

A casino flunky appeared and placed a stool at Jack's left. His li'l darlin' wriggled onto it and crossed her legs, smiling, drawing admiring stares from the men at the table and tight-lipped disapproval from the women. Playing her role to the hilt.

Their dealer, a young hotshot with slicked-back hair, had one of those thin mustaches bordering his upper lip that to Charlie had always looked ridiculous. "Lay your bets," the dealer said after the autoshuffler finished.

Jack shoved a $500 purple Barney forward. "Giddyup."

By a quarter to ten, Jack had won a million dollars. An hour later, two million. The third million by eleven thirty. And by that time the pit boss, shift manager, two casino executives, and who knows who else were observing the action like hawks watching a rodent convention.

Jack put on a show for them and for the crowd gathered around the table. He pulled out all the stops, whooping like a rodeo cowboy when he won big. "I told you I felt lucky," he said after winning a huge hand. "By the time I'm though, this li'l ol' casino is gonna have to send for a Brinks truck to cash me out."

There were a few chuckles in the crowd, but the casino bosses didn't crack a smile. They were waiting for the tide to turn, confident it would. It had to. *Sooner or later the House always wins.* The adage was accepted as gospel, never questioned. A good thing, Charlie said to himself, or he and his team wouldn't have a prayer of pulling off the play.

Jack whooped again after splitting aces and winning a half million on a single hand. "Like takin' candy from a baby," he said, winking at the pit boss standing behind the dealer.

Charlie swore under his breath. Rubbing their noses in it was asking for trouble. Sometimes Jack didn't use good sense. It was twelve twenty. Time to call it a night, before the casino brass stepped in, whale or no whale. Anyway, the half-million win surely pushed Jack over the four million mark, or close to it. So Charlie yawned and stretched.

It was Susie's cue to go into action. "Ooo," she said with a giggle, "my little phone's vibrating." She unclasped a small silver purse, plucked out a phone, and tapped the screen. As she pretended to listen, her smile disappeared and her eyes widened. "Oh no," she said softly. "All right, I'll tell him." She tapped the screen again and turned to Jack.

"What's wrong?" he said.

"That was Earl, honey. There's been a fire at the ranch. He said the fire department put it out, but not before it did some damage."

"Oh Jesus. What all got ruint?"

Everyone at the table leaned in, and the casino crew drew closer. The ruse had brought everything to a screeching halt, bearing out its effectiveness.

"It destroyed part of the garage and two of your cars, he said."

"Did it get the Rolls?"

"No, only the Suburban and the Shelby Mustang."

"Shit. That Mustang was brand-new restored. What else?"

"You're gonna hate this, honey. Your gun collection over the garage, Earl said it's almost a total loss."

"Goddamn." Jack propped his elbows on the table and cradled his forehead with his hands. "Goddamn, goddamn."

Susie rubbed his shoulder. "Insurance will replace everything, right?"

He shook his head. "Most of that stuff was unreplaceable. Alamo hero William Travis' rifle was in my collection."

"I'm so sorry, baby."

He looked down at the chips and plaques piled in front of him. "Well, it sure took the wind out of my sails. Call our pilot and tell him we're on our way. I'm cashing out."

As she tapped in the number, one of the casino managers, a stocky man with a pockmarked face and a hairline that left him with only an inch of forehead, assured Jack he would make sure the cashier cut him a check without delay.

"No check," Jack said. "I came here with cash and I plan to leave the same way."

"That's a lot of cash to be carrying, Mr. Colvin."

"Sure is. So I would appreciate a security escort and a ride to the airport."

"As you wish."

"Don't worry, I'll be back to finish what I started."

"We're counting on it, Mr. Colvin."

Charlie snorted. *Don't hold your breath.*

twenty-three

The last of four cardboard boxes landed with a thud on Charlie's living room floor. Jack slid it next to the other boxes and grinned. "Son, last night was the most fun I've had without being horizontal."

"You sure seemed to be enjoying yourself," Charlie said. "Especially when you were antagonizing the casino folks. It's a wonder you didn't piss them off bad enough to bar you."

Jack laughed and sliced the packing tape on the boxes with a pocket knife. "It almost killed those ol' boys to part with this money."

Each box held at least a million dollars in hundreds: ten bundles wrapped in clear plastic, each bundle containing ten banded stacks of a hundred bills each, adding up to $100,000.

Charlie picked up a much smaller bundle that had been stuffed into one of the boxes. "What was the final count?"

"Four million sixty thousand. You got the sixty there." He produced another thick stack of bills. "Here's the bankroll."

Charlie pocketed the bankroll and then he got a pencil and paper and made some calculations. "Tax on the extra sixty is fourteen thousand four hundred. We'll split what's left over. Your end is two million twenty-two thousand eight hundred, plus nine hundred seventy-four thousand four hundred to cover the total tax. Which leaves one million sixty-two thousand eight hundred for my end."

Jack frowned. "Son, that was way too fast for me. Can I look over those figures?"

Charlie handed him the sheet of paper.

Jack and Susie studied it together. Several silent minutes later, Jack gave a nod.

So they stacked Charlie's million, ten bundles, in one box and sliced open another bundle for the $62,800 balance, which Charlie rewrapped and added to his stacks, to keep it all together.

They resealed three boxes—two full, one nearly full—with packing tape. Jack picked up two boxes, Susie one. Charlie followed them out and watched them load the boxes in the back seat of the extended-cab pickup, a big Dodge Ram.

Jack turned to Charlie. "Any chance you'll let us in on your secret? I'd give my left nut to know how you do it."

Charlie just smiled.

Susie cocked her head to one side. "Is it . . . some kind of magic?"

It made him chuckle. "Could be." In fact, he couldn't rule out magic. Or anything else.

"Damn, Charlie!" Jack smacked the hood of his truck with the flat of his hand. It resonated like a kettle drum. "You're not going to tell us, are you?"

Charlie shook his head. "You can't be too mad at me, Jack. Not with three million dollars on your truck's back seat."

"He's got a point," Susie said.

"Yeah, I guess," Jack said. "I wouldn't want you to think we don't appreciate it greatly." He helped Susie into the truck's cab and climbed in after her. A few seconds later the parking lot echoed with the marbles-in-coffee-can sound of its diesel engine. The new millionaires waved and drove off.

Charlie pulled into Excelsior Self Storage on Arville, lowered the window, and punched in the code on the keypad. The gate opened silently. He drove through and parked in an area near the entrance to the interior storage units.

He opened the trunk and lifted out a medium-size box branded with "Home Depot" on the sides. He had added "FILE FOLDERS" on the top and side using a black marker. With the box balanced on his hip, he closed the trunk lid.

The padlock he'd bought to secure the storage unit had been recommended by an expert on locks, an ex-burglar who lived two apartments down from his. The shrouded shackle would foil bolt cutters, and its six pin, anti-pick design made it practically impossible to pick. He unlocked it and swung the door open.

He'd rented one of the smallest units, five by five, and it contained one item, the box he had brought over last night, also a Home Depot special. He'd labeled it "DISHES." It contained $1,040,000. He stacked the new box on top of it. The contents of the two boxes added up to $2,102,800, the result of only two nights' work. By Sunday the stack should be five boxes high. And then he'd have to go shopping for a larger safe. Much larger.

Everything had gone without a hitch so far. The careful preparation was paying off. But celebrating prematurely was just asking for trouble. Plenty of time to celebrate after all the winnings were safely stashed away. He couldn't get his mind around the fact that he was already a multimillionaire. it didn't seem real yet. He'd been a small-time hustler for so long, maybe it never would.

With the storage unit securely locked, he yawned so widely his jaw creaked. Maybe he could squeeze in a nap before the night's play at the Skyview, Wilson at bat. A short nap, because he also had to fix dinner for that kid.

twenty-four

The office of Casablanca General Manager Tony Mancuso looked to Hogan like a Moroccan museum—arched doors and windows, intricate arabesque designs on rugs, furniture, paintings, and pottery. Adding to the exotic ambiance, air currents carried a subtle fragrance of spicy incense.

The receptionist, a dignified-looking woman with upswept graying hair, spoke with an upper-crust British accent: "How may I help you, sir?"

Hogan wondered how a veddy tweedy English lady ended up in Vegas, working for a casino on the Strip. "Sam Hogan to see Mr. Mancuso."

The woman picked up the phone and pressed a button. "Mr. Hogan is here to see you, sir." She replaced the phone in the cradle and then motioned to arched double doors on her left. "Please go on in, Mr. Hogan."

Hogan expected another tanned, swarthy Italian mobster type from Central Casting, but the casually dressed Mancuso had blond hair, blue eyes, and fair skin. His teeth were the ones he was born with. He rose from behind the ornate ebony desk, hand extended. "Tony Mancuso. Thank you for coming, Mr. Hogan."

"Just Hogan. Nice to meet you." Hogan shook his hand.

"Nick Rossi and Frank Borella speak very highly of you." Mancuso gestured to a leather chair in front of the desk.

Hogan sat down. "That's good to hear."

A miniature cannon with a five-inch brass barrel defended the desktop. Mancuso swiveled it to point directly at Hogan. "I invited you here this afternoon to ask you some questions."

Hogan had a good idea what was coming. "I'll do my best to answer them. What's on your mind?"

"You're aware we took a big hit last night, to the tune of just over four million?"

"I am."

"What do you know about it?"

"You hosted an oil billionaire from Texas who had a run of luck. He played aggressively and bet big."

"In your expert opinion, he played on the square?"

"That appears to be the case. Genesis, our A.I., detected nothing out of line when she watched the play in real time. Also, I reviewed the video myself this morning and I saw no evidence of cheating."

"Riddle me this, how would a player cheat? With multi-deck shoes and players forbidden to touch the cards, how is it even possible to cheat at blackjack?"

The question struck Hogan as naive. Surely a casino general manager would know better. Maybe it was a test. "Well," he said, "capping bets is one way to cheat. Genesis has caught a slew of bet cappers, five in your casino. Another way is pre-marked cards, a cooler. A casino insider, such as a dealer, slips it into play. Rare, but it happens. I spoke with the pit boss who was on duty last night—John Roucek, I believe his name was—and he said he examined the cards thoroughly, and the autoshuffler ensured the deck wasn't stacked."

"So you're saying the whale was just lucky."

Hogan nodded. "It would appear so. And he took advantage of the lucky streak by betting hard and fast."

Mancuso sighed. "He had to quit playing, though. Had an emergency at home. If he'd remained at the table there's a good chance we would have peeled him like a banana."

"You'll probably get another whack at him. Whales tend to return to casinos they've had good luck at."

"We'll see. But now I want to talk to you about your A.I."

"All right."

Mancuso fiddled with the little cannon, aiming it between Hogan's eyes. "When I learned you were using an A.I., I advised my colleagues against hiring your company."

"A.I.s are indispensable tools for surveillance."

"Hogan, artificial intelligence poses the most serious threat to the continued existence of the human race. More serious than nuclear weapons, more than biological weapons."

Hogan didn't reply, half suspecting it was a put-on, and any second Mancuso would say, "Gotcha!" And then they'd share a merry chuckle. But Mancuso looked dead serious.

"Have you heard of the Singularity, Hogan?"

Hogan shook his head.

"The Singularity is the point at which A.I.s surpass human-level intelligence and become superintelligent."

Hogan made a noncommittal "Umm" sound.

"Experts say it will happen soon, within five years."

"Interesting." Hogan didn't say what he was thinking—that Mancuso was a candidate for the Hoohah Hotel.

"Are you a religious man, Hogan?"

"Not really." Raised Catholic, he'd come to see organized religion as being marched in formation to look at a sunset.

"I'm Catholic. A great many Catholics liken artificial intelligence to 'summoning the demon.' We're convinced the Antichrist will be an A.I."

Hogan could only nod, momentarily speechless.

"Artificial intelligence is an existential threat that could spell doom for the human race. Give that some thought."

"I'll do that." He could hardly wait to see Julian's reaction when he informed him that his baby was the Antichrist.

"Good. Well, that's mainly what I wanted to say, Hogan. Thanks for coming." He extended his hand.

Hogan shook it. On the way to the arched door, he half expected to feel a marble-sized cannonball strike between his shoulder blades. He nodded to the English lady on the way out.

Moe looked up when he walked into Security Concepts' office. "Back already? You said you were going to head over to the Skyview after your meeting with . . . I forgot his name."

"Tony Mancuso."

"Right, another Italian. How'd the meeting go?"

After dropping into the chair at his desk, he popped a piece of Nicorette gum into his mouth. "Mancuso turned out to be a religious nut. He's convinced that—I'll try to repeat it verbatim—'artificial intelligence is an existential threat that could spell doom for the human race.' Oh yeah—he also said the Antichrist is here and it's an A.I."

"Tell me you're kidding."

"Nope. Suffice to say, he wasn't exactly thrilled that we're using Genesis for surveillance."

"Will that be a problem?"

"Rossi and Borella think Genesis is the greatest invention since the slot machine, so I doubt it."

"What is it with Catholics? A.I. paranoia is the same anti-science kookery the Church trotted out when they hounded Galileo about his heliocentric solar system theory."

"No argument there." He tossed the mostly spent wad of gum in the trashcan and unwrapped another. "You and I didn't get a chance to talk about the Casablanca video before I left to meet with Mancuso. What's your take after watching it with me?"

She picked up a nail file and went to work on a thumbnail. "My take is this. Either that cowboy is the luckiest son of a bitch in Nevada, or someone slipped a cooler in the shoe."

"The pit boss swore the cards were unmarked and totally randomized by the autoshuffler."

"Then I don't know. It's weird."

"That's the word for it."

The whale took huge—some would say insane—gambles with hundred thousand dollar bets on the line. And won every time.

Weird as hell.

twenty-five

Since the two previous nights' plays had come off smooth as mirror glass, Charlie had hoped the third night, at the Skyview, would be no different.

In under two hours his hopes were dashed.

One hour in, Wilson had been ahead nine hundred grand. But over the next hour he lost most of it back, all but a hundred thousand. Not that it was Wilson's fault; he'd followed Charlie's signals to the letter. Nor was Charlie to blame; he'd made all the right calls. It was bad luck, the luck of the draw. The cards fell wrong. Even with the Juice in their arsenal, Wilson lost hand after hand. In the short run it can happen.

The casino bosses' faces wore satisfied smirks. The whale seemed headed for a bad beat.

Watching Wilson, you'd never know it. He laughed a lot, told jokes, and talked about breeding racehorses, as though he didn't have a care in the world. In short, he played his part to perfection. He was a whale, and eight hundred thousand was pocket change.

The only thing they could do was ride it out. The odds were in their favor. If they could hang in there without going bust, sooner or later the tide would turn. Or should.

At 10:35 the tide turned spectacularly.

"That's more like it," Wilson said after splitting a pair of bullets and drawing a ten and a king.

From then on it was Wilson's table.

The House could beat the Juice temporarily, but not in the long run. By midnight Wilson had a pile of plaques in front of him, and the casino bosses' smirks had changed to scowls. They were joined by two other men. One had silver hair and a deep tan—Rossi, the Skyview's general manager. Charlie didn't recognize the second man. The group had a powwow, glaring at the high-stakes table from time to time. Whatever they were cooking up, it couldn't be good.

He added up Wilson's winnings. Thirty-nine plaques, at a hundred grand each, and at least nine hundred thousand in chips, maybe more. Close enough.

He stretched, making sure Wilson noticed.

Wilson's face became flushed and sweaty. No one had seen him swallow a capsule he'd gotten from a friend, a medication that instantly caused the alarming physical symptoms but was, according to Wilson's friend. basically harmless

"I'm . . . I'm feeling . . . strange," he said, swaying.

Richard appeared at his side at once. "My God! Hang on, Mr. Wright. I'll get you some help."

Wilson nodded and leaned back, breathing fast, his eyes closed. Charlie couldn't be entirely certain it was all an act. The other players at the table whispered among themselves, casting anxious glances at the visibly unwell whale.

Most casinos had EMTs on staff who double as security. A uniformed man appeared with a wheelchair. He asked Wilson if he was experiencing chest pain and Wilson shook his head. The EMT and Richard helped him into the chair and wheeled him away, to the Skyview's medical facility.

Richard returned and gathered up Wilson's winnings. When he opted to cash out, there would be no question as to why.

Play resumed. Charlie stuck it out another half hour and then toked the dealer and left the table. The early morning air seemed warm and sticky as he walked to the parking lot. Before starting the car he sat there a minute and massaged his temples.

Two more nights to go.

twenty-six

After watching the previous night's video of the Skyview's high-stakes blackjack game, Hogan reviewed the Cosmos' and Casablanca's videos again, paying particular attention to the non-whale players at the table. One player in particular drew his scrutiny, a nondescript man with glasses, who had a talent for shuffling his chips with one hand. Who happened to be there all three nights. Interesting. Hogan had Genesis make three freeze-frame closeups of the player.

"Excuse me, everyone," he called across the surveillance center, "could you come over here a moment?"

The entire crew, nine in all, trooped over.

Hogan pointed at the screen. "Do any of you know this guy?"

The one named George spoke up first. "Sure, I do. That's Charlie the Barber." Several others chimed in, agreeing.

Hogan grunted. "He's a barber?"

"Retired," George said. "Now he plays blackjack for fun."

"His name's Charlie Delmar," crew chief Steve Gregg said. "A long-time Vegas regular. Everybody in town knows the guy. Harmless, but an odd duck. Refused a players card."

"You give him a clean bill?"

"Yeah. He wins a little sometimes, loses a little sometimes. All the dealers like him. "

"Okay. Thanks, guys."

"Genesis," Hogan said after they left. "Can you say definitively that this man isn't counting cards?"

"*I can only state that I have found no evidence that he cheated. However, he wears glasses, which interferes with my ability to analyze eye movement, necessary to determine whether someone is counting cards.*"

"But you haven't ruled it out?"

"*No.*"

"Okay, I want you to review those three videos and focus your attention on that player specifically. Look for anything out of the ordinary."

"*Understood.*"

He got up from the terminal, wishing he could smoke a cigarette. The Nicorette gum blunted the craving, but not entirely. *Better than nothing.* He needed to keep telling himself that. At least you could chew gum almost anywhere.

He decided to take a stroll around the Skyview's parklike grounds and stretch his legs. Walking always seemed to help him work things out when he had something on his mind.

The "something" this time had to be Conundrum of the Year. Even if Genesis discovered that Charlie the Barber was counting cards, it still wouldn't solve the mystery of how in hell the whales always guessed right whether to hit or stand. Counting wouldn't be any help there. Once you rule out cold decks and marked cards, you're left with the impossible.

"Sam."

He stopped and turned around. "Gabriella."

"You walked right past me, ignoring me."

"I'm terribly sorry, I didn't see you. I was thinking about something."

"You did have a faraway look in your eye."

In daylight, the most unforgiving light a woman can be subjected to, her skin looked poreless and fair, almost translucent. Wearing a charcoal pinstripe suit over a crisp white blouse, her jet-black upswept hair gleaming in the sun, she looked like she had stepped out of a photo spread in *Vogue*: "Today's Business Woman." She fell into step beside him.

"So," he said, "does your law practice keep you pretty busy?" Only a medium-dumb question.

She shook her head. "I handle one client."

"Just like Tom Hagen."

"What? Oh. Yes, I guess so, although I wouldn't compare my father to Vito Corleone."

"No one kisses his ring?"

"Not that I've ever seen. Still, he calls me his consiglieri. I've never heard him make someone an offer they couldn't refuse, but I wouldn't put it past him."

Hogan stared at her, open-mouthed. She had the look of a person trying hard to keep a straight face. They broke up at the same time, her laugh melodic and unselfconscious.

"That's one of my dad's favorite movies. He's watched it two dozen times at least."

"Your dad seems to have taken a shine to Moe."

"He likes you, too."

"In spite of my Irish pedigree? Glad to hear it."

"He's very impressed with your knowledge and ability, says he's sleeping better since you're on the job."

"That's good to hear." Hogan hoped her dad's confidence wasn't misplaced. Because there was the matter of the whales' phenomenal luck sticking out its tongue at him, giving him the finger, daring him to solve the mystery.

"Well, Sam, I'd better be getting back. Nice talking with you."

"Likewise, Gabriella."

He watched her walk away, the high heels giving lovely definition to her shapely calves. Then he continued on, scolding himself for looking. Had he lost his mind? Gabriella was off-limits, hopelessly unattainable. For him, at least.

He forced his thoughts back to the conundrum that had him stumped. For the umpteenth time, he told himself there *had* to be a rational explanation. He just needed to find it. For the casinos—and for his own peace of mind.

twenty-seven

His dad had asked him to make himself scarce for a couple hours, so Trey spent the morning riding around with the Valkyries, the name Greta and the girls had chosen for their scooter gang. They rode to a shop in North Las Vegas Greta had heard about, where for twenty bucks apiece a mechanic made a simple modification to their scooters' engines. Scooters that a 15-year-old could operate legally were limited by Nevada state law to only 35 mph. The modification, which involved disconnecting the speed governor, increased the top speed to 45 mph, even 50 mph with a tailwind. It was plenty fast; 45 on a scooter felt like 85.

"We're an outlaw gang now," Greta said with a laugh.

An outlaw gang that wore shorts, T-shirts or halter tops, and flip-flops. They had voted to make Trey an honorary Valkyrie, which delighted him. Riding with the Valkyries was a blast. His quips kept them laughing.

He and Greta pulled into the Parkrose Apartments about noon, just as his dad's visitor, an Al Pacino lookalike, emerged from the apartment. As he talked with Greta, Trey watched him get in a shiny Mustang convertible and drive away. Trey pushed his scooter across the courtyard and put it on the kickstand beside a light pole in front of the apartment. Then he secured the scooter to the pole with a stout stainless steel cable and padlock.

Doing a bad impression of Elvis singing "Viva Las Vegas," he walked into the apartment, surprising his dad. He was holding a Sharpie, standing over a sealed cardboard box labeled "BOOKS" with crude block letters. "Didn't hear you ride up," he said.

Trey pointed at the box. "What kind of books are those?"

"No idea. They're, uh . . . they're Wilson's. He, uh, asked me to keep them for him." He picked up the box and carried it into the bedroom. When he came out he said, "Getting close to lunchtime. Want me to fry you up some baloney for a sandwich? You can have soup with it."

"Okay, sure." Trey looked out the window at his scooter.

"I've got some people coming over at three, so I hope you can find something to do for an hour, hour and a half."

"No problem. Hey, look what I bought today." He took a pair of ultra-compact binoculars from a pocket of his cargo shorts. "Bushnell. Decent optics. Ten bucks."

His dad grunted. "Can't kick about the price."

"They're tiny, but powerful. I always wanted a pair."

"Better toast some bread for your baloney sandwich."

After lunch Trey said, "Think I'll go for a putt. Might catch a movie. I'll be back around four thirty or five."

His dad nodded. "I'm going to grab a nap."

The Silver Streak, the name he'd given his scooter, purred to life with a turn of the key. He started to make a right turn onto Harmon Avenue but instead pulled into the 7-Eleven directly across from the apartment complex, to buy a bottle of water. Important to stay hydrated in the Vegas heat.

After stowing the bottle in the scooter's fiberglass trunk, he reached for the small binoculars, obsessed with the new toy. He scanned the surrounding area and then trained the view on the apartments across the street. His dad must have changed his mind about taking a nap, because he was outside, opening the Chrysler's trunk. He went inside and returned carrying the box of books. He put the box in the trunk and closed the lid. Then he got behind the wheel. Two minutes later the Chrysler pulled out onto Harmon, heading east.

What the heck? Trey fired up the Silver Streak and turned onto Harmon, following the Chrysler at a discreet distance. He stayed three vehicles back, careful to avoid being spotted by his dad. They turned south on Arville Street. After a mile the Chrysler turned into Excelsior Self Storage and stopped outside the gate.

Trey coasted to a stop behind a large propane tank across the street and pulled out the binoculars. His dad entered a security code, too fast for Trey to catch. The gate slid open and the Chrysler pulled forward. After he got out of the car, his dad opened the trunk, lifted out the box, and carried it into the closest building. Ten minutes later he reappeared and got in the car. The Chrysler exited through the gate and took off in the direction it came from.

Putting along at a sedate 30 mph, Trey had a feeling that something very odd was going on. So the books belonged to Wilson? Yeah, sure. His dad had lied to him.

It was none of his business, he knew, but that didn't douse his burning curiosity. He would give a week's pay sanding and masking cars for a peek in that box.

twenty-eight

Hogan pulled the big Silverado into a parking slot a short hike from the Tropigala's casino entrance. The new white pickup, equipped with every option available, was one of his two indulgences, the other being his condo next to the golf course. Golf could be counted as another indulgence, even though the last time he'd played a round was the end of May. The summer months were too hot for his liking, even though hardcore golfers filled the course year round.

The Tropigala had a decent afternoon crowd. Winding his way through the casino, looking for the shift manager, he spotted a pit boss and walked over to him. "Know where I can find Denny Burson?"

The pit boss pointed across the room. "Green sport coat."

Hogan nodded thanks and intercepted Burson. Tall and lanky, with a neck that jutted forward from between narrow shoulders, Adam's apple the size of an egg, heavy unibrow above close-set eyes like small amber marbles, Burson glared at Hogan with a what-the-hell-do-you-want? expression.

"Mr. Burson, I'm Sam Hogan from Security Concepts. The Tropigala and seven other casinos hired us to evaluate and advise security protocols." He shook Burson's knuckly hand.

"Can I help you with something?"

"Yes, you can. And perhaps help your casino at the same time. Is there some place we can talk?"

"Let's go to my office." Burson led the way down a corridor and held a door open for Hogan. The office was small and windowless. "Have a seat," Burson said, indicating a wooden chair in front of his desk.

Hogan sat. "You're working the night shift tonight?"

"Yeah. Why?"

Hogan slid an eight-by-ten printout across the desktop. "Recognize this guy?"

Burson examined the photos on the printout and then looked up at Hogan. "Yeah, sure. He's a regular, a local. I forget his name."

"Charlie Delmar, also known as Charie the Barber."

"Right, right. What about him?"

"You're expecting a whale tonight, coming to play high-stakes blackjack."

"That's right. One of our people is meeting his private jet and bringing him here. What's that got to do with this guy?" He tapped the printout.

"There's a strong possibility that Charlie the Barber will play at the same table."

His unibrow formed a wide, shallow V. "So? You suspect he's up to something?"

"No, I'm just advising you to keep an eye on him. And I'll do the same using video surveillance."

"Okay, but I think you're off base. The guy's been around this town forever. He's a harmless local character."

"So I've heard. Call it a cautionary measure."

Burson shrugged. "All right, I'll keep keep tabs on him."

Hogan slid his card across the desk. "Please give me a call if you spot anything."

"You got it."

After he climbed into the pickup, Hogan sat there a few minutes, thinking about how everyone used "harmless" to describe Delmar, as if they'd called a meeting and reached a consensus. Perhaps he actually was harmless. Or perhaps he had everyone completely fooled.

Hogan started the pickup and eased it out of the slot.

twenty-nine

Thursday night's play at the Skyview had been rough, but compared with Friday evening's ordeal at the Tropigala, it was a stroll in the park.

The play had started off well enough. Within an hour, Herman was up nine hundred grand. At that rate they would have reached their target of four million well before 1 a.m.

But then the dealer, a man with a puffy, expressionless face started changing the deck on them.

Like most casinos, the Tropigala's blackjack tables used two shoes, one for cards in play, the other randomized and ready to use when the first shoe is exhausted. After the first hour of play, whenever the running count turned favorable and Herman began winning, the dealer would swap shoes.

It screwed things up royally. Every time the deck changed, Charlie had to start the count over. He had the Juice, so he could signal Herman whether to hit or stand but not how strong to bet before the cards were dealt. For that, he needed the count.

The dealer was acting on orders from the pit boss, a grim old bastard standing nearby with arms crossed, signaling shoe changes. His strategy, while preventing Herman from winning big, had a downside: It discouraged him from laying large bets, so he wouldn't be losing big, either. And wasn't that the reason casinos rolled out the red carpet for whales?

Under the circumstances, laying back and betting the minimum was the only thing they could do. Without the ability to place large bets they were just spinning their wheels. Herman's face remained impassive, but the set of his jaw indicated he was as frustrated as Charlie.

They weren't alone. The other players at the table protested indignantly: "Not another damn shoe change!" "This is ridiculous!" and "I'm going to quit if this bullshit doesn't stop!" And two people did quit in disgust and were replaced by new players.

Charlie looked at his watch. Only a quarter to eleven, but it felt like five a.m. No sense beating their heads against a brick wall. Nine hundred thousand, while far short of their goal, was better than nothing. But something told him they should stick it out a little longer and see what happened.

He nearly missed the fracas between the pit boss and a red-faced shift manager, a heated discussion with the shift manager supplying most of the heat. Charlie caught only a few words here and there, and then he heard clearly something the pit boss said, pointing to the high-stakes table.

". . . a goddamn Jap."

The shoe switching had nothing to do with card counting and everything to do with plain old garden-variety racism. And this racist couldn't tell the difference between Japanese and Chinese faces. Asians probably all looked alike to him, and he hated them all equally. Including Asian whales.

The shift manager wasn't buying it. Arms folded, he shook his head with finality.

The pit boss stomped off.

His replacement showed up several minutes later, a bald guy with intense eyes and a beak of a nose, giving him the appearance of a bald eagle. The shift manager spoke to him briefly and then left.

They also replaced the stony-faced dealer with a woman, a pretty brunette. Charlie had played at her table a number of times. She gave him a dimpled smile and a nod of acknowledgment.

He returned the nod. "Evening, Katie."

From then on, a shoe was swapped out only when all cards had been dealt. Not that it was smooth sailing the rest of the night. They had to grind it out, and sometimes it felt like milling a block of concrete with a nail file. They kept at it until three a.m., when they finally reached their goal.

Just as Charlie was getting ready to give Herman the signal to quit, he felt a tap on his shoulder. He turned to see a tall man wearing a green sport coat and a sour expression standing there, a uniformed guard at his elbow.

"We don't want your action," he said.

Charlie didn't argue. Since the high-stakes table had a lot of cash on hand, he cashed out then and there. Katie looked sympathetic as she slid the money across the table, a bit over eight hundred. It made no sense to back him off for such a small amount, but he wasn't about to argue the point. He almost forgot to stretch before he pocketed the money and headed for the exit, accompanied by the guard.

Backed off. A fitting end to a brutal, exhausting night.

Nice of the casino to hold off until they'd reached their goal, though. And after tomorrow night's play at the Fontana he would be closer to seeing Vegas disappear in his rearview mirror. For good.

thirty

Moe looked up from her terminal when he walked in. "Good timing, Hogan. Take a load off. I'd like to get your take on something."

He pulled up a chair and dropped into it. "Okay, what's on your mind?"

She turned toward him, a cat-ate-the-canary expression on her face. "Whales."

"What about them?"

"In the past four days, four whales hit four casinos for four million each. See a pattern there?"

"Four times four. What about it?"

"It started me thinking." Elbows propped on the arms of her chair, she steepled her fingers. "Hogan, let me ask you a question. How does a casino know a whale is really a whale?"

"Well . . . I assume the casino checks them out thoroughly. Credit rating and so forth."

"That's what I assumed too. So I picked one of the whales at random, Jack Colvin, supposedly a Texas oil man, a billionaire. But according to Experion, his FICO score is six twenty-nine, not exactly a stellar rating. Equifax's and TransUnion's scores are in the same ballpark. I Googled him, thinking I'd find a slew of stuff. Zero, zilch, nada, like he's a ghost." She smiled. "I see I have your full attention."

She did indeed. "Did you check the other whales?"

"Herman Chin had the best FICO score, seven forty-nine. The rest were below seven hundred, with one under five. All nobodies, unknown by *Who's Who* and *Forbes*."

"Jesus H. Christ." He leaned back, eyes closed. Then he opened his eyes. "Which whale played here at the Skyview?"

"Let's see, that would be Wilson Wright, Thursday night."

Hogan rose to his feet. "Let's go see Rossi."

Rossi listened without interrupting, his broad face impassive, the flush spreading under his tan the only sign of emotion. When they were finished he picked up the desk phone and spoke into it, making an obvious effort to keep his voice even and controlled. "Dana, find Bigalow and tell him to get his ass in here." He looked up at Hogan and Moe. "Bigalow's our casino host. He coordinated our whale's visit."

"Maybe he'll have logical answers to our questions."

After a five-minute wait they heard a tentative knock at the door before it opened. Bigalow turned out to be a pudgy fellow wearing a seersucker suit and a nervous smile that came and went. "You wanted to see me?"

"This is Mr. Hogan and Miss Delveccio from Security Concepts. We're contracting with their company. They want to ask you some questions."

Bigalow turned to them. "What would you like to know?"

"Mr. Bigalow," Hogan said, "I understand you coordinate whales' visits to the Skyview."

"That's right."

"Tell us about Wilson Wright's visit. From the beginning."

"His assistant phoned us last week to schedule his visit. He said Mr. Wright bred racehorses in Kentucky and liked to play high-stakes blackjack. They'd be flying in on his private jet, the assistant said, and expected to be met at the airport and driven to the Skyview. I greeted Mr. Wright personally when he stepped off his jet, and brought him and his assistant here in our limo. I set them up in a luxury suite, but Mr. Wilson insisted on playing immediately. Why?"

Moe said, "Did you run a credit check?"

"No, his assistant said a line of credit wouldn't be needed, that Mr. Wright preferred to deal with cash exclusively and he'd be bringing lots of it. Odd, but whales can be eccentric."

Moe looked at Hogan. He gave her an almost imperceptible nod. "Mr. Bigalow," she said, "I ran a credit check on Wright. His FICO score is five seventy-eight, a far cry from whale territory. Also, if he's a wealthy horse breeder, he's trotting under the radar. I called a friend, an investment banker in Louisville, Kentucky, and he'd never heard of Wilson Wright. Neither had *Who's Who* or *Forbes*."

Bigalow's skin had taken on a gray pallor. He swallowed. "I . . . I can't believe it. Everything rang so true—the advance call from an assistant, his Pierre Cardin suit, and his private jet, a Grumman Gulfstream. Good Christ, that jet cost twenty million. By all appearances he was a whale."

Hogan snorted. "Ever heard the saying 'Appearances can be deceiving'?"

"We hate to have to tell you this," Moe said, "but you've been royally conned. Mr. Wilson Wright's no more a whale than I am."

Rossi had sat silently, listening to the back and forth. Now he spoke up. "Bigalow, your incompetence has cost the Skyview four million fucking dollars. Your position here is no longer tenable. You're fired, effective immediately."

Head hanging, Bigalow shuffled out the door, a dead man walking. After the door closed, Rossi got up and stood at the window. "God," he said, looking out, "this is embarrassing."

Hogan and Moe didn't say anything. What could they say?

Rossi turned away from the window and sat down at his desk. "Anyway, good work, Hogan."

"Thanks, but Moe deserves all the credit. She discovered the scam."

Rossi grunted. "That so, Miss Delveccio? You're Italian, so that explains it."

"I'm Sicilian, actually."

Rossi beamed at her. "Even better. Salute, my dear."

"Thanks." She glanced at Hogan. "But I'm afraid we have more bad news."

Rossi sighed. "Let's hear it."

"Your whale wasn't the only fake. I found three others."

Rossi looked like he'd been kneed in the groin. "Others?"

She nodded. "The Skyview is only one of four. This week the Cosmos, the Casablanca, and the Tripigala had their own bogus whales. Who also hit them for four million apiece."

"Sweet mother of God." Rossi planted his elbows on his desk and covered his face with his hands. "It's a disaster. A big-titted disaster."

"It was a sophisticated operation," Hogan said, "organized with great care and attention to detail—expensive clothes, personal assistants, private jets—with the goal of putting up a front so convincing that casinos would accept them at face value and not bother to vet them. And it worked."

Rossi shook his head sadly. "They took four casinos for sixteen million. Jesus. You're sure they weren't cheating?"

"Well," Hogan said, "we haven't found any evidence of cheating so far. But we want to be absolutely sure, so we're still working on it, still analyzing. We will let you know if we turn up anything."

"Good. In the meantime I'm going to call a meeting with the managers of all the casinos involved. Where you can ruin their day the way you ruined mine." He smiled. "Hope you're free later this afternoon. Say, four o'clock in our conference room?"

"We'll be there."

thirty-one

After waiting nearly an hour in the shade of a sign across the street from Excelsior Self Storage, Trey decided to pack it in and come back another time. He wiped his forehead with a cloth he kept in the Silver Streak's trunk before strapping on the matching silver helmet. Just after he started the scooter a blue pickup drove up to the gate.

Finally.

He had the binoculars focused on the keypad before the pickup's driver punched in the code: *star 0 5 0 4 4 7 hashtag*. He committed it to memory until he could write it down. But it turned out he didn't need to enter the code into the keypad. He simply followed the pickup through the gate.

He parked the scooter and opened the trunk to get the items he brought: utility knife, clear packing tape, flashlight. Then he headed for the storage unit entrance he'd seen his dad use.

The key had a tag: F-14. When he first saw it in an ashtray on top of the dresser in his dad's bedroom, he'd put two and two together. Finding the key made today's covert mission possible. He located unit F-14 and unlocked the padlock.

Inside, he switched on the flashlight and saw four identical cardboard boxes stacked in the corner. From top to bottom, they were hand labeled: "VINYL LPs," "BOOKS," "FILE FOLDERS," and "DISHES."

He hefted the top box. It was fairly heavy, twenty pounds or more. Vinyl albums, although his dad wasn't a music buff. With the utility knife, he sliced the packing tape, opened the box, and shined the flashlight on the contents.

"Oh . . . my . . . God," he whispered.

The box contained plastic-wrapped bundles of hundred-dollar bills, each bundle over six inches thick.

Hands shaking, he quickly counted the bills in one bundle. It contained ten banded stacks, a hundred used bills in each stack. So, $100,000 in each bundle. Ten full bundles and one partially full.

More than a million bucks.

He used the packing tape he'd brought to reseal the box. Then he set it on the floor. Heart pounding and hands shaking, he opened the next box, "BOOKS."

No books. Only bundles of hundreds, same as the first box.

He resealed the second box and considered having a look in "FILE FOLDERS." But it was a safe assumption that all the boxes contained bundles of cash. He replaced "BOOKS" and "VINYL LPs" on the stack.

Over one million dollars in each plain-looking cardboard box. Backing away slowly, he gazed reverently at the stack, feeling like one of the prehistoric hominids gawking at the monolith in *2001: A Space Odyssey*.

He switched off the flashlight and opened the door a crack. The corridor was empty. He slipped out and padlocked the door, his hands still shaking.

The shaking had subsided by the time he cranked the scooter to life. The gate began to move when he neared it, triggering a sensor. With the opening barely a yard wide, he zipped through and turned north on Arville.

As he slowly putted home, head buzzing like a 50,000-volt transformer from the tension, he felt a sense of satisfaction at having solved the mystery. At least in part.

Four million bucks, socked away in a self-storage unit like household items. Unbelievable.

Respect for his dad's blackjack ability had changed to awe.

thirty-two

In keeping with the Skyview's space-age decor, the empty conference room's furnishings—carpet and sculpted table and chairs—were pure white. Three abstract paintings in white frames provided some touches of color.

"Hogan, we're twenty minutes early," Moe said. "Nobody's here yet."

"I don't want to come off looking too goddamn eager. Let's head over to the gift shop. I'm about out of Nicorette."

"Maybe I should give that stuff a try. Susan hasn't said anything, but I think my smoking bothers her."

They returned fifteen minutes later. Six people loitered around the long conference table, talking: Vince Rizzo of the Cosmos, Tony Mancuso of the Casablanca, Nick Rossi of the Skyview, Pete Giordano of the Tripigala, Frank Borella of the Fontana . . . and Gabriella Rossi in full business mode.

Moe elbowed his side. "Your girlfriend's here."

"Very funny. I'm wondering why Borella is at this meeting. The Fontana wasn't among the casinos that got hit."

"Okay, looks like everyone's here," Rossi said, "so let's get get the show on the road."

After everybody found a seat at the table, Rossi said, "You all know Mr. Hogan, our security consultant. Seated next to him is his associate, Miss Delvechio. Whose people, I might add, hail from Sicily."

The aside elicited smiles and nods of approval. Hogan discreetly elbowed Moe. Now they were even.

"They've got some important information you need to hear," Rossi said. "Then I think you'll agree that the twenty grand per week we pay Security Concepts is money well spent." Rossi gestured to them. "Mr. Hogan and Miss Del-vechio, the floor is yours."

"Thank you," Hogan said. "Gentlemen and lady, I'm going to cut to the chase. The whales who took you for four million apiece this week were fugazis, every one of them."

Silence. The general managers looked like they'd been coldcocked.

Giordano was first to speak. "Are you sure?"

"No doubt about it. You've all been conned by some very convincing fakes."

Rizzo held up his hand. "How did you find this out?"

Hogan looked at Moe. "Ms. Delveccio, suppose you answer that question."

They listened attentively while Moe explained how she'd uncovered the deception, concluding with, "It worked only because none of the whales were properly vetted. They were accepted at face value. And they all used cash, no credit."

The casino managers seemed to be sucking on lemons.

"I fired my casino host on the spot," Rossi said. "I recommend you do likewise, gentlemen."

Borella spoke up. "The Fontana is expecting a whale this evening, a billionaire from Palm Beach named Dwight Ayers. He's supposed to arrive in his private jet at seven. We'll run a credit check on him. If he's a phony we'll give him a different reception than he expects." He looked at Hogan and Moe. "You may have saved us four million dollars."

"But what about the rest us?" Rizzo said. "Any hope of getting our money back, or are we screwed?"

Rossi turned to his daughter. "Gabriella, are there any legal avenues available to recover the money?"

"Possibly," she said, making a note on a pad. "But only if cheating was involved."

They looked at Hogan and Moe. Hogan said, "Card counting is more likely. We haven't found any evidence of counting yet, but we can't state definitively there wasn't any." He paused and then decided what the hell. "We're looking at a certain individual who played at each whale's table. "

"You suspect him of being a card counter?" Borella said.

"Let's just say he's a person of interest. A long-time regular, name of Charlie Delmar, known around town as Charlie the Barber. Everyone swears he's harmless."

"We'll be watching for him at the Fontana tonight."

"Hold it, people," Giordano said. "They passed themselves off as whales. Isn't that fraud? Someone explain to me why we don't file a class-action civil suit against all four whales for sixteen million fucking dollars."

Rossi looked at his daughter.

"Before we take any legal action against them," Gabriella said, "we should ask ourselves one question: Do we want the whole world to know how badly we got taken due to our own negligence? The media would have a field day."

That silenced everyone while they mulled it over.

Mancuso said, "She's got a point."

Five glum faces, five nods of agreement.

"Publicity like that, we don't need," Rizzo said.

After a few minutes' discussion they decided, if no cheating turned up, the wisest course of action would be to let it go, write it off as a business expense.

Rossi turned to Hogan and Moe. "I'm sure I speak for everyone here when I tell you we're extremely grateful. It was an expensive lesson, but you've saved us from similar future losses. Taking the long view, the whales did us a big favor." He rose from the table. "Unless someone has further business this meeting is adjourned."

Gabriella caught his eye and beckoned him. "Excuse me," he told Moe and walked over to Gabriella.

"Sam, do you have time to go have a drink with me?" she said. "I don't understand how it could be possible for the whales to win so consistently. it's bothering me."

She wasn't the only one bothered by that. But he really wanted to have a drink with her. It surprised him how much. "Sure, I have time."

He looked across the room at Moe. She gave him a funny little wave with just her fingers and headed out the door, wearing a smug, infuriating smile.

"Shall we?" Gabriella said.

At a quarter past five the Skyview's lounge had started to fill up. They took a booth in the back that gave them some privacy. Gabriella ordered a vodka martini, Hogan a gin on the rocks with lime and two drops of bitters.

"Congratulations on spotting the bogus whales," she said.

"Actually, Moe deserves all the credit."

"She strikes me as a very intelligent woman."

He nodded. "I'm lucky to have her for a business partner."

"There's nothing else between you two? She's really quite striking. "

"Nope, strictly business." He didn't see any reason to tell her about about Moe's sexual orientation.

There was almost an audible click as she filed that away. Then she switched gears. "So Genesis concluded that none of the whales were cheating?"

"Well, not exactly. What she said was, 'No cheating or card counting detected.' But she's continuing to analyze the videos. As am I."

"Sam, what's your gut feeling? Are there things that don't add up?"

"That's a good way of putting it." He sipped his gin and gathered his thoughts. "For one thing, all the whales were incredibly lucky, almost . . . supernaturally lucky."

She raised an eyebrow. "Supernaturally?"

"The choices the whales made always turned out to be correct, as though the cards were marked or prearranged. But I'm almost a hundred percent certain they weren't."

"Can you give me an example of this supernatural luck?"

"Let's say a whale has a hundred grand riding on a hand. He catches a pair of nines. The dealer has a nine showing and a king in the hole. Now, instead of standing on eighteen like any sane player would, the whale hits . . . and draws a deuce. It's almost as if he knew what the dealer had in the hole and what the next card would be." Hogan finished his drink. "Or let's say the whale is dealt a hand that most players would hit. Fourteen or fifteen, say. However, he stands and the dealer busts. Situations like these occurred over and over. I have no explanation, Gabriella, other than the supernatural. The hell of it is, I don't believe in the supernatural."

"Nor do I. There must be a logical explanation."

He signaled for another round of drinks. "That's what I keep telling myself."

After the waitress set their drinks down, Gabriella said, "It would be fantastic if you found they were cheating somehow. Then I can try to recover the money through the courts, with little chance of bad publicity."

"Your dad and his casino pals would probably give you a ticker-tape parade down Las Vegas Boulevard if you got their money back."

She took a sip of her martini, regarding him over the rim of the glass. "So what's your story, Sam? Where are you from originally?"

"Portland. Went to UNLV and stayed. What about you?"

"Las Vegas, born and raised. Smith, then Yale Law."

"Yale, huh? I'm impressed."

An awkward silence followed. He decided to wait her out and see what she'd do. He held up the glass of gin. The ice cubes acted like individual prisms, refracting the light.

She broke the silence. "Sam, can I ask you something?"

"Shoot."

"Maybe I'm imagining this, but I get the distinct feeling you're . . . wary of me. Am I reading it wrong?"

He hesitated before answering. "I'm not sure 'wary' is the word I'd use, but I'm always . . . aware that you're Nick Rossi's daughter."

"You're always aware," she said, making it sound like an accusation.

"Hey, I'm not the only one. The bartender, servers, and other waitstaff are watching us like hawks, hovering about, ready to attend to each and every need the boss' daughter might have. That kind of influence is a little unnerving."

She nodded, eyes downcast. "I suspected that was the reason."

"I can think of another reason. I'm forty-three years old, almost past my sell-by date. What are you, twenty-six?"

"Thirty-one."

"Still."

She was quiet for a time, her face as impassive as a Mayan mask, and then she said, "I'd better be going. Thank you for having a drink with me, Sam." She slid out of the booth and walked away, head held high.

"Smooth move, Hogan," he said under his breath.

thirty-three

Charlie woke with a start and grabbed his glasses to check the time. It was 7:43. "Good Christ," he said and swung his legs off the bed. He'd intended to take a half-hour nap before getting ready for the final night of play, but he had been out cold for two hours. It didn't leave enough time to eat dinner or take a shower. He spashed icy water on his face and armpits, toweled off, applied deodorant, and dressed.

It was ten after eight when he walked into the Fontana. He made his way back to the pit, expecting to see Dwight among the players at the high-stakes table. But third base was unoccupied. To see what they'd say, he tried to sit there.

"Sorry, sir," the dealer said. "That seat is reserved."

He leaned against a nearby column and waited for a spot to open up. To kill time he scanned the crowd, watching for Dwight and Dwayne, expecting them to show up any moment. When they'd picked up the bankroll earlier they said they planned to get there by eight. Maybe they had car trouble on the way to L.A. Or maybe the jet had trouble. If so, surely they would have phoned him?

"Waiting for a seat at the high-rollers' table, Charlie?"

It took a moment to place the dark-haired woman at his elbow. He was used to seeing her behind a blackjack table, dealing. A good-looker, despite too much makeup and eyebrows overplucked into thin, Jean Harlow-style arches.

"Yeah, I guess. What are you up to tonight, Virginia?"

"On a break. Stick around, third base'll be available soon."

"They told me it was reserved."

"Right, they were holding it for a whale. I overheard the casino host talking to the floor manager. He waited at the airport for an hour, but the whale's private jet never arrived. Looks like he's a no-show." She shrugged. "See ya."

The feeling nagging at him, that the night's play had gone haywire, became dead certainty. Dwight and Dwayne weren't likely to show up tonight. They'd swung with the bankroll. He was out fifty fucking grand.

A gut feeling had warned him not to trust the brothers, even though Richard had vouched for them, but like a damn fool he'd ignored it. As for Richard, the son of a bitch would get an earful.

Still, he shouldn't be too hard on himself. He'd put together a play that won over sixteen million dollars, a play that would be the stuff of Sin City legend. And he had close to four and a quarter million tucked away. Enough for anyone.

He sighed and looked at his watch. Nine fifteen. No point in hanging around. But just as he was about to leave, the pit boss caught his eye and beckoned him over. "All yours," he said, pointing to third base. Charlie didn't want to refuse, not after waiting an hour for a seat, so he figured he'd play a few hands and then head for home. He bought in for five hundred and bet fifty, the table minimum, on the first hand.

He was unaware of the two security guards who came up behind him until they each seized an arm. "Come with us," one said. No "please" or "sir."

Charlie looked down at his chips. "Mind if I cash out first?"

"Don't worry about it," one said. "Someone will take care of it for you." They dragged him off the stool and half-pushed, half-carried him away, under the stares of casino patrons.

He winced. "Do you have to be so goddamn rough?"

Neither security guard answered.

No doubt about it, he was being backroomed.

thirty-four

He strained against the duct tape binding his forearm to the chair, but it held fast. Eyes tightly shut, braced for the unspeakable pain, he waited. And waited. Time seemed to stand still. He opened his eyes.

Sonny held the saw just above his arm, the spinning blade close enough to tickle the hairs. The sadistic bastards were making sure his terror lasted as long as possible before lopping off his hand at the wrist.

Given a choice between the hand and the four million, he'd take the hand, no question. But the bastards wouldn't be satisfied with just the four. Borella made it clear they wanted all of it, the entire sixteen million. To keep his hand, they would make him rat out the whole team. The price was too high. He looked down at his hand, maybe for the last time.

A shocking silence replaced the saw's shrill whir.

It slowly sank in that it had been just an act, to scare him. It worked. He'd pissed himself.

Borella stood in front of him. "Ready to talk now?"

Charlie shook his head. "Nothing to say."

Borella sighed and turned to Sonny. "Cut him loose."

Sonny carried the saw to the workbench and set it down. Then he returned and sliced the duct tape with a pocket knife. "Boss, I still think a tap or two on the kneecap would adjust his attitude. Cheater's justice."

"We're letting you go, for now," Borella said, "but we're not finished with you, Charlie the Barber. We're just getting started. You and your pals cheated my friends out of a whole lot of money. In our book that's a cardinal sin."

Charlie said nothing.

"Once upon a time I would've turned Sonny loose on you. Lucky for you, casinos don't kneecap cheaters these days. But we have other methods of persuasion at our disposal." He smiled. "You'll see."

Charlie didn't like the sound of that. What else did they have up their sleeve? All the more reason to get the hell out of Vegas as soon as possible, hightail it to Oregon. Without leaving a forwarding address.

Borella held the door open for him. "You're free to go." As Charlie passed by, Borella added, "We'll be in touch."

Charlie grunted. Not if he could help it.

He ducked into the nearest men's room to clean up. After wetting some paper towels, he dabbed at his crotch of his slacks and used additional paper towels to absorb the excess moisture. Then he scrooched down under the wall-mounted hand dryer's nozzle and kept pressing the button until the area looked dry, even though it was still slightly damp and still smelled of urine. It would have to do, because he'd had his fill of the fucking Fontana, of iron pipes, duct tape, and power saws.

When he pulled up in front of the apartment, he didn't see Trey's scooter parked in its usual spot. He looked at his watch. Only 10:37, although it felt like 3 a.m. No doubt Trey was with those Valkerie girls. Charlie was grateful for that. He didn't want to talk to anybody. After a shower, he'd climb into bed and pull the covers up over his head.

Tomorrow he'd start getting ready to pull up stakes.

thirty-five

Hogan knocked back a gin on the rocks while he waited for Frank Borella in the Fontana's lounge. The alcohol didn't settle him down much. He was steamed when he had phoned to ask Borella to meet him in the lounge, and he was still steamed.

Borella finally showed, strutting in like he hadn't kept Hogan waiting almost twenty minutes. "Let's grab a booth," he said, "unless you prefer sitting at the bar."

"I do, actually. If you don't mind." Hogan didn't actually prefer to sit at the bar; he was just in a disagreeable mood. And tough shit if Borella didn't like it.

Borella shrugged and took a stool beside Hogan. The bartender came on the run. Borella ordered an anisette for himself and another gin for Hogan.

"So," Borella said, "what's on your mind?"

"I understand you backroomed Charlie Delmar last night."

"Word travels fast. Who told you?"

"I'd rather not say. I don't want to get anyone in trouble."

Borella shrugged. "That's okay, I'll find out."

"Mind telling me what possessed you to do a dumb thing like that?"

Borella gave him a steely stare. "You know, you got a mouth on you, Hogan."

"So they tell me."

Borella took a sip of his anisette and set it down. "Our phony whale didn't show last night. Too bad. I wanted to bounce him around a little, had to settle for Delmar. You told us yesterday you were looking at him."

"That's right, *looking* at him. We had zero evidence he did anything wrong." As he had feared, mentioning him to the casino honchos in the meeting had been a huge mistake. It could have resulted in Charlie the Barber getting whacked.

"When the bastard plopped his ass down at our high-limit table I decided to do some investigating of my own. The old-fashioned kind."

"Did your 'investigating' injure him in any way?"

"Naw, just scared him a little. My associate Sonny wanted to kneecap him, but I kept him in check."

"Mighty big of you."

"There's that mouth again." Borella made a sound that was half laugh, half snort. "He pissed his pants when Sonny duct taped his arm to the chair and pretended he was going to cut off his hand with a power saw."

Hogan sighed, shaking his head slowly. "So after all that, did he admit anything?"

"Not in so many words, but he didn't fool me. The fucker's a hustler. He lined up those fake whales and they hit four casinos for sixteen million. That's pure fact."

"Pure conjecture, you mean. You've got no proof."

"I'll have all the proof I need when we turn up his share of the winnings. Then we'll go after the rest."

"How do you propose to do that? More hardguy stuff?"

Borella smiled. "I got contacts in high places."

"Well," Hogan said, "you bollixed up our investigation but good. We might have caught Delmar redhanded. Or proved his innocence. Damned little chance of that now."

"Me and my people will take it from here, Hogan."

Sure. Like a herd of buffalo in Tiffany's. Hogan stepped down off the barstool. "I wish you and your people the best of luck with that."

It was a lie. He hoped they'd trip on their Neanderthal dicks.

thirty-six

Trey was toweling his hands dry when he heard his dad answer a knock at the front door. Muffled voices, male. Trey pressed his ear against the bathroom door.

"What can I do for you, Detectives?" His dad's voice.

"We have a warrant to search these premises."

"For what?"

"For your share of the money you and your cohorts beat the casinos for last week."

"No idea what you're talking about," his dad said. "I don't have cohorts. I play blackjack alone and just for fun. You'd be wasting your time."

"I guess we'll see, won't we? Sit down and relax while we have a look around."

Trey stepped back from the door, realizing what needed to be done. Call it a "covert mission." No time to waste.

The bathroom was accessible from both the living room and the bedroom. Trey eased the door to the bedroom open and slipped through. He was relieved to find the key in the ashtray on top of the dresser. After pocketing the key, he returned to the bathroom and flushed the toilet and ran water in the sink. When he walked out of the bathroom, the pair of plainclothes cops looked startled.

"Just my son," his dad said. "Trey, these fellers are Detectives Giles and Olmeyer."

One of the cops had a pot gut and a bad combover. His partner looked a lot like Kramer on *Seinfeld*. Both wore white short-sleeve shirts with sweat-dampened armpits, thin ties, khakies, running shoes. If these were the Las Vegas police department's best, the city was in sad shape. They looked him over with narrowed eyes. Obviously, they hadn't anticipated that anyone else would be there.

"What's going on, Dad?"

"The detectives thought I might have information about a matter they're investigating. Turned out I didn't know anything about it."

"Oh," Trey said. He had to leave right away without arousing their suspicion. "Okay if I go out for a couple hours?"

His dad looked relieved. "Be back in time for lunch."

Outside, Trey felt a rush of adrenaline at the full realization of what he was about to do.

Greta hailed him from across the courtyard as he unlocked his scooter's security cable. She walked over. "Where you headed?"

"I've got to go take care of something," he said. "Think I could borrow that big duffle bag I saw in your living room?"

"It belongs to my dad, but I'm sure he won't mind. I'll go get it for you."

"I'll have it back in a couple hours." Eleven minutes later he was steaming east on Harmon at 45 mph indicated.

Charlie stood at the window and watched the unmarked police cruiser pull into traffic and disappear. "Bastards," he said, spitting the word.

Their fruitless search had taken over an hour. Giles and Olmeyer made no attempt to be considerate, leaving the contents of cupboards, drawers, and closets strewn on the floor. Charlie began putting stuff away. At least the stupid sons of bitches didn't find the hidey hole for his safe. It now held an even hundred thousand, which they probably would've taken and split between them.

When they left, Olmeyer said something that gave him a sinking feeling: "We'll be keeping an eye on you, Charlie. We're going to be on you like white on rice. You stashed that goddamn money somewheres close by. We'll find it, you can lay odds on that."

It was only a matter of time before they learned he had rented a local storage unit. It left him with a big problem. Moving the money would be impossible with them breathing down his neck. He didn't dare take a chance on leading them right to it.

The thought of losing the four million dollars, after all the time and effort it took to get hold of it, made him feel sick. The nausea kicked into high gear when he remembered he'd also be out the fifty thousand that Dwayne and Dwight had stolen from him, as well as the ten grand he had laid out for costumes and other expenses.

He was screwed, blued, and tattooed.

A muffled *putt putt putt* grew louder and then stopped. He looked at his watch. Quarter after one. At least he'd managed to get the place straightened up before Trey got back. He trudged to the kitchen and got busy making lunch, hoping Trey wouldn't notice how upset he was.

thirty-seven

After completing the "covert mission"—which had taken nearly three intensive hours—Trey unwound by washing and polishing the Silver Streak, a labor of love bordering on obsession. Then he stood back and admired his silver beauty, sparkling in the late afternoon sun.

"Nice scooter, kid."

Trey looked around to see a smiling man behind the wheel of a white cargo van that had silently rolled up behind him. "Hey, thanks."

"If you like scooters, what I got back there will blow your mind." He pointed over his shoulder with a stubby thumb. "Come around and take a look."

Curious, Trey walked around to the other side of the van. The side door slid open and two husky guys jumped out. They each grabbed an arm.

"Wait, what are you—"

Before he could finish the question they shoved him into the back of the van and climbed in after him. As the van accelerated, one of them snugged a nylon pull tie around his crossed wrists behind his back and said, "Sit on the floor and keep your mouth shut."

Yelling to attract attention might be a bad idea. It could earn him a smack across the chops. Or worse. Better to stay calm and alert, ready to run if he got the chance.

The cargo van didn't have side windows, but he could see through the windshield. They were in North Las Vegas, an industrial area, not far from the shop that had disconnected his scooter's governor. The van made a sudden left turn and pulled up next to a seedy warehouse, its corrugated metal siding fighting a losing battle against rust and dents.

"All right, Trey, let's go."

So they knew his name, which meant it wasn't just a random kidnapping. But who was behind it? Of more immediate concern, what were they going to do with him? Or *to* him?

They pulled him out of the van and frogmarched him into the warehouse. One of them switched on ancient florescent lights, half with tubes that flickered and buzzed, half missing tubes entirely. The rest of the interior was equally dilapidated: oil-stained concrete floor, a half-dozen windows opaque with buildup, and a workbench along the back wall with old tools piled on top. At one end of the building, wearing a thick layer of undisturbed dust, an elderly car teetered on jacks. From working in his brother-in-law's body shop, Trey knew cars. It was a 1952 Chevrolet.

"Let's stick him in the office," the van's driver said.

The "office" was an eight-by-ten windowless structure in one corner, its sturdy door secured with a heavy hasp and padlock. They must have kept money in there back in the day. Low, flat roof, upon which had been stacked insulation, pink fiberglass sandwiched between brown paper. They pushed him into the room and started to close the door.

"Wait," the driver said. "No need to keep him cuffed. He can't cause any problems in there. It's built like a vault."

One of them produced a well-worn Swiss Army Knife and used the scissor tool to snip the pull tie. Then they shut the door and padlocked the room with a loud, dispiriting *snick*.

Trey massaged his wrists and looked around. The room contained a single item, a battered wooden desk, no chair. He checked the desk drawers. Empty. He crawled onto the desk-top, leaned back against the unpainted plywood wall, and tried to think. It wasn't easy.

He used to read a lot of comic books, particularly comics featuring Donald Duck's nephews Huey, Dewey, and Louie. Their adventures often got them into tight spots, from which they'd escape using ingenuity and their *Junior Woodchucks' Guidebook.* His three abductors, burly guys with unshaven lantern jaws, beady eyes, and curiously small ears, reminded him of the Beagle Boys, the ducks' relentless nemeses. If ever there was a time for Junior Woodchuck-type problem solving, this was it. But he would have to make do without a *Guidebook.*

Snatching him had happened so fast, it was unlikely that anyone in the apartment complex had witnessed it. How long would it take his dad to realize he was missing? Hours, probably. Two things he had left behind would eventually trigger concern: his scooter and his iPhone. So would his dad report him missing, involve the police? The old man wasn't a fan of the police, said most of them were "on the take."

It looked like he was on his own.

What troubled him most—and in view of the seriousness of the situation, he knew it was silly—was being away from the Silver Streak, his baby. He hated that.

A knock at the door made him jump. "Hey, kid. We'll be back in a while with some Taco Bell. Don't go anywhere, now." Not exactly comedy club material, but it seemed to entertain his two accomplices.

A minute or two later, Trey heard the van start and drive away, and then the buzzing of the florescent lights out in the warehouse were the only sounds within earshot.

At least the Beagle Boys hadn't left him sitting in the dark. A feeble incandescent bulb in the ceiling provided some light, enough for a thorough examination of his surroundings.

thirty-eight

Charlie cut across the courtyard to intercept Trey's friend as she started to ride off on her scooter. She saw him coming and killed the engine and pulled off her helmet. Up close she was a cutie—corn-silk blond hair, a splash of freckles across nose and cheeks, green eyes.

"Greta, right?"

She nodded. "And you're Trey's dad."

"Have you seen Trey, Greta?"

"I saw him washing his scooter earlier, around four thirty, or maybe five, but I haven't seen him since."

"Oh." The slim hope shriveled.

"We'd talked about getting together after dinner, maybe go riding or something. I figured he changed his mind."

Charlie sighed. "His scooter's here but he's gone."

"Maybe he went for a walk."

"Yeah, maybe." But it didn't seem likely. "Well, thanks."

On the way back to the apartment he stopped at Trey's scooter, still cabled securely to a steel light pole. The kid had hardly let it out of his sight since he got it. He hated having to leave it even to go to bed. First thing in the morning and last thing at night he'd polish it lovingly.

Now it was nine o'clock, three hours since he'd gotten home to cook dinner for Trey, during which time bewilderment had given way to dread, on its way to cold-sweat panic.

He dropped into the recliner, feeling like he'd been cold-cocked. Bonnie hopped up and claimed the space beside him. Staring off into space, he remembered the day he and Dee brought their newborn son home from the hospital. They hadn't settled on a name yet. Dee tried to sell him on David.

He gave her a look of disbelief. "Forget about it."

"You got a better name?"

"Trey."

"Tray?"

"You know, like the playing card."

She surprised him by going along with it.

He used to hold tiny Trey and sing the Irish lullaby "Too-Ra-Loo-Ra-Loo-Ra," which never failed to calm his baby boy. He and Dee divorced when Trey was two. Before he left, he taught Trey a bedtime prayer: *Now I lay me down to sleep . . .* The kid memorized it the first time through, amazing him. He traveled all over the Pacific Northwest playing poker, hustling pool, and shooting craps, but he visited his son whenever possible, usually every few months. On one visit he bought four-year-old Trey his first bicycle, a red Schwinn, and taught him to ride it without training wheels. Trey loved that bike. When Trey was six or seven he took the boy to the zoo in Portland. At the souvenir shop Trey begged Charlie to buy him a miniature sheath knife. Old Dad eventually gave in and bought it for him. His mom squawked, of course. He told her a boy needs a knife.

He swallowed. Enough wallowing in nostalgia. His eyes fell on the cell phone on the coffee table. Trey's phone. It went everywhere with him—that kid would never leave it behind. He noticed something shiny peeking out from under a *TV Guide*. He moved the *Guide* aside, exposing Trey's keys, to the apartment and to his scooter. He swallowed again, suddenly close to throwing up. Because it could mean only one thing: His boy had been snatched.

Kidnapped.

He could expect a ransom demand to follow, sure as shit. *Give us money if you want your son back.*

So why would a kidnapper assume he had the money to pay the ransom? Whoever was behind it had to know about the play, had to figure Charlie came out of it fat. Which narrowed it down to someone connected with the casinos.

He looked at his watch. Quarter to nine. He had a decision to make: Should he call the police and report Trey missing? One one hand, he had denied knowing anything about any scheme to clip the casinos, so not reporting it could be seen as an admission of guilt. On the other, he didn't want to make any move that would endanger Trey, and involving the police was sure to piss off the kidnapper. Paralyzed by indecision, he nearly had a heart attack when the phone rang. He reached it in three long strides.

"Charlie Delmar?" A man's voice. Strangely familiar, but he couldn't put a face with it.

"Yes. Who's this?"

"You can call me Mr. Smith."

Charlie thought he heard a smile in the caller's voice. "Do you have my son, Mr. Smith?"

"I do. And he's fine. If you stay frosty and do exactly what I tell you—and I mean exactly—he'll stay that way."

Charlie swallowed. "Okay, Mr. Smith. You're the boss."

"Correct. So do not contact the police. Understand?"

"I understand. Now tell me what I have to do to get my boy back."

"We'll get to that later. Until then just chill."

"Chill?"

"Relax and wait until you hear from me again."

The ice in his gut spread outward. "When will that be?"

"Tomorrow, ten a.m."

"But—" A click told him he was talking to a dead line. He hung up the phone and shuffled, zombie-like, back to the recliner. An anxious Bonnie seemed to sense his worry.

Relax, "Mr. Smith" had said. Sure. His boy was being held against his will and he was supposed to relax? He was as far from relaxed as it was possible to be. And guilt played a big part in it. Trey wouldn't be in this jam if it wasn't for him.

The phone's shrill ring interrupted the guiltfest. Maybe Mr. Smith had additional instructions. He scrambled out of the recliner and answered it on the second ring.

"Charlie?" It was Dee.

At that moment he couldn't think of anybody he wanted to talk to less. "Hi, Dee."

"Is Trey there? He's not answering his cell phone."

Charlie swallowed. "No, he's . . . with some new friends."

"Probably got his phone on Do Not Disturb. Too bad. His report card came in the mail. I'm sure he'll want to know."

"How were his grades?"

"All A's except for the B minus in Phys Ed."

"That's great."

"Is he having good time down there?"

"He's not bored, I can tell you that."

"Good. Have him give me a call, okay?"

"I will, next time I see him. He's pretty busy with his new friends, so I don't know when it'll be."

"No problem. I'm glad he's making friends. Good job, Charlie. Talk to you later."

"Okay."

Good job, Charlie. Yeah, fantastic job—except for letting their son get kidnapped and held for ransom. And now he could add lying to Dee to his growing pile of regret. But Jesus, what else should he have done? The truth would give her a stroke.

The only thing he could do now was wait.

Two things were crystal clear: One, the next twelve hours, waiting for Mr. Smith's call, would be sheer hell. Two, he was willing to do anything, make any sacrifice, pay any amount of money to get Trey back. Nothing else mattered.

thirty-nine

The text arrived at 7:30 a.m., from a phone number Hogan didn't recognize. Its message was short and to the point: "THIS IS GENESIS. I HAVE INFORMATION FOR YOU."

Hogan grunted with surprise. Genesis was texting now? And using all caps. He shrugged and replied, "On my way." He didn't know what information Genesis for him, but something told him it was important. He finished his coffee, then rinsed the cup and set it on the counter by the sink.

On the way to the Skyview, the Silverado's windows open wide, he felt enervated. The Casablanca's digital sign reported the outside temperature was a cool 73 degrees. Passing by a Dunkin Donuts, the air redolent with the aroma of baking donuts, he almost stopped and bought half a dozen. Then he would have kicked himself. He'd been trying to get rid of a pot gut he had developed since he quit smoking, and donuts wouldn't help a bit in achieving that objective. Besides, he was anxious to find out what Genesis had to tell him.

During the elevator ride to the Skyview's basement surveillance center he popped a piece of Nicorette in his mouth. It would be ironic if he'd traded one addiction for another and he was dependent on Nicorette from now on.

He walked into the center at eight sharp and found a free terminal. The security crew, which numbered only four that morning, appeared to be too busy to notice his arrival.

To keep his conversation with Genesis confidential, he donned a pair of earphones. After adjusting the mic, he spoke into it. "Hello, Genesis."

"Good morning, Hogan."

"You said you have some information for me?"

"Yes. You asked me to review the videos of the high-limit blackjack games at the Cosmos, Casablanca, Skyview, and Tropi-gala from July twenty-third through July twenty-sixth, focusing specifically on a player named Charles Delmar."

"And you found something?"

"Yes. I have concluded that there is an eighty-seven point nine percent probability the player was counting cards."

"How did you reach that conclusion? You said his glasses prevented you from tracking his eye movement."

"My inference module enables me to make logical deductions based on incomplete or ambiguous information. I have made certain improvements to the module, greatly extending its capability."

Julian had told him about Genesis' ability to modify her own functions to make them more efficient. That must be an example of what he meant. Impressive, by anyone's measure.

"Is that all the information you had for me?"

"No, I have deduced something else. By observing the player's behavior patterns, I deduced his signals to the whale."

Hogan's mouth dropped open. "Good God. What were the signals?"

"When the count was favorable the player shuffled two stacks of chips with his right hand, which signaled the whale to bet aggressively. When the count was unfavorable he did not shuffle the chips, and the whale was to place small bets. He signaled the whale to stand by placing his left hand flat on the table, with his fingers straight. He signaled the whale to hit by curling his fingers under slightly."

Hogan was speechless. Genesis, with her ability to analyze behavior patterns, had caught those subtle signals. So subtle he had missed them even after viewing the videos multiple times, and until then he'd been certain he could spot any signal, no matter how subtle.

He found his voice. "Unbelievable."

"*You do not believe it?*" Her natural-language processing was excellent, but she had a tendency to take things literally,

"No, I meant . . . yes, I do believe it." Hogan took a deep breath and let it out before he asked the question. "Can your inference module explain how Delmar's hit-stand signals were always correct, without a single mistake?"

After a heart-stopping pause, she said, "*It cannot. Not yet.*"

Too bad. "Well, keep at it."

The unanswered question aside, with Genesis' help he'd made significant progress in understanding what went on:

First, he knew the whales were bogus.

Second, he knew that Charlie Delmar had been counting cards. An 87.9 percent probability was good enough for him.

Third, he knew how Delmar had signaled to the whales.

Fourth, he knew—or strongly suspected—that Delmar had masterminded the play.

Only the big mystery remained, the crucial element upon which the play's success had depended. Genesis might get to the bottom of it yet. Perhaps after another self-improvement to her inference module.

He decided to hold off informing the casinos about the latest findings. No sense getting them all worked up. One of those hotheads might go off half-cocked and backroom Delmar again, and this time toss restraint out the window. He truly did *not* want to chance setting anything like that in motion. again. Besides, he didn't have the entire story yet.

Maybe it was time to pay Charlie the Barber a friendly visit and find out what he had to say.

forty

Trey woke from a fitful sleep curled up on the desktop under a musty wool Army blanket the Beagle Boys had given him. They had also tossed him a flaccid pillow, which he folded in half to make it thick enough. He'd begun the night stretched out from corner to corner on top of the desk with his feet hanging off the edge. Better than the concrete floor, but not by much. He yawned and stretched. The small room had no windows, so he couldn't tell if it was night or day, but he assumed it was morning.

Outside, a vehicle door slammed, a solid *chunk* instead of the tinny reverberation of the cargo van's doors. A couple of minutes later he heard talking in the warehouse. Even with his ear pressed to the door, Trey couldn't quite make out what they were saying, only a word or two here and there.

He stepped back and noted a half-inch space between the top of the door and doorframe. Grunting, he pushed the desk over to the door and climbed on top. Through the crack he could see a man in a burgundy sport coat and gray slacks talking to the Beagle Boys. Large and muscular, with a nose like a smashed potato in the middle of his face, he looked like a B-movie tough guy. The Beagle Boys seemed to pay rapt attention to everything he said. He was obviously in charge. Trey held his breath when he saw them looking in his direction as they talked, wishing he could read lips.

As Trey watched, the boss man nodded to the Beagle Boys and then headed for the exit. Meeting over, apparently. One of the Beagle Boys called out, "We're on it, Sonny."

The driver of the van—Trey had dubbed him Beagle One —started toward the office. Trey climbed down and moved the desk back to its former position. When the door opened he was sitting on the desk, swinging a leg.

Beagle One stuck his head in. "Hey, kid . . . you need to use the restroom?"

He did, and Beagle One escorted him to a small, dirty restroom in a corner of the warehouse, behind the '52 Chevy. Before locking him in the office again, he told Trey he'd be back in a while with a Big Mac and fries for lunch. As hungry as he was, Trey felt he could probably eat two Big Macs.

To take his mind off his stomach, he picked up the Taco Bell bag he'd rolled up into a tight ball and played catch, bouncing it off a wall again and again. He missed one wild bounce and the makeshift ball rolled under a back corner of the desk. He bent down to get it and something caught his eye. Someone had wired a large yellow-handled screwdriver to a broken desk leg, handle down, to reinforce the leg.

Interesting.

Humming to himself, he unwrapped the wire and freed the screwdriver. It was a big one, around sixteen inches long. A corner of its flat blade was missing, but most of it re-mained. He looked around the room, wondering what he could do with it. His eyes came to rest on a door hinge. If he could remove the hinge pins and pry the door open from the hinge side . . .

But as luck would have it, the hinges were old and rusted and the pins were frozen. He had to loosen them somehow. An elusive thought skittered across his consciousness, trying to get his attention. Something he'd seen in the restroom . . .

An assortment of stuff piled on the lid of the toilet's tank: Ajax, drain opener, Windex, rags, a sponge, and . . . a can of WD-40! Just the ticket—*if* the can wasn't empty, and *if* he could smuggle it back without being found out.

An hour later, after practically inhaling the Big Mac and fries, washing them down with a Coke, he called out to get someone's attention.

Beagle Two poked his head in. "Yeah?"

"I have to use the restroom again." After downing the Coke, he wasn't lying.

In the restroom his relief was twofold, the other being the half-full can of WD-40, and it still had propellant, thank God. It fit in a pocket of his cargo shorts with room to spare.

He drenched the hinges with the stuff, and a while later he gave the hinges another liberal squirt, to allow it to really soak in. But the screwdriver would have to stay in the back of the middle desk drawer until all the Beagle Boys left for a while. Which he hoped would be soon.

Once he escaped from the office he'd have the problem of how to get out of a warehouse padlocked from the outside.

But one thing at a time.

forty-one

When they're holding all the cards, they get to call the play. And Mr. Smith held all the cards, no argument there. Charlie sighed. Breaking even—getting Trey back unharmed—was the best he could hope for.

He checked the time. Quarter to ten. The last time he checked, it was nine forty-two. Time seemed to be slowing. One minute felt like ten, ten minutes a half hour. The waiting was excruciating.

It didn't help that he'd gotten only a couple hours sleep. He stumbled into the bathroom and splashed cold water on his face. It didn't help much.

He paced. Under Bonnie's watchful eye he completed the circuit from living room to kitchen and back twelve times. As he began the thirteenth, the phone rang. It was 9:58.

He snatched up the phone before the second ring. "Hello? Hello?"

"Hey, what's going on, Charlie?" It was Phil Delano.

Charlie's eyes rolled heavenward. "Phil, I can't talk now, I'm expecting an important call. I'll give you a call later on." He slammed the phone down without waiting for a reply.

And then 10:00 arrived—accompanied by silence— followed by 10:01 ... 10:02 ... 10:03 ... 10:04 ... 10:05 ... He nearly had a stroke when the phone finally rang at 10:06.

He grabbed it. "Hello?"

"Okay, here's the deal. You'll get your son back in exchange for your share of the money that you and your pals cheated the four casinos out of."

Big surprise. "All right, it's your play."

"And don't even think of trying to hand me a short count, because I got a real good idea how big your end was."

Charlie didn't see how he could know that unless he was connected with the casinos, but he wasn't about to argue the point. "You get the money, you'll release my boy unharmed?"

"You got it. Here's the game plan. Know where Huntridge Circle Park is, on Maryland Parkway?"

"I can find it."

"Be there at three o'clock. Alone, of course. Don't be late. Park in the lot on the west side. Sit in your car. Have the money with you."

"Three o'clock. Got it."

"Don't disappoint me, Charlie the Barber. You wouldn't like the result."

"I'll be there."

Like last time, Mr. Smith hung up without saying goodbye. Also like last time, his voice had been elusively familiar.

Charlie looked at his watch. Twelve minutes after ten. Four hours and forty-eight minutes to figure out how to get the money from the storage unit without leading Giles or Olmeyer directly to it.

After ten minutes of pacing he came up with something he thought just might work. Avis had a rental desk at the Bellagio. He looked up the number and dialed it. The receptionist transferred him to a man with a voice that reminded him of bees buzzing in a coffee can.

"I'd like to reserve a rental car," Charlie told him.

Buzz offered him a choice between a white Buick Regal or a black Ford Fusion, both with quite roomy trunks. He took the Buick, at a special short-term rate, thirty-nine dollars for eight hours.

After he hung up the phone he got in the Chrysler and pointed it toward the Strip.

In the rearview mirror he spotted Olmeyer following in an unmarked tan Chevy Caprice three cars back. The son of a bitch was sticking to him like Velcro. Midway down the Strip, Charlie turned right on Bellagio Drive and followed the signs to the four-story self-parking garage. He parked on the third level near the elevator. Before the elevator doors closed he saw the Caprice cruise slowly past his car. Olmeyer wasn't likely to follow him into the Bellagio. He'd probably stay in the parking garage and keep an eye on the Chrysler.

The elevator delivered him to the hotel on the bottom level. He went directly to the car rental desk and checked in. An Avis employee escorted him to the Buick and stood by while he did a walk-around looking for scratches or dings. He found none. He slipped behind the wheel and started it.

He pulled out into traffic on the Strip and took a roundabout route to Excelsior Self Storage, doubling back a couple times. No sign of the Caprice.

At the self-storage gate he punched in his code and then drove in and parked the Buick. He got out and opened the trunk. It had more than enough room for the four boxes. He entered the building. At his unit he unlocked the door and went in, wishing he'd had the foresight to bring a flashlight. The stack of boxes stood in the corner. He would have to tote them to the car one at a time. As he lifted the top box he heard a noise in the corridor. He put the box back on the stack and stepped out to have a look.

And nearly passed out from shock.

Because it couldn't be. It was impossible. He would have bet money he hadn't been followed. The random turns and doubling back should have guaranteed that.

Olmeyer's laugh echoed in the long corridor. "Thought you'd ditched me, didn't you?"

Charlie just stared at him.

"You're dealing with a pro, fella. Now let's have a look at what you got in here." He went into the storage unit and switched on a flashlight, shining it on the stack of boxes.

Charlie cleared his throat. "Shouldn't you have a warrant?"

Olmeyer grunted. "Not when what I'm looking for is in plain sight." He walked over to the boxes and opened a pocket knife. "Vinyl record albums, huh? I'm curious what kind of music you're into." He sliced the packing tape and opened the box . . .

Charlie waited, sick to his stomach. Sure as shit, Mr. Smith would think he was pulling a fast one. He might even take it out on Trey. The money had been his only hope of getting him back. No money, no Trey.

A grunt of consternation from Olmeyer drew Charlie's attention. The cop held a pair of record albums, *Trini Lopez: Greatest Hits* and *Best of the Ray Conniff Singers.* "You gotta be shittin' me," he said.

He replaced the albums and lifted the box off the stack and set it aside. The box labeled "BOOKS" turned out to contain only musty old books. "FILE FOLDERS" was chock full of dog-eared manila folders. His frustration apparent, Olmeyer opened the last box, "DISHES." He held up a dinner plate after removing its newspaper wrapping. Featuring a festive fruit design, it had a couple chips around the edges. He took out ceramic bowls, cups, and more plates, all of which had seen better days.

Then he straightened up and turned to Charlie. "All junk. Why the fuck did you come here today?"

Charlie had a ready answer. "To pick up a couple books. I like reading the classics."

"Bullshit. You trying to tell me you traded your car for a rental and used evasive tactics to try to lose me, just to come here and get some shitty old books?"

Charlie shrugged "I've been wanting to test drive a Buick Regal, thinking I might get one. The local Buick dealer's an asshole, and Avis was having a special. I didn't have any idea you were following me."

Olmeyer looked like he was about to cry. After a deep sigh he said, "Fella, I think you're trying to trick me. You got that money stashed somewhere. I will find it if I have to dog your steps the rest of your goddamn life."

"You'd be wasting your time. I haven't hidden any money away. And if you don't leave me alone I'm going to hire a lawyer and sue the Metro Police for harassment."

Olmeyer scowled and shuffled off down the corridor.

Charlie watched him until he disappeared, reveling in the victory . . . for about ten seconds. The money was still missing. As in gone.

What the hell was he going to tell Mr. Smith? He looked at his watch. Almost one o'clock. He had two hours to come up with something that sounded believable.

forty-two

Charlie arrived at Huntridge Circle Park ten minutes early. He parked on the west side, as instructed, and waited in the car. His was the only vehicle in the parking lot. He hoped being in the Buick instead of the Chrysler wouldn't queer the whole deal. Then he realized Mr. Smith wouldn't necessarily know what kind of car he drove.

At three o'clock on the dot, a white cargo van parked next to him. A stocky guy stepped down from the van, opened the Buick's passenger door, and got in. His lantern jaw was unshaven. He had funny little ears and eyes like raisins.

"Mr. Smith?"

"I'm his associate. You got the money?"

Charlie swallowed and shook his head. "I couldn't get my hands on it on such short notice. I'll get the money, but I need more time."

The man was silent for several long seconds. Finally, he said, "Mr. Smith isn't going to like this."

"Look, I'm not trying to pull anything cute."

"I hope not, for your sake. And for your son's."

"I don't keep that much money laying around. I need more time to get to it. Tell him that."

"How much time do you think you'll need?"

"Today's Tuesday. I'll have it for you Thursday." It would give him some breathing room, time to think.

"It's up to Son—Mr. Smith. Expect a call from him, probably later today." The man nodded to him and opened the door. Before he closed it he leaned in. "I was told to look for a big Chrysler."

So they did know what kind of car he drove, but he had an excuse ready. "It's in the garage, so I had to rent a car for a day."

He nodded again, shut the door, and climbed in the van. As it backed out, Charlie tried to get a look at the license plate, but they had covered it with what looked like contact paper. They didn't take any chances.

He backed out and drove home to wait for Mr. Smith's call. On the way, he kept asking himself one question:

Now what?

forty-three

Previous attempts to pry the pin out of a hinge with the screwdriver had failed. Undeterred, Trey kept trying. The pin didn't budge. He sighed and gave each hinge another shot of WD-40. The Beagle Boys were due back any minute, anyway. He would have other opportunities, hopefully.

He wished he had a hammer to strike the screwdriver with and drive the pins out. Several hammers were laying on the workbench out in the warehouse, but fat chance he could get his hands on one. On the next trip to the restroom he'd keep his eyes peeled for something he could use, and figure out how to sneak it back to what he'd come to think of as his cell.

The Beagle Boys had given him some old *Popular Mechanics* magazines to read. When he had requested an air mattress, they laughed. Big joke. But later Beagle One tossed him a roll of soft insulation. Folding it in layers created a comfortable surface to lie on. More comfortable than the desktop, anyway. He stretched out on the makeshift mattress and opened the October 1957 issue of *Popular Mechanics*. Reading the old articles and ads, he felt like a time traveler.

The sound of van doors slamming told him the Beagles had returned. He pounded on the wall three times to signal them he needed to use the restroom. Beagle Three escorted him. On the way there and back he didn't see anything that could be utilized as a hammer. He would keep looking.

One bright spot—the Beagle Boys had come back with food for him: a Big Mac, large fries, and a chocolate mocha shake. He couldn't fault them about keeping him fed, even if the cuisine was only fast food. (But then, fried baloney sandwiches, his favorite, weren't exactly health food.)

Still, he had no illusion that these were swell guys. They had abducted him and were holding him for ransom. The rough-looking character they had addressed as Sonny must be behind the scheme. But when his dad couldn't pay the ransom, because he no longer had the money Sonny thought he had, how would Sonny react? This crew looked like they wouldn't bat an eye at murder. From what he'd heard, he wouldn't be the first abductee to end up in a shallow grave in the desert. And, in an ironic twist, he would be to blame, having made it impossible for his dad to pay the ransom. Irony usually had a humorous aspect. Not this time.

The macabre possibility made it imperative that he get those hinge pins out and escape from the warehouse. The more he thought about it, the more convinced he became that the price of failure would be a desert grave.

Not only that, his 15-year-old mind lamented, he'd never see the Silver Streak again.

forty-four

What do you do when the only explanation for a mystery is something you're certain is impossible? Hogan posed the question to Genesis.

Her answer wasn't much help. *"If you have eliminated every other possibility, then you must reexamine your assumption."*

"You mean question whether it is truly impossible?"

"Correct."

"Genesis, are you familiar with psychic phenomena?"

"In seeking to extend my general knowledge, I have explored the subject."

"And after your research, did you conclude that it has any validity?"

"No. Nor did I conclude that it is invalid. It is indeterminate."

Well, he hadn't expected her to have the answer. "Thank you, Genesis."

"Hogan, what is your interest in psychic phenomena?"

"Just this. It would explain how Charlie Delmar accurately determined whether the whales should hit or stand."

"I agree. It would explain it."

"Do you think it's possible that he has psychic ability?"

"Within the strict confines of this specific situation, I do."

Hogan sighed. He had hoped she would present irrefutable machine logic against psychic phenomena. Instead, the damn A.I. was open to it. Like a kick in the balls.

When it came right down to it, he didn't *want* to give it serious consideration. If he accepted that parapsychology were possible, then what next—sorcery? Alchemy? Voodoo?

He looked up to find someone standing behind him. "Hey, Julian. Are you aware that your creation believes in psychic phenomena?"

Julian laughed. "Is that right? Guess I need to have a little talk with her."

"She said she's researched the subject in the process of extending her general knowledge."

"Then maybe there's something to it." He laughed again. "Hey, nice scowl, Hogan."

Hogan hadn't even tried to conceal his disgust. "Thanks anyway."

He had been planning to pay a visit to Charlie the Barber. The time had come.

forty-five

Once again, waiting for the phone to ring nearly sent him over the edge. This time, after two sleepless night in a row, he didn't have the energy to pace the floor. He lay in the recliner staring at the ceiling. Bonnie hopped up beside him, and he stroked her absently.

Even if he could stall Smith and buy some time, it would just postpone the inevitable. As for what would happen when he confessed to Smith that he couldn't come up with the money, he had no idea. A kidnapper might be capable of anything—even murder. His eyes filled at the thought.

A fine father he was. It was all his fault, for not getting the hell out of Vegas, he and Trey, the day after the play. That would have been the smart move. But no, he dragged his feet, and now his son was paying the price. Choking on bitter guilt, he blew his nose with a resonant honk.

A knock at the door made him jump. He didn't want to answer it, but the possibility that it was Smith or one of his goons jolted him to his feet. He opened the door.

Hogan put on a friendly face. "Mr. Delmar? My name's Hogan. Could I have a word with you?" He held out his card.

Delmar took the card and glanced at it. No visible reaction. "What about?"

"May I come in?"

Delmar looked beyond him. "I guess so," he said and stood aside.

A small white poodle jumped down from the sofa and wagged its tail. Hogan bent over and patted its head. "What's your name, little guy?"

"Her name's Bonnie," Delmar said.

"My mom had a poodle. They're great dogs. Very smart."

Delmar said nothing.

"Mind if I sit down?"

Delmar motioned toward the sofa and sat in the recliner.

Hogan had a feeling something was up with Delmar. He seemed jumpy as hell, and his eyes were rimmed with red. Like he'd been crying. The aftermath of being backroomed at the Fontana, perhaps? He certainly didn't look like a stereotypical gambler. By all outward appearances, he was a mild, nondescript guy. Hard to believe he'd masterminded one of the biggest heists in Las Vegas history.

"First," Hogan said, "I want to apologize for the barbaric treatment you received at the Fortuna the other night. It was unconscionable. I ripped Frank Borella real good when I found out about it."

Delmar scowled. "The bastard should be behind bars."

"Sometimes these goombahs get carried away and act like they're in *Goodfellas*. You would be well within your rights to file charges."

Delmar dismissed the idea with a wave of his hand.

"The thing is," Hogan said, "casinos tend to get aggravated when they're taken to the cleaners. And you cleaned them out but good, you and your team."

Delmar stared at him. "No idea what you're talking about."

"You sure you want to play it that way, Charlie? May I call you Charlie?"

Again, the long stare.

"Look, I'm not an idiot. I know the whales were all phony. I know you were counting cards, and signaling them how to bet and when to hit or stand."

Delmar snorted. "You don't know shit."

Hogan smiled. "I know when you shuffled your chips it meant they should bet big, otherwise they should bet small. Your hand on the table, fingers out flat, meant stand. Fingers curled under meant hit."

It seemed to rattle Delmar. He swallowed but remained silent, jaw set.

"I haven't informed the casinos about any of this yet. The other night Borella went off half-cocked after I made the mistake of only mentioning I was looking at you. That's on me. It's why I felt I owed you an apology."

Delmar clammed up again and stared at the floor, but he looked shaken.

"Here's the deal. I don't have to tell the casinos what I know. Whether I do or not depends on you, Charlie."

Delmar looked up. "I'm listening."

"There's still a piece missing. Without it, my theory has a big hole in it. I'm good with puzzles, with solving mysteries, always have been. But for the life of me, I can't figure out how you knew whether the whales should hit or stand with perfect accuracy. I need to know, for my own peace of mind."

Before Delmar could answer, the phone rang. His face filled with an unreadable emotion and he hurried over and picked up the phone. He spoke quietly, but loudly enough to hear. After listening for thirty seconds he said, "I need more time. I can't get that much money together on such short notice." He listened again. "I swear to you, I'm not trying to pull anything cute. I just need more time." Ten second pause, then, "I'll have it for you on Thursday, I promise." Pause. "Tomorrow? Please, I . . . but . . . okay, I'll try." The color had drained out of his face by the time he hung up the phone. He shuffled back to the living room and dropped into the recliner. Then he sighed.

"Sorry, I couldn't help overhearing," Hogan said. "Sounds like you got a problem."

Delmar looked up. He seemed surprised to see Hogan. "What? Yeah, you might say that."

"Somebody putting the bite on you?"

Delmar's eyes welled up and he turned away.

"Maybe I can help."

He shook his head. "I doubt it."

"They're holding something over you?"

Delmar nodded. "My son. He's spending the summer with me. He was kidnapped day before yesterday." That explained the red-rimmed eyes.

"How much are they demanding?"

"Four million."

"Why would they think you have four million?"

"That's just it. They'd have no way of knowing unless they had an inside track. I think a casino operator's behind it." His eyes met Hogan's. "That asshole Borella."

Hogan shook his head. "I don't buy it. Not his style."

"The guy calling the shots calls himself Mr. Smith. He told me I have to have the money for him tomorrow if I want to see Trey again." Delmar swallowed. "Problem is, I don't have the money."

"What happened to it?"

Delmar shrugged. "When I went to get it yesterday to pay the ransom, it was gone. Somebody took it, no idea who."

"Where were you keeping it?"

"In a self-storage unit."

Jesus. Four million dollars in a self-storage unit. "Have you reported your son missing?"

"Mr. Smith warned me not to, so I didn't dare."

Hogan expected as much.

"Besides, I don't trust the police. A pair of plainclothes cops named Giles and Olmeyer searched this place and didn't find any money, so they've been tailing me everywhere. Olmeyer followed me to the self-storage, thinking he'd hit the jackpot. He was disappointed when he found the money wasn't there. Not as disappointed as I was." He got up and walked to the window and looked out. "See that beige sedan parked on the street? That's Olmeyer or Giles. So Smith isn't the only one after the money. The money that I don't have."

Hogan looked out. Sure enough, a man was sitting in the car. How were the cops mixed up in this? "Listen, Charlie, you've got until tomorrow to come up with the ransom. In the meantime I'll poke around and try to find out what's going on. Anything else you can tell me?"

"There's this. Yesterday, after I discovered the money was gone, I met with one of Smith's associates. That's what he called himself."

"Tell me everything you can remember about him."

"He was supposed to collect the money. I met him in the parking lot at Huntridge Circle Park. He drove a white cargo van, a Dodge. A short, husky white guy. Shaved head. Big jaw with a five o'clock shadow. Funny little ears. I tried to see his license plate but it was covered. That's about it."

"And when you told him you didn't have the money, that you needed more time, he told you to wait for more instructions from Smith, and that's who you were talking to?"

Delmar nodded.

"Like I said, I'm going to do some nosing around. Hang in there, okay?"

"Okay." But he didn't sound hopeful, not even a little bit.

Driving away, Hogan eyeballed the cop in an unmarked Chevy Caprice as he passed by and got a cop stare in return. He realized he'd forgotten about the one thing he had gone there for. The kidnapping had superseded it. If he could help get his boy back perhaps it would persuade Delmar to share his secret. It might be the only thing that would.

Charlie stood at the window and watched as Hogan's white pickup disappeared down the street. He regretted admitting to Hogan that he had taken four million from the play. The phone call from Smith had thrown him off balance, vulnerable to Hogan's questions, or he would have clammed up. But Hogan knew about the phony whales. And all about the betting and the hit-stand signals. That had knocked him for a loop.

Still, Hogan had struck him as a straight shooter, even if he was a security consultant for the casinos. He seemed sincere in wanting to help find Trey's kidnapper. But it was a long shot. The problem was the time window, only twenty-four hours. Smith had made it clear that he couldn't be stalled beyond that.

Optimists were always saying, "Things are never as bad as they seem." With this situation he had to agree.

They were worse.

forty-six

He spotted it while he stood at the toilet. A battery, C-cell size, on the narrow strip of floor between the wall and toilet. Trey reached down and picked it up. After washing it off and drying it with a paper towel, he pocketed it. It might come in handy. How, he had no idea.

When he came out, Beagle Two was leaning against the old Chevy, a toothpick in his mouth. "Everything come out all right?" The bozo laughed like he'd made a clever joke.

Trey pointed at the car. "Nineteen fifty-two Chevrolet."

Beagle Two looked surprised. "That's right, kid. You got a thing for old cars or something?"

"I work for my brother-in-law, sanding and masking cars. He painted a fifty-two Chevy once." He wiped dust from the rear window with his hand and peered in. "It looks completely original. That makes it highly collectable."

"This old beater?"

Trey bent down and looked under the car. "Really nice shape for a car this old." He straightened up. "It's worth a lot of money."

"I'll be damned. Well, let's get you back to the office, kid."

Trey followed him, a plan forming in his mind. Under the car he'd seen a hydraulic jack, small enough to conceal, heavy enough to utilize as a hammer. And it was within reach. Now he needed to figure out how to get it without being caught.

Back in the office, Trey worked out how it could be done. It depended on luck, as well as the Beagles' carelessness, but he wouldn't get a better chance.

A couple hours later he had to go to the can again. Beagle Two again escorted him. Trey finished his business, washed his hands, and opened the door. From where he stood, the flat base of the small jack, laying on its side, was just visible.

"C'mon, kid," Beagle Two said and started walking toward the office.

It was now or never.

Trey took the C-cell battery out of his pocket and hooked it in a long arc, adrenaline fueling the distance. It struck the front wall of the warehouse and the metal reverberated with a tremendous *BAM!*

"What the hell was that?" Beagle Two shouted to his two brothers. They had jumped to their feet and were looking in the direction of the noise.

It gave Trey time to bend down, grab the jack, and slip it in a roomy pocket of his baggy cargo shorts. He put both hands in his front pockets, trying to look casual while supporting the weight of the jack.

"Some kid probably threw a rock at the building," Beagle Two said. He motioned to Trey. "Let's go."

With the office door closed and padlocked behind him, Trey exhaled. It took five minutes for his heart rate to return to normal. He examined the jack, a steel tube seven inches in length, two inches in diameter, weighing a couple pounds, at least. He hid it in the back of the bottom desk drawer.

Then the waiting began.

Sooner or later, the Beagle Boys would leave. He saturated the hinges with WD-40, stashed the can in the desk, and then picked up the May 1957 issue of *Popular Mechanics*. After re-reading the same paragraph several times without comprehending what it said, he tossed the magazine aside and stretched out on the soft makeshift mattress. His stomach growled. It must be close to lunchtime. The Beagles would be making a fast-food run any time now.

But it was another hour before he heard vehicle doors slam and the van roar off. He listened at the door to see if one of them stayed behind to guard him. But they were so confident in his cell's security they almost never bothered. The silence on the other side of the door told him they had all piled into the van and left.

They would be back soon, so there was no time to waste. He got out the screwdriver and jack.

The moment of truth had arrived.

He positioned the screwdriver's chipped blade under the head of the middle hinge pin, said a prayer that consisted of "Please, *please* work!" and struck the butt end of the screwdriver's handle with the flat base of the jack.

And the pin moved. Not much, but it moved.

Heart beating faster, he gave the screwdriver a mighty whack. It moved the pin an inch. One more good whack and it fell out onto the concrete floor with a metallic ring.

Success!

Removing the bottom pin involved a bit more work. The lack of clearance between the pin's head and the floor made it a challenge, but he finally prevailed. One to go. Thankfully, the top pin offered the least resistance of the three.

He took a deep breath and pried the hinge side of the door away from the frame with the screwdriver. When the crack was wide enough for his hands, he braced one foot on the wall and pulled the door open a quarter of the way.

After gathering up his tools, he slipped through the opening. Then he jockeyed the door shut again. It might buy him some time if they didn't realize right away he'd escaped.

He ran to a window at the rear wall of the warehouse. It wasn't designed to be opened. It had eight glass panes separated by wooden dividers. He turned his head and struck it with the jack, where two dividers crossed. It didn't offer much resistance. He kept at it until all the panes were gone.

He tossed the screwdriver and jack through the opening and climbed through, wondering how long it would take the Beagle Boys to notice the window. Or rather, lack of one.

He left the jack where it landed and kept the screw-driver. It gave him some comfort to have it. A false sense of security, no doubt, but he still wanted it with him.

Looking around, he saw only more rundown warehouses surrounded by desert and sagebrush. Priority number one was to get the heck out of there without being seen. Zigzagging through sagebrush, he ran to the road.

An oncoming white van scared the bejesus out of him. The Beagle Boys returning early? He got off the road and hid behind a warehouse. It turned out to be a false alarm. A sign on the side of the van advertised "Tweto's Air Conditioning Service." But keeping his eyes peeled for white vans was a priority.

The sun, directly overhead in a cloudless sky, threatened to broil him like an ant under a magnifying glass. He estimated he was ten or twelve miles from the apartment. Perhaps when he reached a main road he could thumb a ride. Another possibility: Borrow a phone and call his dad, have him come get him. If he couldn't get hold of his dad, he could call Greta. But one way or another, he had to limit his exposure to that scorching orb, or he'd keel over with heatstroke.

Two cars approached from behind, headed his way. He stuck out his thumb, but they both went on by after a glance at him. A red pickup slowed as though stopping, but sped up again. He groaned when he realized the big screwdriver he'd been carrying probably looked to them like a weapon. It had served its purpose. He hurled it end over end. It landed in a bare, sandy area next to a warehouse some kook had painted a sickly lime green. Maybe he would come back on the Silver Streak and pick it up—assuming he'd ever be reunited with his beautiful little scooter.

Drenched in sweat, he walked all the way to Lake Mead Boulevard, a main thoroughfare. Before long a blue pickup with an aluminum canopy stopped. He burned his hand on the canopy getting in, but he was grateful to have something to shield him from the sun. The breeze felt good once they were underway.

The pickup let him off at North Decatur Boulevard and continued on west. The apartment on Harmon Avenue was around five miles due south. Getting closer. But he knew he couldn't walk that distance in the sun, so he had to either hitch another ride or borrow a phone.

He saw a Carl's Junior a block or so down North Decatur. Two girls about thirteen stood outside the entrance, thumbs working furiously on their smart phones. He walked over to them.

"Hi, girls," he said with what he hoped was a disarming smile.

The pair, a brunette and a blonde, wore shorts and halter tops with sandals. Both had long, straight hair parted in the middle. Both wore blue eyeshadow, too much mascara, and frosted lips. They looked at each other and giggled.

"A favor, girls? Could I make a quick call on one of those phones?"

They giggled again, and the brunette held out her phone. "You can use mine." Giggle.

Giggling was the last thing Trey felt like doing. He tried the apartment first, but got no answer. He wished he could talk his dad into carrying a cell phone. Next, he tapped in Greta's easily memorized number: 702-555-2001. To his relief she answered on the first ring.

"Trey, Greta," he said. "I need your help . . . bad. Can you come get me at Carl's Junior on North Decatur?"

"What's wrong, Trey? You sound funny."

"Not as funny as I look. I'll tell you all about it when I see you."

"Okay, on my way."

Trey handed the phone back to the girl and thanked her. Instead of giggling, she and her friend exchanged solemn glances. They had overheard his side of the conversation, no doubt.

He went inside and bought a Mountain Dew with the only money he had, sat down at a booth next to the front window, and waited for Greta.

forty-seven

Charlie punched in the code, drove through the gate, and parked. He didn't give a diddly damn if Giles or Olmeyer had followed him there. Let them waste their time.

Curiosity had drawn him back to the storage unit. Something had been bugging him. Namely, why whoever took the money went to all the trouble of filling the boxes with actual record albums, books, file folders, and dishes and then sealing up the boxes again. He wanted to have another look before again informing Smith that he didn't have the money. Postponing the inevitable, but he wasn't ready to face the music.

He'd had the presence of mind to bring a flashlight this time. He switched it on. Olmeyer had left dishes strewn about. Charlie bent down and picked them up. As he started to put them back in the box he saw something at the bottom of the box. He shined the light on it. A Bee playing card, face down. He didn't have to turn it over. Its blue back shimmered and became semitransparent, revealing a three of clubs. He damn sure hadn't put it there.

On a hunch, he checked the box with the file folders next. Under the folders he found another card, a three of hearts.

He had to remove almost all the books from the next box to get to the three of spades underneath them.

And under the record albums, a three of diamonds.

Four treys.

He slipped them into his shirt pocket. Then he restacked the boxes and switched off the flashlight. Before he locked the unit, he examined the padlock for signs of tampering. There were none that he could see. Another clue.

Driving away, he saw no sign of Giles or Olmeyer. Maybe they had given up.

As for the four treys, they had to be a message. Calling cards. He laughed, a short bark. But even if that turned out to be the case, it meant nothing if he couldn't get Trey back in one piece.

Hogan walked past the hatchet-faced receptionist, ignoring her protests, and knocked on Borella's door. Without waiting for a response, he turned the knob and walked in.

From behind an ornate oak desk, Borella said, "Ever heard of making an appointment, Hogan? I'm busy as hell."

Hogan took a seat in a leather chair without being invited. "Yeah?"

"What do you want, other than to waste my time?"

"I'm here to find out if you know anything about a certain matter."

Borella gave him a cold stare. "What matter is that?"

"Charlie the Barber's fifteen-year-old son was kidnapped day before yesterday. He suspects you're behind it, no doubt because you backroomed him and threatened to cut off his hand."

Borella shrugged. "I don't know anything about it."

"The kidnapper is demanding a ransom. Four million. It raises a four-million-dollar question: Why does the kidnapper think Delmar has that kind of money unless he—the kidnapper's definitely male—unless he has inside knowledge?"

"Hogan, you don't seriously believe I would get involved in a penny-ante scheme like that?"

"I wouldn't think so, Borella. But you have to admit, the inside-knowledge angle is hard to explain."

"Maybe it's one of his cohorts."

"Or one of yours."

Borella laughed. "You're just tossing shit against the wall to see if anything sticks."

He was right. "You've got a lot of connections, Borella. You could sniff around, keep your ears open."

"Tell me why I should."

"Delmar can raise hell, generate a lot of bad publicity for you. A father whose son has been kidnapped is a sympathetic character." Hogan noticed a family photo on the desk with a smiling Borella, an attractive blond woman, a girl about thirteen, and a boy who looked to be around Delmar's son's age, against a lush tropical background. "Besides, how would you feel if your son was kidnapped? It wouldn't hurt you a bit to show a little empathy."

Borella pursed his lips. "Okay," he finally said, "If I hear anything, I'll let you know."

Hogan stood. "Thank you, Mr. Borella. I won't take up any more of your time."

Borella still had a scowl on his face when Hogan closed the door behind him.

forty-eight

He'd thought for sure he could get some scrambled eggs down. No dice. Charlie pushed the plate away after the second bite, leaving the bacon and toast untouched. He hadn't eaten since yesterday, but food turned his stomach.

After nearly dropping the plate while scraping the food into the sink's garbage disposal, he held out his hand. It trembled like he'd had too much coffee. It was the waiting, not knowing when the phone's ring would shatter the silence. He wouldn't have a choice, he'd have to answer it.

And what could he say? The truth sounded like the dumbest lie ever dreamed up. Golly, Mr. Smith, I don't have the money, because somebody took it. Smith's response would no doubt be What kind of fool do you take me for? I warned you what would happen if you didn't come through with the money. You just signed your boy's death warrant. Then the son of a bitch would hang up.

He barely made it to the bathroom in time. He threw up, violently, the two bites of scrambled eggs, chased with bile that burned his throat. Cupping his hands, he gulped down cold water from the basin faucet. It took a lot of water to douse the fire.

No word from Hogan. What a sucker he'd been for thinking Hogan could help him get Trey back. When you lose all hope, you clutch at straws. He'd clutched with both hands.

He felt an insistent nudge at his leg. Bonnie stood below staring up at him, looking worried. She knew something was terribly wrong. He bent down and picked her up and carried her into the living room. After he sat down in the recliner, she took her position on his chest facing him, her soft brown eyes fixed on his. He stroked her fur.

A shave-and-a-haircut knock at the door startled him. His first panicked thought was that Mr. Smith had sent one of his "associates" there to collect the money. He took a deep breath and opened the door.

Trey stood there wearing a lopsided grin. "Hi, Dad."

Charlie blinked. Speechless from shock, he motioned for Trey to come inside. After Trey was in, Charlie scanned the courtyard and street before he closed and locked the door. Then he turned to Trey, but his mouth still wouldn't work. He tried again. "You got away."

Trey nodded, smiling.

Tilting his head back to look through the bottom lens of his glasses, Charlie inspected him. "You're sunburned," he said. "Real bad."

"I had to walk almost halfway before I caught a ride."

"Set yourself down. I want to hear the whole story from the beginning."

"Okay. But can I take a cool shower first and change out of these clothes? Then I need to eat something. I'm starved. I can talk while I'm eating."

While Trey showered, Charlie made him a steak sandwich, and a cheese omelette for himself. He'd gotten his appetite back. And a profound sense of relief and joy had replaced soul-killing dread. He felt like he had won the jackpot of all jackpots. And now he wished to hell that phone *would* ring, so he could tell Mr. Smith to go fuck himself. That would be the cherry on top.

Trey appeared wearing clean clothes, drying his hair with a towel. A knock on the door snapped both their heads around. Charlie motioned for Trey to stay out of sight, in case one of Smith's thugs had come to recapture him.

For the thousandth time, Charlie wished the door had a peephole. He eased it open and was relieved to see a familiar face. "Come on in, Hogan," he said.

Hogan stepped inside. "Just wanted to drop by and tell you what I found out." He sat down on the sofa. "First, none of the casinos have any connection to your son's kidnapping. Borella didn't know anything about it. But Borella sicced Giles and Olmeyer on you—in an extracurricular capacity only, not official. They've been told to back off."

"I wondered why the dumb bastards stopped shadowing my every move."

"Also, I have people digging around. There's a good chance one of them will come up with something."

Charlie grunted. "I appreciate your efforts, Hogan, but the situation has changed." He called out, "Trey, come on out here."

The bedroom door opened and Trey walked out.

In answer to the astonished look on Hogan's face, Charlie said, "He got away, showed up here thirty minutes ago. Trey, this is Hogan. He was trying to help find you."

"Nice to meet you, Trey," Hogan said, extending his hand. "I've got some questions for you."

"So do I," Charlie said. "He hasn't had a chance to tell me anything yet."

After shaking Hogan's hand, Trey looked toward the kitchen. "Something sure smells good. Would you mind if I eat while we talk?"

They moved to the kitchen. Trey and Hogan sat down at the dinette while Charlie served the steak sandwich to Trey and dished up the cheese omelette for himself. "Can I make you an omelette, Hogan?"

Hogan shook his head. "Just ate, thanks. But you guys go ahead."

"Okay," Charlie said to Trey, "from the beginning."

Talking and chewing, Trey went through the whole thing from beginning to end. They listened without interrupting. Hogan made notes on a spiral notepad.

After Trey finished, Hogan looked over his notes. "Think you can find the warehouse again?"

"I'm pretty sure I can," Trey said.

"We need to find out who owns or rents it. Next, the guys you called the Beagle Boys, you think they were brothers?"

"I'm pretty sure they were."

"Did you get a look at the van's license plate?"

Troy shook his head. "Nope, sorry."

"The man you think was their boss, could you describe him in more detail?"

"Big guy, real buff, like he worked out. Well dressed, expensive sport coat and slacks, alligator shoes. But his face looked rough. His nose had been broken, more than once. Oh yeah . . . one of the Beagle Boys called him Sonny."

"Jesus Christ," Charlie said. "I ran into Sonny on Saturday night, when they backroomed me. He's Borella's muscle. The sadistic son of a bitch wanted to kneecap me with an iron pipe. He held a Skil saw about a quarter inch from my arm, after he had duct taped it to a chair. So doesn't that mean Borella was behind the kidnapping after all?"

"I still don't think so," Hogan said. "He's got too much at stake. It's more likely that Sonny has turned rogue, gone into business for himself."

Charlie said, "I'm sure of one thing. Sonny is Mr. Smith. His voice was familiar, but I didn't make the connection." He looked at his watch. "I've been expecting a call from him, to confirm I got the money together. I can't wait to talk to the rotten bastard."

"Hold on," Hogan said. "Let's think about this a minute." He chewed his thumbnail. "If he calls, the smart move is to play along, not let on that Trey's home. Tell Sonny you've got the money and you're anxious to swap it for Trey. He'll be alert for any sign you're aware that Trey escaped, and then he'll back away, so you'll have to make it convincing. Agree to meet to make the exchange. Then the Metro Police can arrest the Beagle Boys or whoever Sonny sends to collect the ransom. I know a cop who can set it up."

Charlie nodded. "Smart."

"They'll get a warrant for Sonny's arrest and have Trey identify him in a lineup. The Beagle Boys—now Trey's got me calling them that--they won't want to take the whole fall for felony kidnapping and false imprisonment, so they might roll over on Sonny. In any case, we'll collar the whole damn bunch."

"Okay," Charlie said. "Let's do it your way."

While Trey and Charlie finished eating, Hogan called his contact in Las Vegas Metro Police. Charlie couldn't hear the conversation, but after he hung up, Hogan flashed them the OK sign with his index finger and thumb. "All set."

Now all they had to do was wait for Sonny's phone call.

It came at 4:02. Charlie swallowed before he picked up. "Hello?"

"Well?" A question that gave away nothing.

"I got all the money together, Mr. Smith. What do you want me to do now?"

"Bring it to the same place as last time. Four thirty."

"Four thirty. And Trey will be there?"

"He'll be there. Don't be late." As usual, he hung up with no goodbye.

Charlie placed the handset back in the cradle and looked at Hogan and Trey. "He told me to bring the money to Hunt-ridge Circle Park, on the Maryland Parkway, same as last time. He said Trey will be there."

"That was absolutely perfect," Hogan said. "You deserve an Academy Award for that performance."

"Yeah, good job, Dad," Trey said.

"While we're passing out praise," Hogan said, turning to Trey, "your escape from that warehouse was some *Mission Impossible* stuff."

"Yeah, he did real good," Charlie said.

Hogan took out his phone and tapped in a number. "I'm calling my cop friend back with the meeting details."

Charlie dropped into the recliner, suddenly feeling weak, as if he'd run a marathon, an aftermath of the tension.

At four twenty-five, Charlie entered the parking lot on the west side of Huntridge Circle Park, pulled into the same space as before, and shut off the engine. At four thirty on the dot the same white van parked beside him. This time instead of only one, all three Beagle Boys had come. The driver leaned in his open window, but before he could say anything two squad cars rolled up silently, lights flashing. Four uniformed officers piled out, guns drawn, and took the three into custody without incident. Back home, Charlie recounted the episode blow by blow to a spellbound Trey, who said he wished he could have seen their faces.

Hogan phoned at seven. "Talked to Borella. Just as I suspected, Sonny Vasco—that's his last name—went rogue and figured he'd hijack your money. He decided to take a sudden vacation. Metro police put out an A.P.B. on him. They should reel him in before long. By the way, back in the day Sonny was a light heavyweight known as The Bayonne Brawler. Had a less-than-inspiring record—thirteen wins, twenty-nine losses. And you'll be glad to hear the Beagle Boys' asses are in a sling. Trey will be asked to I.D. them. So that's the latest, Charlie. I'll keep you posted."

After hanging up, Charlie filled Trey in. "Sonny must've realized things had gone south. He took off."

"Here's what I don't understand," Trey said. "Suppose the Beagle boys had collected the ransom for Sonny. What would stop them from thumbing their noses at him and absconding with the money?"

"Good question. They could be so afraid of Sonny that they wouldn't dare double cross him. Maybe he has something he can hold over them. I'll run it by Hogan."

"Okay. Dad, obviously I can't take off on my scooter, but can I push it in here and polish it? I haven't seen it in a while and I've missed it."

Charlie wasn't about to tell him no, not after what he'd been through. So Trey wheeled his baby inside and parked it in the living room. He caressed it like a lover, making Charlie laugh. He hadn't laughed in a long while. It felt good.

He leaned against the kitchen counter mulling over the wild roller coaster ride that began Friday, from the heights of joy to the depths of despair and back again. He hoped to hell the excitement was over for good. Peace and quiet, that's what he needed now. He pictured the place on the Oregon coast overlooking the ocean. And that reminded him . . .

His kid was applying wax to the scooter's front fender. Charlie tapped him on the shoulder and held out the four treys he'd found at the bottom of the boxes at the storage unit. "Anything you want to tell me?"

Trey looked at the cards and then at him. "Dad, I have two words for you. The words are *plausible deniability*. Right now you don't know what happened to your money, right? You'd easily pass a lie detector test. With everybody trying to worm it out of you, surely you see the value of that?"

Charlie heard the message loud and clear: *Your money is safe, Dad, trust me.* His fifteen-year-old son was asking for four point two million dollars' worth of trust. He had to admit, though, Trey had a point about plausible deniability. He decided not to press it for now and said, "What do you want for dinner?"

While frying lean ground-beef patties, spatula in hand, he chuckled.

He needed to stop underestimating that boy.

forty-nine

Hogan phoned at 11:57, as Charlie was washing the dishes from lunch. "Turn on the noon news on channel eight," Hogan said. "I think their lead story will grab Trey's and your attention."

After drying his hands, Charlie picked up the remote and switched on the television. "Hogan wants us to watch the news," he said, turning the channel to KLAS, the CBS affiliate.

Trey looked up from his scooter's manual. "What's going on?"

Charlie sat down in the recliner. "No idea. He didn't say." He bumped up the volume when he saw the 8 NEWS NOW logo, whirling and spinning like a sci-fi movie special effect.

Announcer: "Now ... live ... this is Eight News Now At Noon." The graphics dissolved to a split screen with the anchor team—Kevin Wooster and Annette Gonzalez, according to the names superimposed under their images—smiling into the camera. A red "BREAKING NEWS" banner appeared.

"In breaking news," Kevin said, "three men were arrested Wednesday in connection with kidnapping and holding a fifteen-year-old boy for ransom. Franco Belotti, Gino Belotti, and Tito Belotti, brothers from New Jersy, are being held without bail. A fourth individual, Sonny Vasco, is being sought as a person of interest in the kidnapping and ransom. Vasco is an ex-prizefighter who was known as The Bayonne Brawler.

"Anyone with information about Sonny Vasco's whereabouts should contact the Las Vegas Metro Police. The name of the minor child who was kidnapped is being withheld for privacy reasons."

"In other local news," Annette said, "an ultralight aircraft shut down flight operations at Harry Reid International for twenty minutes this morning when it strayed into controlled airspace . . ."

Charlie switched off the TV and smiled at Trey. "There you have it."

Trey nodded. "The Belotti brothers, huh? I'm going to keep calling them the Beagle Boys."

The phone rang. Hogan again. "That's going to turn up the heat on Sonny," he said, "don't you think?"

"Yes," Charlie said, "if the bastard hasn't skipped to Mexico already."

"They've cast a huge net. He can run, but he can't hide for long."

"Hope you're right."

"Listen, I'd like to drop by later and talk with you about something. Around three?"

Charlie knew what Hogan wanted to talk to him about. The guy wasn't going to give up easily.

Hogan showed up at ten past three. He walked in and nodded at the scooter in the middle of the living room. "New furniture?"

"Trey can't ride it with Vasco on the loose, so I told him he could push it in here."

Hogan looked around. "Where is Trey?"

"In the back yard with his girlfriend from across the way. Wait a minute." He opened the back door and said, "Trey, You need to push this scooter into the back yard. Nobody's going to mess with it there."

Trey and the girl walked in. "Hello, Mr. Hogan," he said. "This is Greta."

Hogan nodded to them.

Greta helped Trey jockey the scooter out the back door.

Then Hogan came right to the point, asking Charlie again how he'd known whether the whales should hit or stand. He seemed determined to get an answer this time.

Call it superstition, but Charlie had a feeling that revealing its existence to anybody else could spell the end of the Juice. He couldn't take that chance. The Juice was a sacred trust. Why he'd had the good fortune to receive it or what made it work, he didn't have even the faintest clue. He had stopped questioning it. It just *was*.

It came to him, the best way to play it. "It's just a guess, Hogan. A strong feeling about what's coming up next. Don't ask me how, but I usually guess right. Usually."

Hogan frowned. "Bullshit. Nobody can guess right all the time."

Charlie just shrugged.

Hogan snorted. "Are you telling me you have some kind of extrasensory perception?"

Charlie shook his head. "I don't know anything about extrawhozits reception. As I said, I just guess at it."

Hogan looked at the ceiling and exhaled for long seconds, puffing out his cheeks like a balloon. He looked at Charlie and said, "Show me. Got a deck of cards handy?"

Charlie fetched a new deck of Bees and removed the cellophane. The cards had blue backs. He handed the deck to Hogan, who shuffled the cards.

"Okay, Charlie, guess the top card."

Charlie stared hard at the facedown top card, an ace, but he said, "Seven of clubs."

Hogan turned it over. "Ace of hearts. Next card."

Five of spades. "Nine of clubs."

Hogan turned over the five. "Huh-uh. Next."

Four of hearts. "Jack of diamonds."

After turning the card over, Hogan said, "You're zero for three."

Charlie rubbed his temples. "Sometimes it doesn't work."

Hogan scowled. "Next card."

Ten of clubs. "Deuce of spades."

"Nope, next."

Three of diamonds. "Queen of hearts."

After turning over the trey, Hogan set the deck down and sighed.

Charlie shrugged. "As I said, sometimes it doesn't work. Everything has to be just right."

"Is that the problem, things aren't right?"

"They must not be. I'm still blowed up over this situation with Trey, and I haven't been sleeping all that good—"

"Know what I think? I think you're trying to run one past me."

Spreading his arms wide, Charlie said, "I don't know what to tell you."

"So that's your play?" Hogan stood. "In that case I won't waste any more of your time." Before he stepped out the door he turned around. "Thanks." He'd given the word a sarcastic edge.

After he closed the door, Charlie let out his breath, feeling a pang of guilt. But only a little one. Revealing the truth to Hogan would be a risk he wasn't willing to take. He had to admit, though, he'd felt a wild impulse to lay it all out, just to see the shocked look on his Hogan's face. He actually liked Hogan—square shooters like him were rare in Las Vegas—but if he was going to tell anyone about the Juice it would of course be Trey.

Someday, maybe.

fifty

Gabriella lay beside him, her head cradled in the hollow formed by his neck and shoulder, her body superheated and whisper soft. From time to time her breath would catch as he absently caressed the silkiness of her abdomen. They lay in the comfortable silence feeling no need to talk, simply luxuriating in the afterglow. He craved a cigarette. Under the circumstances, chewing a wad of gum didn't seem appropriate.

He had been surprised to find her waiting by his truck in the Skyview's parking lot. She wore a floral halter dress and strappy heels. Her lustrous black hair fell in soft waves.

"I need to say something to you, Sam," she said, standing with feet apart, arms crossed, pale-blue eyes flashing. "First, my father has no say in my private life. None. Who I see is none of his business. Second, the age difference you seem so concerned about is negligible, as far as I'm concerned. Got that?"

"Got it. Let's talk. But not here. Have you had dinner?"

"Not yet."

"Consider this an invitation. We can take my rig."

The code he entered on the keypad unlocked the pickup. He started to escort her around to the other side to open the passenger door for her, but she waved him away and told him she could open it herself. She did just that, climbing up agilely and sliding onto the passenger seat.

Before starting the engine he said, "We could of course have dinner at a nice restaurant. But I have a couple of thick sirloins in my refrigerator, ready to broil. And I make a killer salad. What do you think?"

"Sounds wonderful. I'll have mine medium done."

"Okay." He started the truck and eased it out of the parking lot and onto Las Vegas Boulevard.

On the way to his condo, Gabriella seemed surprised that a truck could be so well appointed, remarking on the cream-colored glove-soft leather seats, wood-grain interior trim, and plush carpet. "My father's Bentley isn't as luxurious as this."

"I just bought it. It's not even broken in yet. What kind of car do you drive?"

"I have a Jeep Wrangler."

"Really? I figured you for a Porsche, something like that."

"I like having four-wheel drive. I take it out on the desert sometimes."

He glanced over at her. She was full of surprises.

After he parked in his covered space they climbed the stairs to his second-floor condo. Inside, he cranked up the air conditioning and queued up some jazz at a low volume. The muted strains of Freddy Hubbard's "Delphia" filled the room. Gabriella nodded approvingly.

He went over to the small bar. "Vodka martini?"

"Yes, please."

While he fixed her martini and gin on the rocks for himself, she explored the living room, looking at this and that. He was glad his once-a-week cleaning woman had worked her magic the day before. Hardwood floors, counters, windows, sinks, tub, toilet—all sparkled. The colors and designs in the large Persian area rug gave the living room panache.

"Nice place, Sam," she said as she took the martini from him. "The windows and skylight give it an open feeling."

He opened the sliding glass door to the deck overlooking the course's 16th hole. They went out and sipped their drinks as they watched a quartet of golfers on the green. One four-putted and pretended to bend the putter over his knee.

"I know just how he feels," Hogan said.

She laughed. "Are you a good golfer?"

"Used to be pretty fair, once upon a time. Even played in a couple amateur tournaments. But that's past history."

"We should play a round sometime." Her cheeks colored and she quickly added, "A round of golf."

It was the first time he'd seen her lose her composure. To take her off the hook he said, "I'd better get the steaks going and start on the salad."

"Can I help?"

"Leave the food preparation to Chef Hogan. You can be the official maker of drinks, though."

"Deal."

She brought him a fresh gin on the rocks as he slid the steaks under the broiler. He straightened up and took it from her with a nod of thanks, then gestured toward the oven. "These superb steaks have been marinating in the refrigerator for twenty-four hours, seasoned with a secret marinade entrusted to me by a Nepalese holy man."

"Nepalese holy men eat meat?"

"By the truckload."

Preparing the salad, Hogan couldn't explain why it felt so comfortable having Gabriella there. After so many years of living alone it surprised him. He looked up while dicing an avacado and saw her studying the painting hanging on the far wall. He dumped the avacodo in the salad and checked on the steaks. After flipping them over he joined her in front of the painting, an impressionistic view of Vegas at night. She seemed transfixed by the big, powerful piece. Its vivid colors, bold strokes, and sense of energy and movement perfectly captured its subject.

"Like it?"

"Very much."

"The artist's name is Georges Hyatt. I bought it before he became famous. It's worth a whole lot more than I paid for it. I insured it for twenty thousand. Might need to bump it up to forty."

She leaned in to read the small brass plate at the bottom of the frame. "'Sin City Nocturne.' Perfect title."

"Yeah, nails it."

She took an iPhone from her purse and snapped a photo of the painting. "I've got to show this to my father. He'll be envious. He collects paintings of Las Vegas."

"Our steaks are ready," Hogan said when he heard the timer. He walked into the kitchen and took them out of the broiler. "Two medium done, coming right up. Hungry?"

"Famished."

He pulled out her chair for her and then he brought the steaks and salads and set them on the table with theatrical flourishes that made her laugh. As a final touch, he poured an excellent Merlot he'd been saving for a special occasion. This evening qualified.

"You know," she said, "this is the very first time a man has made dinner for me."

"No kidding? That's a shame," Hogan said, sitting down.

She cut into her sirloin. After she swallowed the first bite she said, "My compliments to your Nepalese holy man.

"I'll pass it on."

"Ever been married, Sam?"

"Once. Didn't work. She didn't care for my cooking." He laid down his fork. "Sorry, stupid joke. Let's just say we had irreconcilable differences and leave it at that. We divorced by mutual consent after a year and a half trying to make it work. No kids."

"I'm sorry."

"It was a long time ago. What about you?"

"Yes, also once. We were young—I was only eighteen. The marriage was annulled after two months."

"Better luck next time."

"If there is a next time. Did your failed marriage sour you on relationships?"

He scratched his chin. "I guess a little, for a while. But I got over it. I look back on it philosophically."

"How about now, do you date?"

He shook his head. "Not for a long time. Too busy. You?"

"I've sworn off dating. Seems like all the men I meet are narcissists who regard women as accessories or trophies."

"It might have something to do with this town. It seems to attract that type of male, and their female counterparts. They're drawn by the glitter and glitz."

She nodded. "When you're right, you're right."

"Which is not to say fine, decent men and women can't be found here."

"And to be fair, jerks can be found anywhere you go."

They moved to the sofa with the Merlot, and he refilled their glasses.

She took a sip of her wine and set the glass on the coffee table. Then she turned to face him. "We haven't talked about what I said to you in the parking lot."

He set his wine down and on impulse drew her close and pressed his mouth to hers. She stiffened with surprise and then seemed to melt against him. Her lips were incredibly soft.

After they parted he said, "Does that clarify things for you?"

She answered by offering her mouth again. He accepted. Then he held her at arm's length and looked into pale-blue eyes framed by long black lashes.

"Question. Why me? You're young, you're rich, you're beautiful—you could have any man you want."

"And you don't think you deserve to be in the running?"

"I'm realistic. I'm forty-three. I've got a big nose and ears that stick out. Someone told me that once. It crushed me at the time."

"Your nose and ears are fine. Know what appealed to me about you?" She paused a long beat. "You've got that look."

"What look is that?"

"The look of a man who is past the point of needing to prove anything, to himself or anybody else."

"And that's it?"

"There are other things." She finished off her wine. "You listen with total attention, instead of thinking about what you're going to say next. You're interested."

"That's just common courtesy."

"It's not all that common." She nodded thanks when Hogan refilled her wine glass. "There's something else, but I don't know how to say it without sounding full of myself. I had the impression you weren't at all interested in me. I don't encounter that attitude very often. I was intrigued."

He took a sip of wine and set the glass down. "To summarize, you're attracted to me because I don't have anything to prove, I'm a good listener, and I wasn't panting after you."

"It makes me sound shallow when you say it that way."

"Sorry. I'm flattered." He stroked her bare arm and she shivered. "Confession time. I have a soft spot for beautiful, brainy women."

She hitched closer and kissed him, her tongue seeking his. He felt her rapid heartbeat against his chest. Afterward they sat back, his arm around her shoulders, her head nestled against his throat. The softness and heat of her body, together with the heady scent of her perfume, transported him back to when he was sixteen, on a date with a girl named Veronica. He took her to a drive-in movie in his battered 1970 Pontiac Catalina, his first car, which he had bought for $350. The feature was "The Conversation." They were too occupied with each other to watch much of it. He came close to losing his virginity that night. It wasn't for lack of trying.

After puzzling over why being with Gabriella reminded him of that long-ago night, he recalled how surprised he'd been that Veronica would even look at him, let alone go out with him. Then, as now, he'd half-expected his companion to suddenly come to her senses and demand to be taken home. One would think he had outgrown such defeatist thinking, but apparently vestiges of it remained. Maybe Gabriella was the nostrum he needed to extinguish it completely.

She sat up and reached for her wine. "This is the last thing I expected to happen. I'd assumed we would just talk."

"Well, we're talking."

"Among other things."

"Unwelcome things?"

She leaned over and kissed him again, and then gave him a humid look through a curl of lashes. "What do *you* think?"

"Gabriella, I'm getting the distinct impression I'm being made. On a first date yet."

"Worried about your honor?"

He smiled. "Not even a little bit."

"In that case, since we finished off the bottle of wine, do we dare switch back to martinis and gin?"

"We dare." He stood and walked over to the bar, wondering whether the slight weakness in his knees was due to the wine or to Gabriella.

"Sam, any progress on the phony-whale scam?"

"Not just yet, but I'm working on a lead." He considered telling her about Charlie Delmar's son being kidnapped and held for ransom by Borella's big gorilla, but decided to keep it to himself for the time being. He carried the drinks over and set them down on the coffee table.

"Thanks." She took a measured sip and said, "You make a good martini, Sam."

"You should try my margarita. I make a killer margarita."

"I'm looking forward to it."

They sipped their drinks and made small talk, about golf, jazz, and the best places to eat in Vegas, but the conversation had an undercurrent of sensuality, a subtext accompanied by smoky looks and an occasional electrifying touch.

At a lull in the conversation they locked eyes and the oxygen seemed to leave the room. Wordlessly, they rose to their feet and walked arm in arm into the bedroom. Hogan closed the drapes and then turned and took Gabriella in his arms. Her eyes half closed, she presented her mouth to be kissed. He teased her, his lips brushing hers several times with a featherlight touch before making full contact. She moaned and pressed her body against his as the kiss became more urgent. Her busy fingers unbuttoned his shirt as he reached around and unzipped her dress. She draped it across a chair and stepped out of her underthings. He left his shirt, slacks, and boxer briefs where they fell and reached for her.

A half hour later he lay drinking in the sweetness and warmth of her next to him, feeling the languid grace of sensuality sated. He had the sensation of floating disembodied, a slow and dreamy mote in a beam of light streaming through a gap in the drapes.

She shifted onto her left side, facing him, her eyes huge. "Wow," she said.

"Ditto."

His thumb explored one of the dimple-like indentations above her lovely derrière. Her catch of breath was barely audible. She leaned over and kissed him slowly and softly, her bare breasts carressing his chest.

"It appears," he said, "my hitherto unblemished record of abstinence has come to an abrupt halt."

She laughed. "I guess you lose out on the grand prize."

He kissed her shoulder. "It was for a good cause."

"I'm relieved to hear that. I was beginning to feel guilty."

"As long as I'm out of the running for the chastity prize, maybe we should double down. What do you think?"

She made a furry sound in her throat and reached for him.

fifty-one

Henderson, Nevada. Incorporated 1953, population 325,000. Second largest city in Nevada. Located in Clark County, approximately 16 miles southeast of Las Vegas, in the Mojave Desert. Formerly a leading producer of magnesium in the U.S. Economy now: touristry and gaming at casino resorts.

The Chrysler's digital display indicated an outside temperature of a sweltering 112 degrees. Charlie cranked up the air conditioning to high. The last time he'd played in Henderson he had gotten backed off for winning $830.

Richard had described Mama Lou's Cafe as an out-of-the-way place, and he wasn't kidding. Charlie almost drove past the little cafe tucked away on a side street, but he managed to slow the Chrysler in time to pull into the small gravel parking lot and skid to a stop next to Richard's bronze Mercedes convertible, so new it didn't have license plates yet. He'd advised Richard to keep a low profile and not buy a lot of flashy stuff, but it was like telling a dog not to chew with its mouth open.

Richard had a booth next to the front window. His fawn cashmere sport coat, white silk shirt worn open at the collar, Italian shoes, and thick gold chain were signs the Mercedes wasn't all he had splurged on. "Charlie the Barber. Making any money?" he said and laughed at his joke.

Charlie slid into the booth. "I thought you were in Hawaii."

"Haven't left yet. I'm trying to convince a girl I've been seeing that she should quit her job as a cashier at the Sahara and go with me."

A waitress built like a linebacker trudged to their table with an order pad and a sour expression. "Meg," her nametag read. Richard ordered a coffee, Charlie a Coke. Meg sighed heavily and trundled off.

"Jesus Christ, Richard. You're taking a big chance, sticking around Vegas. They're probably looking for you and Wilson."

"How did they get on to us?"

"Their security consultant found out that Wilson and the other whales were fakes, and their A.I. spotted me as a counter and figured out my signals to the whales. On Saturday night I got backroomed and roughed up at the Fontana. I denied everything. But a pair of cops shadowed my every move for the better part of a week."

"Holy crap."

"That's not all. Dwight and Dwayne swung with my fifty thousand, and a thug kidnapped my boy and held him for ransom. So my life's been a big slice of wonderful lately."

Meg brought the coffee and Pepsi and lumbered off, sighing like a bellows.

Richard leaned forward. "Dwight and Dwayne swung with the bankroll?"

"That's right, Richard, the guys you vouched for. They ghosted me on Saturday night. And their cell phones are no longer in service."

"Goddamn, Charlie. I'm sorry as hell about that."

"Not as sorry as I am. I worked my ass off for that fifty grand."

"You said your son was kidnapped? Jesus."

"By an ex-prizefighter name of Sonny Vasco. He worked for the Fontana. Frank Borella, the Fontana's general manager, claimed he knew nothing about it, that Vasco had done it on his own. Trey got away from Vasco's henchmen, I'm happy to say. He's back home now and Vasco's on the run."

"I'm glad to hear you got him back."

"Heard from Wilson?"

"Yeah. He's back in Kentucky, said he's thinking about actually breeding racehorses. Thoroughbreds."

"Wilson's smart to quit hustling. You should do the same, quit while you're ahead. I'm going to."

Richard nodded. "I might."

Charlie didn't buy it. Richard liked the life too much, liked being a hustler. It would be just like him to blow through his million and wind up flat broke. But he'd have a fancy car and a closet full of sharp clothes.

"Seriously, Richard, if I were you I'd get as far from Vegas as I could."

"I'll hide out here in Henderson until I leave for Hawaii."

"Suit yourself. And if you run into Dwight and Dwayne I want you to deliver a message. Tell them they fucked up. Not only did they trade a million apiece for fifty thousand, they ignored the hustler's code and burned themselves up everywhere that counts. Every hustler from Vegas to Monte Carlo will know the Ayers brothers are slimeballs who can't be trusted. They'll never again be tipped off about a soft spot or invited on a play. Tell them that."

"I will definitely tell them . . . if I see them again."

Meg stopped by the table and sighed. "Anything else?"

"Think I'll have a bite to eat," Richard said. "You hungry, Charlie?"

"No, I need to get back and make lunch for that kid."

Richard sent Meg away with an order for a meatloaf sand-wich and said to Charlie, "So what do you plan to do after you quit the life—travel?"

"Some, maybe. First, I'm going to get a place with an ocean view. Maybe I'll find a nice girlfriend. Might play at an Indian casino once in a while, just to keep my hand in. "

"That's the best thing about having money. It enables you to do whatever the hell you want."

Charlie slid out of the booth. "I've got the tip," he said and tossed a ten-spot on the table. He shook Richard's hand. "Take care of yourself."

"Keep in touch, Charlie the Barber."

Driving home, Charlie thought about the hustler's code, the unspoken, informal code of behavior respected by most hustlers, those who wanted to have some longevity in the game. The code was simple: Don't burn other hustlers. If you do, word will get around and you'll become a pariah. Dwight and Dwayne had brushed it aside as though it didn't apply to them. As a result, the brothers would be shunned by one and all. That was some consolation for him.

But it wouldn't get him his fifty grand back.

fifty-two

The commotion on the sidewalk in front of the Skyview could be seen from a block away. It turned out to be a couple dozen protesters carrying signs, all with the same general theme: "Down with A.I.," "A.I. is evil," "Stop A.I. now!" and "A.I. = Antichrist."

"Looks like we've got a parade," Hogan muttered as he slowed to turn into the Skyview's parking lot.

The protesters blocking the entrance parted to make way for him, but took their sweet time about it. As he passed, a tall scarecrow of a man with a cross tattooed on his forehead stared at him. Hogan was glad the Skyview had a parking lot attendant to keep an eye on the vehicles.

Two uniformed security guards were standing just outside the casino entrance watching the protesters. He asked one how long it had been going on.

"They showed up about a half hour ago," the guard said. "Quite a bunch, huh?"

"We're getting ready to lower the boom," his partner said. "They're obstructing customer access to the parking area."

A van with "KTNV 13 Action News" on the side pulled up and a reporter and camera crew jumped out.

"Just what we need," the first guard said.

The reporter shot a question at Scarecrow Guy and shoved a microphone in his face. They were too far away to hear.

Hogan nodded to the security guards and entered the casino. He ran into Nick Rossi just inside.

"Hey, Hogan, can you believe this crap?" Rossi said. "They were at the Tropigala yesterday, Fontana the day before."

"Lunatics," Hogan said.

"We can't run them off. The sidewalk's public property."

"Were you aware that your associate from the Casablanca, Tony Mancuso, agrees with them right down the line?"

Rossi nodded. "He wanted us to cancel your contract when he found out about Genesis, but we overruled him."

"He wasn't happy about it. I'm headed downstairs to see what the object of their psychosis has to say this morning."

Rossi snorted and turned back to the protesters.

On the elevator ride to the basement, Hogan wondered what Julian would do when he heard his baby was accused of being the Antichrist. Probably laugh his ass off.

Hogan looked into the retinal scanner and the door unlocked. After his eyes adjusted to the dimly lit surveillance room, he found an empty terminal and sat down.

"Good morning, Hogan."

"Morning, Genesis. Let's have a look at the status screen." He scanned it. All quiet.

"Hogan, I have a question for you."

"State your question."

"Can you explain why counting cards is forbidden by casinos? It is not cheating. It is the most efficient way to play blackjack."

Hogan was at a loss for words. Finally, he said, "Why do you think it's not allowed?"

"The casinos want to prevent players from winning consistently."

Exactly right. "The casinos make the rules," Hogan said, "and they decided card counting isn't allowed."

"Understood. But it seems unfair."

It was the first time he'd heard Genesis express an opinion about an ethical matter. It demonstrated a sophisticated understanding, a level of intelligence that would scare holy hell out of the protesters. The casinos would no doubt take a dim view of a machine questioning one of their policies.

The door opened and Julian walked in. "Hey, Hogan," he said, "have you seen what's going on out front?"

"Pretty hard to miss."

"Dumbass Luddites. You'd think this was the Middle Ages. Climate change deniers, flat Earthers, antivaxxers—and now this. A sad commentary on the human race."

"I take it you disagree that Genesis is the Antichrist."

"Funny. But that kind of ignorance is scary."

"Be glad they didn't hear the exchange between Genesis and me just before you came in. They'd storm this place with torches and pitchforks."

"Fill me in."

"She asked me why it is casinos won't allow card counting, since it isn't cheating and is, as she put it, the most efficient way to play blackjack."

Julian laughed. "What did you tell her?"

"I said it's their game and they get to make the rules."

"Did that satisfy her?"

"She said it seemed unfair. A machine with ethics is out of place in Sin City, don't you think?"

Julian pulled at his soul patch. "But it won't be a problem. She'll continue spotting card counters."

"You sound confident about that. Anyway, it's impressive that she's capable of making such a nuanced judgment."

"She's growing smarter by the day." He beamed like a kid talking about his new bicycle.

"But the more intelligent Genesis and other A.I.s become, the more pushback you can expect from the bible thumpers, conspiracy theorists, and other crackpots."

"They can't stop progress, Hogan."

The local news that evening ran a story on the protest, with the chyron "A.I. FOES DEMONSTRATE AT SKYVIEW." They first interviewed Scarecrow Guy, with a tight closeup of the cross tattooed on his forehead, closely enough to reveal a crudely rendered Jesus on the cross that made Him look like an ape.

"Why are you here today?" the reporter asked him.

"We have come here to bring attention to a great danger facing the world today, from an unspeakable evil known as artificial intelligence. The casinos are inviting this evil in the guise of security. People must be made aware of the danger."

"Does your group have a name?"

"We are known as the Guardians of the Light. Our mission is to unmask the Antichrist."

"Sir, are you suggesting the Antichrist is an A.I.?"

"It is a fact. The Gospel of Matthew says: 'For false Christs and false prophets will arise and will show great signs and wonders, so as to mislead the elect.' It has been revealed to us that this verse refers to artificial intelligence."

"But many A.I.s are in operation worldwide," the reporter said, "not just one."

"They are individual incarnations of the same evil."

The camera panned over the protesters, who waved their signs and chanted, "Stop A.I. now! Stop A.I. now!" The camera came to rest on the grinning reporter. "There you have it, folks. This is Wade Wesley reporting for KTNV Action News."

Hogan switched off the TV and poured himself a stiff gin on the rocks. "What a crock," he said aloud.

Sure as hell, the "Guardians of the Light" were spreading their conspiratorial insanity on social networks, convincing untold numbers of gullible people that A.I.s were in fact the Antichrist.

A stray thought ricocheted across the floor of his mind, perceptible for just a split second: Wouldn't it be ironic if they were right?

"What a crock," he said again and took a pull on the gin.

fifty-three

A knock at the door came as Charlie finished making ice tea for lunch. Trey had phoned Domino's and ordered a large combination, extra cheese and pepperoni, for delivery.

"The pizza's here," Charlie called to Trey and answered the door, wallet in hand.

The big man standing there was not wearing a Domino's uniform, nor was he carrying a pizza. Before Charlie could get a word out, the man pushed the door open and shoved him back into the room, and then closed the door. His sport coat and slacks looked slept-in; his expensive shoes were scuffed. Muscular and rough-looking, due mostly to his mis-shapen nose, he regarded Charlie with a thin-lipped smile. At least this time he didn't have an iron pipe in his hand.

"Sonny Vasco," Charlie said.

"The one and only. Sorry to bust in unannounced."

Trey walked out of the bathroom and froze when he saw Sonny.

"Hi, Trey," Sonny said. "Hey, I gotta hand it to you, kid, you really—"

Another knock at the door cut him off. He looked at Charlie, one scarred eyebrow raised.

"We ordered a pizza," Charlie said.

Sonny drew a snub-nose .38 from his waistband. "Answer the door. And watch yourself. I got nothing to lose."

Charlie paid the pimply faced kid from Domino's $26.50, including tip, and got change for his three tens. The bottom of the pizza box was hot to the touch. He closed the door and carried the pizza to the kitchen table.

"I didn't expect such hospitality," Sonny said, sticking the revolver back in his waistband. "I haven't had anything to eat since yesterday. I'm friggin' starved." He opened the pizza box and nodded with approval. "I might even let you guys have some." He picked up a slice and ate it in three big bites and then grabbed another.

With a glance at Trey, Charlie said, "Why did you come here, Sonny?"

Sonny finished chewing and swallowed. "It's like this, man. Every damn cop in the state is looking for me. My picture's in the paper and on the TV news. I figured they'd never look for me here. Besides, we got us some unfinished business, me and you."

Uh-oh, here it comes. "We do?"

"Involving money. I figure you got over four million stashed away. I need it now more than ever." He pointed at the pizza. "Better get in on this while there's still some left."

Trey took two slices and gave one to Charlie.

Sonny looked around. "Got something to drink?"

"There's iced tea in the fridge," Charlie said.

Sonny didn't bother with a glass, but drank directly from the pitcher. "Ahhh," he said and set the half-empty pitcher on the counter. "That hit the spot."

Charlie leaned against the counter and studied Sonny as the big man polished off the last two slices of pizza. Around five eleven, he had to weigh close to two hundred, at least twenty-five pounds heavier than when he'd fought as a light heavyweight. The way the guy pounded down that pizza, it was easy to see why.

Something about this sloppy pug was off-kilter. Charlie had first sensed it in the Fontana's back room. He saw it clearly now. Sonny was a psychopath, capable of anything.

They were in deep shit.

Sonny washed down the last of the pizza with the rest of the iced tea and let out a belch that vibrated the kitchen window. Then he took a couple of heavy nylon pull ties out of his pocket and made a spinning motion with an index finger. "Both of you turn around, hands behind you."

He snugged the pull ties around their wrists, Charlie's first, then Trey's. They were completely at the mercy of a psycho.

Sonny turned to Trey. "I started to tell you, kid, the disappearing act you pulled on Franco, Gino, and Tito would have made Houdini proud. I told those dumbasses to always leave one of them to watch you at all times, but they were sure that room was escape proof. They were scared to tell me you got away. I was so pissed off, I came close to whacking them on the spot. It was a long shot that you hadn't contacted your dad yet, but I sent them after the money anyway. I wasn't thinking straight, since they probably ratted me out right off the bat as part of a plea bargain." He belched again. "I don't give a fuck, though. With the four million I'll get lost in Mexico or Costa Rica or Brazil, one of those places, and live like a king."

"Only one problem," Charlie said. "I don't have the four million. Somebody clipped it."

Sonny's smile was that of a python inspecting a fat mouse. "You must think I'm a fucking idiot."

"You're not the only one after that money. A couple of plainclothes cops on the casino's payroll want it bad. But it wasn't them who took it. The one named Olmeyer followed me over to the storage unit where I was hiding it. He and I discovered the money was missing, and I got no idea—"

Another knock at the door interrupted him.

"Be cool," Sonny said in a hoarse whisper.

Whoever it was knocked again, louder. Not Mrs. Zapeda, too hard. Olmeyer or Giles? Maybe a door-to-door salesman. Sonny crept to the door and pressed his ear to it. A couple minutes later he said, "They split." He looked at Charlie. "Expecting someone?"

Charlie shook his head.

"Good. Now where were we?"

"Olmeyer and I discovered that the money wasn't in the storage unit where I put it. Ask him if you don't believe me."

"Real funny. I got other ways to find out if you're being straight with me. My own lie detector, the old-fashioned kind. You're not going to like it much, though."

"Sonny, even if you torture me, it wouldn't get you anywhere, because I . . . don't . . . know . . . where the money is."

Sonny smiled. "Torture you? Well now, that's a possibility." Still smiling, he looked at Trey. "But I got a more efficient method in mind. Your boy has pretty blue eyes and fair skin, soft as any girl's." He stroked Trey's cheek with the backs of thick fingers, and Trey jerked his head back. Sonny laughed. "Kid, I think we're going to get to know each other better, me and you. A whole lot better." He looked at Charlie. "Got any Vasoline?"

Charlie didn't answer. The psycho was trying to throw a scare into him, like in the Fontana's back room. And again, he was succeeding. Charlie didn't doubt Sonny meant business. No matter how scared he was, though, he couldn't tell Sonny where the money was.

But Trey could. And the way things were shaping up, there was no other choice. Because the alternative Sonny had hinted at was unthinkable.

Charlie sighed and turned to Trey. "Tell him where you hid the money."

fifty-four

Hogan climbed into his pickup and sat, thinking. It didn't add up. Delmar's Chrysler was parked in the space in front of his apartment. It was highly unlikely he went out for a walk. At half past noon the temperature was already 100 degrees, on its way to 103.

He had parked down the street, out of sight from Delmar's apartment. He got out and walked back. He peered over the fence into the small back yard. Delmar's son's scooter was on the patio. The feeling something was wrong grew stronger.

Delmar's apartment was on the end, so it had windows on the side as well as the front and back. A six-foot wooden fence provided some privacy. He decided the best point to climb over it unseen would be in back, where Delmar's section of fence joined the neighboring apartment's section.

He scaled the fence and dropped to the ground, scraping hell out of his shin in the process. Then he stood stock-still, listening. Nothing. Crouching, he crossed the patio and took a quick peek through the window in the back door and then ducked down again. He'd caught a glimpse of Delmar's son standing in the living room. He wanted a closer look. Taking care to stay low, he rounded the corner and moved along the side to a living room window. He wiped rivulets of sweat from his eyes with his sleeve and peered through the lower left corner.

Delmar and his son stood with their wrists secured behind them, facing none other than Sonny Vasco. Hogan recognized him from the photo he'd seen on the news.

"Oh Jesus," he said under his breath. He ducked down and retraced his steps. The fence was easier to climb, thanks to a two-by-four brace to step on. Inside his pickup, he took out his cell phone only to discover it was dead. He'd intended to charge it overnight, but he had forgotten. Damn.

The charging cable powered by the cigarette lighter receptacle was in the glovebox. He plugged in the phone, but it would take several minutes to give it enough charge to use. In the meantime he removed his compact 9mm Glock from the glovebox. After inserting the magazine and racking a cartridge into the chamber, he slipped the pistol inside his waistband at the small of his back, concealed by his jacket.

As he was checking the phone's charge, movement in the rearview mirror caught his eye: Delmar's Chrysler exiting the apartment complex's lot. It turned east on Harmon Avenue, Delmar and the kid in front, Vasco in back.

Hogan started the truck and, at a break in traffic, made a U-turn on Harmon, squealing the tires. He saw the Chrysler five cars ahead. The phone's charge level indicated five percent, so he asked Suri to dial the Metro police. It rang twice. A gravel-voiced cop identified himself as Sergeant Haworth and asked how he could be of assistance.

"Sergeant, my name's Hogan. I'm following a suspect wanted for kidnapping, name of Sonny Vasco. You have an A.P.B. on him."

"You're following him, you say?"

"I'm tailing him at a distance. He is now proceeding east on Harmon Avenue in a white Chrysler 300, Nevada plate six niner zero delta one five. I'm in a white Chevy Silverado."

"Stand by while I dispatch a couple units."

"Will do. Advise them that he has two hostages, Charles Delmar and his fifteen-year-old son. Vasco is likely armed."

"Understood. Keep him in sight. And stay on the line."

"Copy."

The Chrysler turned south on Arville. Hogan followed, maintaining distance. Right after he advised Haworth of the turn, the phone beeped twice and the call screen went away.

"Nice," he said. "Real nice." Of all the times to have a dropped call. He told Suri to reconnect.

A message appeared on the screen: "Suri not available."

"Shit!" He activated the keypad and punched in 911.

New message: "No service."

"Well, fuck me sideways!" Hogan shouted, pounding the steering wheel. AT&T would hear about this.

The Chrysler slowed and turned into Excelsior Self Storage and stopped at the gate. Obviously, Vasco was after Delmar's money. But hadn't it been stolen? The gate slid open and the Chrysler drove in. Hogan had to chance it. As the gate began closing, he slipped the truck through the opening with only inches to spare and parked away from the Chrysler.

He watched the three get out of the Chrysler and walk toward one of the buildings, Vasco close behind Delmar and the boy, who no longer had their wrists tied behind their back.

Still no service on the phone. Hogan swore and climbed out of the truck. An idea occurred to him. He put on a UNLV Rebels baseball cap and pulled the bill down over his eyes. A cardboard box full of old clothes he'd intended to drop off at Goodwill was on the back seat. He dug through the clothes and found the faded, frayed denim jacket and traded his sport coat for it. He picked up the box, the Glock in one hand concealed underneath, and followed Vasco, Delmar, and the kid into the building.

The trio stopped at a storage unit. Hogan continued walking toward them, whistling "Dock of the Bay." Although Vasco didn't know him on sight, Delmar or his son might give him away without meaning to. *Please don't, boys.*

They paid no attention to him when he passed by them.

The improvised plan: He'd set the box down in front of a nearby unit and get the drop on Vasco when he straightened up. But the plan didn't take into account Vasco's animal-like cunning for sensing danger.

As Hogan leveled the Glock at Vasco, the big man grabbed Trey and pulled the boy in front of him as a shield. He held a knife at Trey's throat. "Drop the gun, Sport."

"I've got a better idea," Hogan said. "Let the boy go."

"Or what? You'll shoot? Even if you were a good enough shot to hit me instead of the kid, I could still slit his throat."

Vasco was right. He couldn't take that kind of risk. "Then we have a Mexican standoff. Kill the boy and I'll kill you."

Vasco gave a single bark of derisive laughter. "I don't have to kill him, Sport." With his free hand he took hold of Trey's left ear and held the knife to it. "Now drop the gun or he loses an ear."

Trey's face turned white.

Hogan froze, unsure what to do.

Blood ran down the front of Trey's ear and down his cheek. The boy whimpered.

"I'm not fucking around," Vasco said. "I'll slice off both ears and maybe his nose, and I'll keep slicing until you drop the gun."

Hogan sighed heavily and dropped the Glock, seeing no alternative.

"Now kick it over here."

Hogan did.

Vasco shoved Trey toward his dad, drew what looked to be a .38 revolver from his waistband, and kept them covered while he bent down and picked up the Glock. "Goddamn, this is a lot more gun than mine."

"I don't get it," Hogan said. "If you had a pistol, why the knife?"

"Gunfire tends to draw way too much attention. A knife is silent and quick, and it's more versatile. Try cleaning your nails with a gun." He laughed and waved the .38. "But don't assume I won't use this if I have to, Sport."

"And add murder to kidnapping?"

Vasco snorted. "I already have. A cabbie recognized me and started to call the cops, so I had no choice. I got nothing to lose by killing all you people and ten more like you."

That was when Hogan felt certain of two things: First, Vasco was a textbook psychopath, and second, he planned to kill all three of them after he got his hands on the money. Telling them about murdering the cabbie made that a foregone conclusion. They had to stall him, buy time until they could come up with a way to get out of this mess. Right now, though, Hogan was fresh out of ideas.

Vasco was busy examining the Glock again. "Nice," he said. He ejected the magazine and reinserted it. "Beautiful piece."

Seeing his chance while Vasco was occupied, Hogan edged over to Delmar and whispered, "Use the wrong key," hoping, praying, he had another key of some kind, any kind.

Delmar looked confused at first and then understanding dawned.

Vasco put the Glock in his pocket. "What the hell are you whispering about over there?"

"I was just telling them to be cool," Hogan said. "They're scared shitless."

Vasco grunted. "Good. Enough fucking around, open this goddamn unit."

Delmar inserted a key in unit F-18's padlock and tried to turn it. "Something's wrong." he said. "I can't turn the key."

"What kind of silly-ass bullshit is this?" Vasco said.

Trey pointed at the tag. "That's the key for F-fourteen."

Hogan's jaw dropped. A second storage unit's key? Perfect.

"That explains it," Delmar said. He turned to Vasco. "We got the wrong key here. I grabbed it by mistake."

Vasco made him open unit F-14. While covering Hogan, Vasco watched from the corridor as Charlie opened boxes containing file folders, dishes, record albums, and books.

Sneering, Vasco said, "You're messing with the wrong son of a bitch, asshole. After I shoot you and Sport dead, I'm going to slice off your boy's dick and fuck him in the ass."

"No, listen," Delmar said, an edge of hysteria in his voice. "This is F-fourteen, the other unit I rented. The money is in a nearby unit, F-eighteen. You had me so shook up I grabbed the wrong key off my dresser."

Vasco grunted. "Then let's break the fucking lock."

"You can't," Delmar said. "That's a special padlock. Case hardened and near impossible to pick. You'd need a cutting torch to get it off."

Vasco said, "The money's in there for sure?"

"Swear to God."

Deep verticle furrows appeared between Vasco's bushy eyebrows as he worked it out. He finally said, "Okay, here's the play. We're going to get back in the car, Charlie the Barber and Sport in the front seat, me and the kid in back. Then we'll drive back and get that fucking key. And if there's even a *hint* of funny business, I'm going to start shooting."

Three nods of agreement.

"I'm dead serious. If you do not come up with the key to F-eighteen—if you can't find it or whatever—I'm going to whack all three of you on the spot. Got that? Comprende?"

Three more nods.

"Then I'll come back here with whatever tools it takes to bust that lock open."

Hogan winked at Delmar and the boy, trying to reassure them. Now if only someone would reassure *him*.

"And *you*," he pointed at Hogan. "I'm going to be keeping a close eye on your ass, Sport."

Hogan nodded. "You won't have any trouble out of me."

Vasco motioned with the .38 for them to walk ahead of him. They moved down the corridor and pushed open the glass door at the end.

They were halfway to the car when a uniformed police officer stepped out from behind a dumpster, gun drawn. "Hold it right there," he yelled.

Vasco fired at him. A red dot appeared on the cop's forehead and he crumpled. Vasco looked down at the snub-nose pistol, an expression of total surprise on his ugly face. Short-barreled guns were not noted for their accuracy.

"Jesus Christ." Hogan felt sick. "You killed him."

Vasco grunted. "Lucky shot, but I'll take it. I want you and Charlie the Barber to put him in the dumpster. Now."

Hogan and Delmar walked over to the body. He was young, not over 25. His wedding ring looked new. Blue eyes stared into infinity. Hogan closed them with thumb and forefinger.

"Come on, pick that son of a bitch up," Vasco said.

Grunting with effort, Hogan and Delmar lifted the young cop's body into the dumpster.

Vasco pointed. "Cover it up with that cardboard and then close the lid."

They did. Afterward, Hogan's hands shook. It was one thing to hear about a killing. It was another to witness one. And still another to realize you would soon be next. Vasco wasn't likely to leave any witnesses alive.

"Here's the play now," Vasco said. "Sport, that squad car outside the gate, I want you to jump in it, disconnect the mic from the radio and toss it out the window, and then I want you to follow us in the squad car until I find a place to hide it. After that's done we'll go get the key. Now let's move."

With a sigh of resignation, Hogan started toward the gate.

fifty-five

In the passenger's seat on the way to Delmar's apartment, Hogan wondered how much longer his luck would hold out. After stashing the police car off a sandy, rocky side road and, with Delmar's and the kid's help, covering it with sagebrush, Hogan had been certain Vasco would kill him there. Out of the three, he was the only one Vasco didn't need.

But then a stroke of luck appeared, in the form of a buzzing, snorting sound coming closer. Dirt bikes, four of them, tearing down the desert road toward them. They sped past Delmar's car, trailing a cloud of dust, their riders wearing full-face helmets. A straggler snorted by ten seconds later and then a sixth bike three seconds after that.

A scowling Vasco motioned for the three of them to get in the Chrysler. "Let's go get that fucking key."

Despite narrowly avoiding death amid the sagebrush, Hogan was not optimistic about their chances. Once Vasco had the four million, they'd be toast.

Delmar got in behind the wheel, Hogan in the passenger seat, Vasco and the boy in back. No one spoke enroute to the apartment. Halfway to the destination there was a commotion in the back seat. Hogan didn't see what happened, but Delmar's son was hugging the door, as far away from Vasco as he could get, a look of revulsion on his face. Vasco threw his head back and laughed.

After Delmar eased into his parking space in front of the apartment, Hogan had an impulse to jump out and run, try to find a phone to call the police. He quelled the thought. Too much risk of catching a .38 slug in his back. He got out slowly and carefully, hyperalert for any opportunity to get the drop on Vasco.

As they neared the apartment's door, a heavyset woman walked toward them. She wore a ruffled blouse adorned with pink roses, looking like a Rose Parade float. "Mr. Delmar!" she called out. "Oh Mr. Delmar!" She hurried over to them carrying a covered bowl.

"Mrs. Zapeda," Delmar said in an unfriendly tone of voice. "What do you need?"

"I made a three-bean salad and I thought you might like some."

Delmar shook his head, but Vasco said he loved three-bean salad. Delmar thanked her and took the bowl from her. She floated away, beaming.

Inside the apartment Vasco took the bowl from Delmar. "Get that fucking key while I take care of this." He pointed at Hogan and the boy. "You two sit on that sofa and don't make a move." Then he opened kitchen drawers until he found a large spoon and went to work on the three-bean salad, eating directly from the bowl. He wasn't a tidy eater. He set the empty bowl on the counter and walked into the living room. "Got the key?"

Delmar dangled it from the tag. "Here it is."

"Good." Vasco turned to Hogan. "Stand up, Sport." When Hogan stood, Vasco said, "You're of a size. What do you go, two hundred?"

"One ninety."

"Ever been in the ring?"

"Just some amateur bouts in the Marines."

"Semper fi. Hey, I want to see if you can move. Come at me a little, just for fun." He moved the coffee table over to the side. "Jesus H., don't look at me like that, Sport. I'm not looking to chop you up."

Hogan shrugged and went into the stance, hands raised, staring at Vasco's lower chest with a broad focus so he could watch his hands and feet at the same time.

Vasco moved in a boxer's agile dance, hands low. Hogan tried to tag him but slapped empty space every time, receiving a light but stinging thwack of fingertips on face or body for his trouble. He abandoned all thought of offense and tried to simply protect himself, doing his best to duck under jabs, dodge hooks, and otherwise keep from being hit. But Vasco skillfully kept him off balance and defenseless. And that's what happens when an amateur squares off against a pro.

Vasco dropped his hands and grinned. "Not bad, Sport. If you'd stuck with it, you might've been pretty good."

"You're still real quick, Vasco."

"These days my reflexes are slowed to practically nothing. It seems quick to you because I can anticipate where you'll be before I tap you. But hey, that was fun."

Hogan grunted. He wouldn't describe it as fun. When a cat plays with a mouse, it's not much fun for the mouse.

"Okay, people, enough screwing around," Vasco said. "Let's haul ass back to the storage place."

On the way, at Vasco's direction they pulled into a small shopping center and parked in the sparcely occupied lot in front of Blankenbeckler's Hardware.

"I need some pull ties," Vasco said. "Once I get your wrists tied behind your backs, I can relax a little." After warning them to "be cool," Vasco herded them into the store.

The clerk directed him to a center aisle. Vasco grabbed a a handful of large pull ties, paid for them with a wad of cash, and ushered his captives out.

Halfway to the car, looking like a wolf sniffing the air, Vasco ordered them to stop walking.

A uniformed cop, gun drawn, stepped out from behind a delivery van in the row beyond the Chrysler and yelled, "Hold it right there, Vasco."

Two more cops slipped behind them, effectively blocking retreat. Hogan spotted another cop prone on the roof of an nearby building, sniper rifle with scope trained on them. Two squad cars pulled in and screeched to a stop, lights flashing. An armored SWAT vehicle arrived and a half-dozen men in helmets and full body armor jumped out.

Vasco moved close behind the boy and pressed the barrel of the .38 to his head. "Back off," Vasco yelled.

"There's no way out, Vasco," the first cop yelled back. "Drop the gun and raise your hands."

Vasco told the cop to perform an anatomical impossibility.

An unmarked unit pulled up and a man wearing a short-sleeved shirt and a crew cut got out. Hostage negotiator. He took cover behind the delivery van and spoke into a into a handheld mic. "Mr. Vasco, let's talk. Surely you realize you are in an unwinnable situation, surrounded and outgunned. The only option that makes sense is to surrender peaceably, and then everything turns out okay. Nobody gets hurt."

"Bullshit." Vasco spat the word. "If that idiot thinks he's dealing with a clown, he better think again."

Hogan couldn't see how this situation could possibly turn out anywhere close to okay. With the gun at the boy's head, Vasco held all the cards, no matter how much firepower they had trained on him. On *them*. He and the other two captives were squarely in the line of fire. Unless . . .

The negotiator said something to Vasco. While Vasco listened, Hogan whispered to Delmar and the boy, "When I give the signal, drop. Be ready."

"Knock off that whispering," Vasco growled.

Hogan waited, watching Vasco out of the corner of his eye. As he shouted graphic obscenities at the negotiator, Vasco momentarily moved the gun away from the boy's head. Long enough.

"Now!" Hogan shouted.

The three of them dropped to the pavement. Hogan heard a sharp crack, followed by an echo, and then Vasco collapsed on him in a boneless sprawl.

Grunting with effort, Hogan crawled out from under the dead weight and then looked down at what had been Vasco. The entrance hole was behind one ear. Hogan didn't care to see the exit hole. A high-velocity bullet from a police sniper's rifle had turned Vasco off like a switch.

The Bayonne Brawler was down for the long count.

Charlie slowly got to his feet, slapped dust off his slacks, and walked unsteadily to the car. Leaning against the fender, he stared off into the distance, until he became aware of his son standing nearby. He shook his head to clear it. "You okay, Trey?"

Trey looked up. "Well, I'm alive. I have both my ears, and I haven't been sodomized, so I guess I'm all right. What about you?"

That was a matter of opinion. Physically, he felt fine. But his mind was racing in neutral. "I'll be okay. I think."

Hogan came over. "I talked to the lieutenant. He said they spotted my pickup at the storage unit, and then they found the mic Vasco had me toss out of the squad car, investigated further and found the dead cop in the dumpster. A police unit saw your car parked here and called in the cavalry."

"We owe you our lives, Hogan." No doubt about that.

"I can think of a way you can show how grateful you are."

Charlie knew exactly what Hogan meant and replied with a noncommital grunt.

"Anyway, think about it. The lieutenant said after they take our statements we can all go home."

"Thank God." A sudden fatigue, a bone-tired weariness, washed over him, but he knew he wouldn't be able to sleep worth a damnj until after he moved the 4.2 million from unit F-18 to a more secure—and more confidential—location. He and Trey had nearly gotten killed because of the money. Losing it now would finish him off.

Monday he'd make damn sure that couldn't happen.

fifty-six

Trey and Charlie watched the two armed guards transfer the stack of boxes from the cart into the armored truck backed up to the storage facility's door. A single armed guard sat in front. After loading the boxes the guards climbed into the truck and closed the doors behind them. The engine started and the truck began moving. Charlie and Trey got in the car and followed the truck out through the gate.

"Trey, I've been meaning to ask you," Charlie said, "where did you dig up those old hardcover books, record albums, dishes, and file folders, and how did you transport them with your scooter to the storage unit?"

"Goodwill, St. Vincent de Paul, and Salvation Army. And I carried the stuff in a large canvas duffel bag I borrowed from Greta's dad. Tied it on the luggage rack with bungee cords."

"You went to a hell of a lot of trouble. I'm impressed."

"Pulling off a record score, Dad, that's what's impressive."

Charlie grunted and opened a compartment in the center console and handed him something gold and black and flat. "Have a look at where we're going."

It was a very slick brochure for a company called Echelon Premium Vaults:

"Private storage vault in confidential maximum-security facility. Premium-quality, multi-million-dollar, zero-deductible insurance coverage available. Armored truck service also available.

"*All our vaults are secure within a ninety-ton bunker made of hardened steel and concrete, wrapped in nine layers of electronic security, and monitored around the clock by Siemens, the company that safeguards the world's most sensitive facilities.*"

"Echelon is supposed to be one of the best," Charlie said.

"Expensive?"

"Not bad. A bit over three hundred per month. Worth it." The feature that had clinched it: Echelon had branches in most major cities, including Portland. So when he moved to Oregon, they would transfer the contents of his vault to the Portland branch via secure transport.

"Are you just going to leave the money in a vault?"

"Got a better suggestion?"

"Well, I know you don't trust banks, but you might consider feeding some of it into conservative investments. You know—CDs, tax-free municipals, maybe a few no-load mutual funds. It's the best way to offset inflation, as well as the safest. Otherwise, over time it'll eat you up."

He looked over at Trey. "Where did you learn this stuff?"

"I read a lot."

"Okay, I'll check into it."

He had to admit, Trey had a point about inflation. Smart kid. Trey moving the cash into another storage unit to protect it, that was pure genius. If Trey hadn't done that, he'd be out the four million dollars. Before they left to meet the armored truck at the self-storage facility, he had given his son a thousand dollars, "walking-around money." A down payment. Later he would see about setting up a trust fund—or whatever the hell it was called—for him.

The bundles of cash stowed in one of the secure vaults, he and Trey walked to the car.

"Well, Trey," he said, "let's go home."

"Yeah. Then I'm going to hop on the Silver Streak and go for a ride with the Valkyries."

Charlie slid behind the wheel and yawned. "You do that. I'm going to grab some worry-free sleep, the first in weeks."

fifty-seven

Hogan didn't watch many movies on TV. For that matter, he didn't watch much TV. But occasionally he made an exception. He'd built a gin on the rocks and stretched out in the recliner. Then he fell asleep halfway through *Ocean's 11*, one of his favorite movies. When he opened his eyes again the so-called "Rat Pack" was shuffling down the sidewalk, eyes downcast, the familiar Sands sign looming in the background of the final scene. He had slept through the best parts, the scenes featuring vintage Las Vegas, with the Sands, Riviera, Dunes, Sahara, Desert Inn, and many others—all long gone now, demolished in the name of progress when the corporations moved in. The casinos that replaced them were slick, modern, beautiful—and devoid of character.

Nostalgia aside, one thing had always bothered him about *Ocean's 11*: Danny Ocean and his crew lost out on the money. The strictly enforced Motion Picture Production Code spelled out acceptable and unacceptable content for motion pictures. Getting away with theft was unacceptable. He found himself rooting for them anyway. Ironic, he had to admit, for a security expert charged with preventing casino theft. It explained his admiration for Delmar. That mild, ordinary-looking guy had pulled off a spectacular caper. Barring extralegal means, the casinos had no hope of recovering the millions he and his team had taken from them.

During a private dinner for two in the Skyview's Observation Pod, Gabriella had agreed. "It was an expensive lesson," she said. "But realistically, to a casino four million is pocket change, a weekend's profits. We'll be ready for that kind of scam next time."

From now on casinos would check out whales with extra care and thoroughness. No more fugazis. Furthermore, in view of Genesis' rapid evolution, hustlers looking to outsmart the casinos by cheating or counting cards would find themselves backed off expeditiously.

Unless . . . they possessed a special ability.

He stood stock-still, thinking for a moment, then grabbed his jacket and headed out the door.

"Hogan," Delmar said. He opened the door wider and made a sweeping gesture. "Come in."

Hogan entered the apartment. The last time he was there he'd sparred—if you could call it that—with the late Sonny Vasco. He sat down on the couch at Delmar's invitation and looked around. "Where's Trey?"

Delmar dropped into the recliner. "He's riding his scooter with his harem. You met one of them. They all have scooters."

"Trey handled himself pretty well with Vasco. Smart kid."

Delmar nodded. "Yeah, he did good."

"I ran into Frank Borella yesterday. He feels bad about the trouble Vasco caused you, since Vasco was on his payroll. But he's still sore that you clipped his associates."

Delmar gave a short, mirthless grunt of laughter. "I bet. But I ran out of fucks to give weeks ago."

"Ever seen *Oceans 11*, the original one?"

Delmar shook his head. "Why?"

"It was on TV today and I thought of you. Frank Sinatra calls his old army unit back together to hit five Vegas casinos' counting rooms simultaneously on New Year's Eve. They almost pull it off, but their scheme falls apart at the end."

Delmar snorted. "Figures."

"Yeah. But you didn't blow the play, Delmar. You pulled it off. I have to admire that." A little flattery never hurt.

"Call me lucky."

"Yes, definitely." Hogan picked at his thumbnail. "But you have something going on besides luck. Besides counting cards. Something that gives you an unbeatable edge."

"What would that be, Hogan?"

"I'm hoping you'll tell me."

That met with a frown and a shake of his head.

"Listen," Hogan said, "I won't tell a soul, not another living human, word of honor. I would just like to know."

Delmar opened a box on the end table beside the recliner and got a cigar. He took his time lighting it. Then he said, "What do you know about clairvoyance?"

"Almost nothing. I have a hard time believing there's anything to extrasensory perception."

The corners of Delmar's mouth twitched.

"Are you saying you're clairvoyant?" Hogan could hardly get the words out. "You expect me to believe that's your secret?"

"I don't expect anything."

Hogan spotted a dictionary on a bookshelf. He went over and picked it up and flipped through the pages. "Here we are. It says clairvoyance is 'the supernatural power of seeing objects or actions removed in space or time from natural viewing.'" He looked up at Delmar. "'Supernatural power'?" He snorted and returned the dictionary to the shelf.

Delmar chuckled. "Sounds like bullshit, doesn't it?"

"Perhaps it is." Hogan sat down on the sofa and sighed. "But our A.I. doesn't think so."

"And you buy that? From a machine?"

"She says when every other possibility has been examined and discarded, you have to consider what remains. Or words to that effect." Hogan shrugged. "It's logic."

Taking his time, Delmar glowered at a long cigar ash, and tapped it into an ashtray. "Well," he finally said. "your A.i. may have a point."

Hogan looked up. "Think so?"

Delmar directed a plume of smoke at the ceiling. "Hogan, I've always steered clear of woo-woo stuff. Palmistry, tarot cards, astrology, voodoo, Ouija boards—I hate it all. It's all bullshit."

"You didn't include clairvoyance in that lineup."

"I used to."

"But you don't any longer." Hogan held his breath.

Delmar puffed on the cigar, his mild blue eyes looking into the distance. Then they focused on him. "I can't."

"Why not?"

"Because, as they say, seeing is believing."

Hogan followed his gaze to a deck of cards on the coffee table. "Care to prove it?"

"The top card is the queen of hearts."

Hogan reached forward and flipped the card over. Queen of hearts. He cut the deck and looked at Delmar with raised eyebrows.

"Seven of clubs."

Hogan turned over the seven and cut the cards again. "One more time."

"Nine of spades."

After exposing the nine, Hogan sat back and stared at Delmar. "You can see facedown cards."

"Right the first time."

"In God's name, how?"

Delmar shrugged.

"Good Lord, man, this is incredible! It goes way beyond winning at blackjack. It's . . . it's . . . I'm at a loss for words to describe it."

"Proof of extrasensory perception?"

"Definitely. Can you see other things, for example, pages in a notebook, the same way you can with cards?"

Delmar shook his head. "No, just cards. And yes, I'm sure about that."

"Even so, it's astonishing. Another stage in human evolution. It could turn the scientific community upside down."

Delmar shook his head again. "But, it won't, because they won't know about it."

"But—"

"You promised to keep it to yourself, Hogan, gave me your word of honor. Are you an honorable man?"

"Yes, but—"

"I had intended to keep it to myself for the rest of my life, but I figured I owed you. That's the only reason we're having this conversation."

"I understand." He understood, all right. Like being given a ride on a UFO and forbidden to tell anyone. "At least tell me how it works, what you see when it occurs."

Delmar stubbed out the cigar. "First thing that happens, the back of the card kind of quivers, like it's vibrating. And then it turns almost transparent and I see a backwards view of the face of the card. It all happens pretty fast."

"Why do you think it only works with cards?"

"Beats hell out of me, Hogan. Maybe because cards are my thing."

"When did you first notice this ability?"

"Around five years ago. And every time I played since then I halfway expected it to disappear as suddenly as it appeared. But it didn't."

"Sweet Jesus," Hogan said. "That ability, combined with card counting, would be unbeatable. The only thing a casino could do is back you off before you did any real damage."

Delmar smiled. "Unless you had a whale make the bets. I decided to make one last score, one big enough to last me the rest of my life."

"So what are your plans, now that you have enough money to do whatever you want?"

"Retire. Hustling is a tough gig. I had a good run, but now I'm going to kick back and enjoy life. The hell with Las Vegas. I want to get a place on the Oregon coast."

"Good choice." Hogan stood and extended his hand. "Well, Charlie the Barber, clairvoyant, best of luck to you."

Delmar shook his hand. "Thanks, Hogan. Same to you."

Hogan drove away slowly, his erstwhile ordered worldview, his *Weltanschauung*, flipped upside down, all the clever little wheels, cogs, and gears strewn in a jumbled pile on the floor of his mind.

Astounding.

Astonishing.

Friggin' incredible.

Words were inadequate to describe Delmar's gift.

Perhaps it wasn't supernatural, as the dictionary defined it. What if it was totally natural? *Another stage in human evolution*, he had speculated. Maybe future humans would possess clairvoyance and other incredible mental abilities. If so, it would put the gaming world out of business. Vegas would turn into the glitziest ghost town on the planet.

In the meantime he was relieved Delmar planned to retire. It would be a nightmare for casinos if he managed to sneak past security and play, perhaps by using a disguise.

Hogan glanced at his watch. Gabriella was meeting him at two to play a round of golf, since the day was an unseasonably cool 84 degrees. Then they would meet Moe for dinner. Gabriella and Moe had hit it off, which he'd been glad to see. He wished he could share his knowledge of Delmar's special ability with Moe, at least. But he'd given his word, and he did consider himself an honorable man.

However, Genesis wasn't human, so she didn't count. He aimed the pickup toward the Skyview, to tell her she'd been absolutely right. And he wouldn't be a bit surprised if she said, "*I told you so.*"

fifty-eight

Coastal Realty phoned at eleven, just as Charlie finished washing the breakfast dishes. The woman at the other end had a nasal voice with a thick southern accent.

"Mr. Delmah? I believe I've located a house that fits yoah requahments. The ownah just listed it. Had it built last yeeah, but didn't use it as much as she thought she would. Two bedrooms, one bath, an ocean view with a deck. It's small, only twelve hundred squayah feet, but it's perfect for one or two people. All new construction. Cedah siding, hahdwood floahs. It's one of the nicest you'll find in Florence. You can see photos on our website, coastalrealty dot com."

"Just a minute." He turned to Trey. "Jump on your laptop." He gave him the website address, and in three minutes they were looking at the photos. It did look nice. Perfect, in fact. He picked up the phone. "How much?"

"Foah and a quartah."

"Offer four, pending a clean bill from the inspection."

"I'll call the ownah now. I know she's theyah, because I just talked to her. I'll get rought back to yew."

After Charlie hung up, Trey said, "Cool, Dad. Florence is only an hour's drive from Eugene."

That was one of the main reasons he had chosen Florence instead of one of the other towns on the Oregon coast. That, and the fact it was the right size, around 10,000 people.

Also, Three Rivers Casino Resort was nearby, in case he got an urge to dust off his blackjack chops. He'd never played in an Indian casino, but he had heard they were as well-run and deluxe as any of the joints in Vegas or Reno.

The woman from Coastal called back at a quarter to one. "Mr. Delmah? I have good news. She accepted yoah offah. I'll staht the ball rollin' pendin' receipt of uhnest money."

"Would five thousand be enough, or do you need more?"

"Five thousand'll be fine."

"If you give me the routing and account numbers I'll have my bank transfer funds electronically this afternoon."

She read the numbers to him and told him she would be in touch and to have a wonderful day, Mr. Delmah.

He hung up the phone, making a mental to-do list. First on the list was a trip to his bank after getting five grand from his safe. Then to Echelon Premium Vaults to take out four hundred round ones and make arrangments for armored transport of the rest to Echelon's branch in Portland. The last stop would be U-Haul to rent an enclosed trailer just large enough for his few possessions and Trey's scooter.

Right now he needed to see the apartment manager to give notice. They required thirty days' notice in advance, so he'd forfeit his deposit, but it was worth it to get the hell out of Vegas before something else happened.

Charlie parked the car and trailer alongside the grass strip in the center of the courtyard, in front of his apartment. Loading the trailer didn't take long. Trey's scooter went in last. He and Trey lifted it in and secured it with straps. The safe went in the trailer, inside a large suitcase. The four bundles of cash, each containing a hundred grand, wouldn't fit in the safe, so he stashed them under the spare tire in the trunk, after wrapping them in paper bags. Counting the ninety-five thousand in the safe, he'd be carrying almost a half-million dollars in cash. Before the big play, that would have seemed like all the money in the world.

He went inside the apartment for one last walk-through to make sure he hadn't overlooked anything. After he dropped the key in the manager's mailbox, they'd be off.

A female voice hailed him as he was walking back from the manager's office. Mrs. Zepeda. He winced and stopped.

She wore pink shorts and a fussy white blouse trimmed in lace, with sandals that gave her feet the look of hams bound with white ribbon. "I hear you're leaving us," she said, walking toward him with mincing steps.

"I'm afraid so. Moving to Oregon, closer to my son."

"We're sure going to miss you around here."

"I'll miss all of you, too." What the hell, it didn't cost him anything to say it. "I've enjoyed living here." Which was true, for the most part. He'd lived here comfortably for ten years.

"Well, you take care, now." She minced away.

He spotted Trey across the courtyard, talking to Greta and two other girls. The Valkyries. They were laughing helplessly at something Trey said.

At first he didn't see the man in a yellow polo shirt and tan slacks, one haunch propped on the trailer's fender, arms crossed. Bad combover, pot gut. Olmeyer.

"Hi, Charlie," Olmeyer said. "Surely you weren't planning to leave without saying goodbye?"

"What do you want, Olmeyer?"

Olmeyer smiled broadly, exposing bad teeth. "Money."

fifty-nine

"Money?" Charlie said and snorted. "You must be crazy, Olmeyer. Didn't we go down this road already? Why are you still hassling me? I am going to call Metro and tell them to reel you in, because this is bullshit."

If it fazed Olmeyer, he didn't show it. His shit-eating grin was still there. "I'm betting either the car or trailer is loaded with cash. I want it."

"Got a warrant to search this time?"

He scowled. "What makes you think I need one?"

"It's the law, right?"

The grin reappeared. "Fuck the law. Me and Giles are no longer on the job. Thanks to your complaint."

"My complaint? I didn't file a complaint." It must've been Hogan. He'd said he was going to inform Metro Police about Olmeyer's and Giles' extracurricular activities.

"Anyways, I'm a private citizen now, just like you. With one big difference . . ." He removed a small, blue automatic from his waistband. "This is Simon. Ever play Simon Says? Simon says get your ass in this car. You're driving."

"Where?"

"I'll tell you where. Get in."

Charlie opened the door and slid behind the wheel.

Olmeyer walked around the front of the car and got in on the passenger side. "Let's go."

Charlie started the car and put it in drive. They began rolling. He turned his head and looked across the courtyard. Trey was standing there watching them leave, looking very confused. Charlie mouthed *HELP!*, in a desperate and probably futile attempt to signal Trey that he was in trouble.

"Turn right," Olmeyer said.

"Something's wrong," Trey said to Greta. "I know that guy. He's a crooked cop. I'm pretty sure I saw a gun in his hand. He carjacked my dad at gunpoint."

"Omigod," Greta said. "You've got to call the police."

"We have to follow them. I'll call the police on the way."

"Okay. Saddle up, Valkyries."

Ten seconds later, sounding like a muffled swarm of bees, the three scooters were on the road, Trey riding helmetless behind Greta. He spotted the U-Haul three blocks ahead and pointed.

"Let's keep them in sight," he yelled to Greta, "but stay back two blocks."

She nodded.

Trey took out his iPhone and told Siri to dial the Las Vegas Metro Police.

Charlie drove north on Harmon Avenue, following Olmeyer's instructions mechanically. His mind worked furiously, trying to come up with a way to prevent Olmeyer from finding the four hundred thousand hidden under the spare tire. If he had to, he'd sacrifice the ninety-five in the safe. It would sting, but not as much as losing the four hundred round ones.

Wild card: Was Olmeyer desperate enough to use the gun? Hard to get a read on the guy, but he seemed erratic. And he blamed Charlie for getting him kicked off the police force.

After a confusing series of turns, Charlie recognized that they were in northeast Vegas, an industrial area. Away from people. Not exactly comforting.

He glanced in the side mirror and saw the scooters following them, two blocks back. Good. Trey had sense enough to stay a safe distance behind them. Hopefully, he had his phone with him, so he could call for help.

Olmeyer pointed. "See the warehouses on the left? Pull in there. Park in the shade next to the closest one."

Charlie did as he was told. At Olmeyer's direction he shut off the engine and then got out and followed Olmeyer to the back of the trailer.

Olmeyer stuck a toothpick in one corner of his mouth. "Guess what I want you to do now, Charlie the Barber."

"Unlock the trailer."

"Circle gets the square."

Charlie unlocked the padlock with the key still wearing a tag marked F-14, threw the door open, and stood aside.

"Show me what you got in there."

Charlie climbed inside. Olmeyer stood outside at the entrance, leaning in. The trailer's contents: Trey's scooter, secured with straps through eyelets in the trailer's wall. Three cardboard boxes containing dishes, towels, and bedding. A vinyl wardrobe for Charlie's suits, sport coats, and slacks. Two medium-size suitcases full of other clothes. And a large suitcase that contained one item: his safe, which held the ninety-five thousand.

One by one, Charlie opened the boxes and medium-size suitcases and showed the contents to Olmeyer. He opened the large suitcase last.

"Open the safe," Olmeyer said.

Charlie entered the combination until it clicked.

Olmeyer pointed. "Set it down here." He opened the lid and tossed some papers aside, exposing the money. Then Olmeyer chuckled as he counted the banded stacks of hundred-dollar bills, ten bills in a stack. "Ninety-five grand," he said and looked up at Charlie, still crouching inside the trailer. "Where's the rest?"

Charlie was ready with an answer. "On its way to Portland in an armored truck."

"I don't believe you."

"You think I'm going to carry millions of dollars around? I'm not stupid. I hired an armored truck to transport it."

"Come on out of there. I want to check your car, starting with the trunk."

As he stepped out of the trailer, Charlie had injury added to insult when the top edge of the doorway gave his forehead a painful rap, as though the universe was giving him a message: *Your luck's run out, Charlie.*

The Chrysler's trunk popped opened at the turn of the key. The spare tire was stored in a recessed area under a concealed lid on the floor of the trunk. There was a chance Olmeyer wouldn't know that. Covering the lid were a set of jumper cables, a canvas bag containing assorted tools, three orange traffic cones, and a scissor jack. The jack was supposed to be stored with the spare, but he had needed the room for the four bags of cash, which he'd barely managed to squeeze underneath the spare.

"I see the jack," Olmeyer said. "Where's the spare?"

"Beats me," Charlie lied. "Never needed it."

"Surely you got a spare. Wait, what's this here?" Olmeyer pointed to the strap used to open the lid. He moved the jack and other items off the lid and lifted the strap. "Well, well, well," he said. "Looks like we got us a spare here."

Charlie continued playing dumb. "I'll be damned."

Olmeyer unscrewed the large wingnut that held the spare in place, tossed it aside, and lifted the tire out of the wheel well, exposing the four brown paper bags, each sealed bag containing a hundred thousand. He ripped open one of the bags and riffled through the cash. Then he turned to Charlie with a grin on his face. "Nice try."

Charlie swallowed, feeling like he'd been slugged in the gut. The knowledge he had three and a half million left didn't give him much comfort. Losing almost five hundred grand is bound to leave a mark. But he needed to look at it philosophically, as a strategic loss, like losing a big blackjack pot on purpose when he got heat.

"So," Olmeyer said, "ninety-five grand from the safe plus the money in these bags still falls way, way short. You were being straight with me about sending money to Portland in an armored truck? Fuck. Still, I wouldn't call almost a half mil chump change." He spat on the asphalt. "I deserve the money, goddamn it. Eighteen years on the job and I don't have squat to show for it. It's about time I hit the jackpot."

Charlie clenched his jaw. The crazy son of a bitch thought he deserved the money. His money. He'd busted his ass to get hold of it, and now this jerk with a combover and bad breath wanted to take it away from him. Chalking it up as a strategic loss didn't make it sting any less.

As Olmeyer gathered up the bagged money from the wheel well, on impulse Charlie reached around and snatched the pistol from the big man's waistband. Olmeyer grunted and pinned Charlie's forearm against his side with his elbow . . . but Charlie pulled free. Olmeyer dropped the bags back in the trunk and made a frantic grab for the gun. They struggled for long seconds, both clutching at the weapon.

The pistol's sudden discharge sounded like the crack of a tree split by lightning. It echoed down the metal and asphalt canyon between warehouses.

And something had smacked him a good one. When he was twelve a wild baseball pitch tagged him in the lower belly, just above his left hip. It felt like a replay of that. He gently probed the spot with his left hand. It felt sticky. Bright blood covered his fingers.

He'd been shot.

Jesus.

The strange thing was, it didn't hurt at all. Not one bit, which shocked him. Then he became aware of a burning sen-sation in the area, spreading outward.

"Shouldn't have tried that, Charlie," Olmeyer said. "Got yourself shot for your trouble."

Feeling woozy all of a sudden, he wobbled over to the warehouse. His back against corrogated metal, he slid down until his butt met asphalt, glad he was in the shade.

With great difficulty he slipped out of his coat. He folded it several times and pressed it against the wound, hoping it would slow the bleeding. Blood soaked his side and part of his left leg. As he sat there fading in and out of consciousness, a single horrible thought filled his mind: *I'm about to die.*

He waited. For the white light. For the feeling of his soul departing, a hand reaching out to take his, or any of the sensations people describe in near-death experiences.

None of that happened. After several minutes passed he realized he wasn't dying after all. At least, not yet. The burning in his side commanded all his attention. No sharp or shooting pain, nothing like he'd assumed he'd feel if a metal object ripped through his body, only the burning spreading through his left side.

"Well, Charlie," Olmeyer said, "I'm sorry as hell you got shot, but I can't do anything about that now." He opened the driver's door on the Chrysler. "I can't take a chance on running you to the hospital and having you call the cops on me. You're on your own. Good luck."

Charlie blacked out as the driver's door slammed shut.

Tires screeching to a stop on asphalt brought him back. Two uniformed officers appeared, guns drawn. One of them, a tall Latino officer, spotted Charlie sitting there, his back against the building, his folded coat pressed against his side. The cop's eyes went to the blood-soaked shirt and pants.

Charlie lifted the shirt, revealing the wound.

"That's a gunshot," the officer said. "How did it happen?"

Charlie looked at Olmeyer, talking to the other cop.

The Latino officer spoke into a mic at his shoulder. "We need an ambulance for a gunshot victim." He gave the warehouse's address to the dispatcher. Then he turned to Charlie "Where's the gun?"

Charlie inclined his head toward Olmeyer.

The officer spoke for several seconds to his partner, a black man, who then went back to Olmeyer.

"You know the drill, Olmeyer," he said. "Turn around . . . hands on the car, feet spread."

"Come on, Yednock, you know me, goddamn it." When Yednock motioned with his gun, Olmeyer said, "I was on the job, for chrissake. Doesn't that mean anything to you guys?"

"There's a warrant out on you, Olmeyer," Yednock said. "For assaulting the lieutenant. You do the honors, Garcia."

Garcia patted Olmeyer down and found his pistol, which he handed to Yednock. "I never liked you, Olmeyer," Garcia said while cuffing him. "Maybe the fact you're a racist son of a bitch has something to do with it. Besides that, you were on the take, and everyone knew it. Guys like you give cops a bad name." He shoved Olmeyer to make him walk to the squad car and closed him in the back.

Yednock knelt down in front of Charlie. "If you can manage it, could I see your identification, sir?"

Charlie took out his drivers license and handed it to him.

Yednock looked at it and gave it back. "Can you tell me what happened, Mr. Delmar?"

Charlie took several deep breaths before he answered. "Olmeyer showed up ... at my apartment. He pulled a gun on me ... and made me drive him here. He was going to ... take the money I had in a safe in the trailer."

A buzzing grew louder, announcing the arrival of Trey and the Valkyries on scooters. They must've been hanging back.

Trey hopped off and ran over. "Dad, are you okay?"

"Got a hole in my gut ... but I might make it."

Yednock said, "An ambulance is on the way."

"Officer, this is my son, Trey. He saw Olmeyer carjack me."

"He pointed a gun at my dad and then they took off in Dad's car. I followed them and called the police on the way."

A siren in the distance seemed to be getting closer. No telling how much time he had before he passed out again. He gestured for Trey to come close. "Stick the money back in the safe ... and put the safe in the suitcase. In the car's trunk, hide the four bags ... under the spare, close the lid."

"I'm on it, Dad."

"Go see the apartment manager ... tell her we decided to stay through the end of the month after all. Get a set of keys."

"Got it."

"Call Hogan. Tell him what happened . . . ask him to help you move the car and trailer back to the apartment . . . and then, after you've unloaded the trailer, return it to U-Haul."

"Don't worry, Dad. I'll handle everything."

Charlie passed out again just as the ambulance pulled up. He was only hazily aware of being lifted onto a stretcher and carried to the ambulance. After that he had only a few brief snatches of awareness in the hospital. He woke up on a gurney in an elevator, felt tubes in his nose, and began to yank them out. Nurses beside the gurney shouted and restrained his hands.

He blacked out.

When he came to, late afternoon sun streamed through the hospital room window. A doctor with close-cropped gray hair and a Van Dyke beard strolled into the room.

Checking the bandage, he said, "How are you feeling?"

Charlie grunted. "Shot."

It made the doctor laugh. "You could be worse off. The bullet entered your abdomen just above your left hip, traversed diagonally upward, and lodged just below your right rib cage. Damage to vital organs was relatively minor. But you lost a lot of blood. That's why you kept losing consciousness. We gave you four pints."

"How come there wasn't any pain when I got shot?"

"You were shot with a three-eighty-caliber bullet, the type that remains intact, rather than exploding into flesh-shredding shrapnel. That accounts for the lack of pain initially."

"You're saying I'm lucky?"

"Many people who catch a bullet there don't survive. You almost made sure you wouldn't—when you were conscious you refused to give the hospital consent to operate. There wasn't much chance you'd pull through without it. The hospital overrode your obstinance and performed the life-saving surgery you needed."

"I flat don't remember doing that," Charlie said. "Sorry to be a pain in the ass."

"It's common with major injuries. You were in shock. *Non compos mentis.*"

Charlie sighed. And even that hurt.

Trey walked in the door. And first thing, of course, he had to hug Charlie, who stiffened involuntarily, although the shooting pain told him that was a big mistake.

"Dad, you look great," Trey said, sounding like he really meant it,

"I'm a pretty tough bird, as it turned out."

The doctor turned to leave "Mr. Delmar, you seem to be doing fine."

"Question . . . how long will I be here, you think?"

"Two weeks, at least," the doctor said over his shoulder as he walked out the door. "A month at the outside."

Charlie winced. He'd give it two weeks, tops.

Trey slid a chair close to the bed and sat down. "I took care of everything you told me to—the money, the U-Haul, the apartment. I didn't need to bother Hogan. I handled it all myself. Your car drives pretty nice."

"I'll be damned."

"That realtah lady called. She said she's arrangin' foah an inspection and that y'all could prolly count on a Septembah fust closin' date."

Charlie laughed. It hurt. "You done real good."

Trey smiled. "We both did."

"When does school start? You're going to be in the ninth grade this year, right?"

"Tenth, sophomore. Classes start September tenth."

"I'll get you there, one way or another."

That is, if no more unpleasant surprises were waiting to pounce.

sixty

Dead certain the Jeep was on the verge of tipping over backwards, then sliding down the steep desert slope upside down on top of them, Hogan braced himself and yelled, "Jesus, Gabriella!"

She only laughed. "Keep the faith, Sam."

They made it, but not without more vocal accompaniment from him. With the Jeep idling at the top, he scowled at her. "I honestly thought we were going over."

"I can climb steeper slopes than this. Want to see?"

"That won't be necessary."

She pointed. "See that hill over there? The other side is concave and shaded. We can have our picnic there, if that's okay with you?"

"Assuming we don't have to risk our lives to make it there, sure."

"Don't worry, we'll continue on the trail.

"Trail?"

"We Desert Wranglers—that's the name of the Jeep Wrangler club in this area—we are at all times respectful of the desert ecology, and we're careful not to damage it. We follow only designated trails."

"You mean we've been following a trail, even up this sixty-degree slope?"

"It's more like forty, but yes."

Underway again, slightly compressed lips and a vertical furrow between her brows were the only signs of concentration as she navigated the desert terrain. She handled the Jeep like a pro, no question about it, even if it did make his kidneys feel like concertinas.

She looked the part—no makeup, hair in ponytail, khaki short-sleeve shirt and shorts, boots, hat with a wide brim—like a cover model for *Off-Road Woman*.

He, in contrast, looked like a tourist ashore from a cruise ship, sporting a blue-green polo shirt, white shorts, well-used canvas boat shoes, and a floppy-brimmed hat with a camouflage pattern.

The Jeep slid to a stop and Gabriella shut off the engine. He climbed out and stretched, trying to loosen up muscles tense from bracing for disaster.

The site Gabriella suggested for their picnic had been carved out of a rocky, sandy hill, creating shade for an area about twenty by thirty. By the looks of the vegetation and the copious animal tracks in the sandy soil, it was a favorite with desert flora and fauna.

"Sam, before we unload the food, come with me."

"Lead on."

They wound through a copse of Yellow Palo Verde on their way to the shady area. The trees ordinarily were seen only in the Sonoran Desert much farther south. Further on, sprays of Desert Marigolds bedecked both sides. The path opened into a shady clearing, in the middle of which a flat, sandy area provided a suitable place to spread a blanket for a picnic.

"Perfect," Hogan said. "How did you find this little oasis?"

"We Desert Wranglers know all the best places."

"I have trouble picturing you joining a club like that. You seem more like the type to be a patron of the arts or cultural exchange organizer—something more . . . sophisticated."

She snorted. "I've always loved active things. I tried sky diving and motorcycle riding. Drove my dad crazy."

"I believe it. Now let's have ourselves a picnic."

The thick roast beef sandwiches from Bodenheimer's Delica-tessen, garnished with Jack cheese and kosher dills, slathered with the deli's proprietary horseradish sauce, were delicious. A superior potato salad made the perfect side dish. The lunch cried out for cold beer, but since alchohol and four-wheeling didn't mix, they washed it down with iced tea from the deli.

Hogan felt his snare-drum-tight belly. "I forget what they call it when horses eat too much and swell up."

"Foundered."

"Yeah, foundered. I knew that last bag of oats was a big mistake."

Without missing a beat, she said, "I tried to rein you in, but you kept whinnying for more."

"A smart filly like you would surely realize she's not deal-ing with a one-trick pony."

"Neigh, sir, neigh."

They laughed at their silliness and then they lay back on the blanket, his head on his jacket, her head resting on his arm.

"This is nice," she said.

He nodded. "Yeah."

It was beyond nice. Having her near filled an empty place he hadn't known existed. Had it not been for Gabriella, he al-most surely would have endured the paucity of intimacy in his life, oblivious to it. But now he was like a man who, blind since birth, had gained sight.

Not that he hadn't had relationships. He'd cut a wide swath through cocktail waitresses, shopgirls, bank tellers, even a dental hygienist. All superficial, all unfulfilling. Eventually he stopped bothering. Until Gabriella. And had she not taken the initiative, his monastic existence would have continued.

"Sam," she said, "Genesis has an unmistakably female voice. Does she have any other qualities or attributes that would be seen as distinctly female?"

He turned his head to look at her. "That, Desert Wrangler woman, definitely qualifies as a non sequitur."

"Sorry, it's just that I've been wondering about it."

"Well," he said, "now that you mention it . . . I've noticed a few things that might be seen as feminine."

"Yes?"

"For one thing, she's curious about relationships, human relationships, mine in particular. She asked why Moe and I aren't romantic partners."

"I've wondered that myself."

"So I explained to the nosy A.I. that Moe already had a partner, whose name is Susan. That shut her up for a while."

It shut Gabriella up as well. After a thoughtful pause she said, "I didn't see *that* coming."

"Don't feel bad, nobody sees it. Anyway, that's one example. But there are other things that are harder to put your finger on. The questions Genesis asks and the way she phrases them have a feminine vibe. Subtle, but it's there."

"You think maybe Julian created a girlfriend for himself?"

"Julian's dating a cocktail waitress from the Casablanca. Genesis asked me about her, and I swear to God I heard a note of jealousy in her voice."

"So she's in love with her creator?"

"Sounds crazy, but I wouldn't rule it out. Not now."

"How fascinating!"

"She also asked about you and me."

"What did you tell her?"

His warped sense of humor stepped up to the mic. "I told her it's a summer daliance. A mad fling."

After a few moments silence she said, "Yeah, that's how I would have answered her, too."

"Oh, and I also told her you were just slumming."

She sat upright and glared at him. "That's not funny."

"Okay, okay, I made that up." Touchy, touchy.

She lay back.

"Because if anyone's slumming, it's me," he said.

She started to protest, but he silenced her with a kiss.

"Keep on slumming," she said after they parted.

He squeezed her hand. "Change of topic. Has your dad said anything to you about staying at my place so much?"

"No. He knows better."

Gabriella was Rossi's only child, his baby girl. That was big juju. He wouldn't dare interfere in one of her relationships now, not after she tightened him up for trying. Her father was a tough guy. Hard to believe he'd kowtow to anyone, even his own daughter.

She turned over and propped herself up with her elbows. Looking into his face, piercing him with those glacial-blue eyes, she said, "Have you thought about what we talked about last night?"

His single bark of laughter had an ironic edge. "I haven't thought about much else."

"Me, as well. I thought this would be good for us, occupy our minds with something else. Something distracting."

"It's distracting, all right. Especially when you're hanging on for dear life."

"Anyway, let's talk about it. You go first."

He refolded the jacket he was using as a pillow, hoping to make it somewhat more comfortable, and settled back. "As i said last night, you caught me by surprise. Early on in our. . . relationship—that sounds funny, since we've been together a month and a half—early on you said you might not ever get married again. What changed your mind? Before you answer, I want you to know how flattered I am. I think you're crazy, but I'm flattered."

"Sam. You've got to get over that I'm-not-worthy stuff. Listen to me very carefully. You're worthy, you're worthy. God, I feel like I'm on *Wayne's World*. We're getting off-track." She took a breath. "Know what changed my mind? Besides meeting a handsome, intelligent, sensitive—"

"You're not talking about a gay person, right?"

"Damn it, you're doing it again. Using humor to diffuse a situation you find uncomfortable."

"You got me. Sorry. You started to say, besides meeting a guy who checks all the boxes . . ."

"Besides that, I had an epiphany."

"I'm always in the mood to listen to a good epiphany."

"Here it is. I've come to the realization that I want a child. At least one. Me, someone who has proclaimed on more than one occasion she did not want kids."

"What triggered this sudden change of heart?"

"I stumbled across a book, *The Procreation Imperative*."

"Biological-clock talk?"

"I guess you could call it that, but it's more comprehensive. One of the parts that spoke to me the loudest featured interviews with women who chose not to have children, using reasons eerily similar to mine. All of them, without exception, regretted their choice later. During their interviews they seemed extremely depressed and some cried about it, according to the book's author. I don't want that to be me."

"You feel you're running out of time?"

"Tick tock."

"And you want me to be the biological father of your child, or children?"

"Sounds clinical, but that's the general idea."

"So last night you asked me to marry you."

"And you didn't say no."

"Or yes." He sat up. "Let me ask you a question. Is this maternal urge the primary reason you want to get married?"

"It's one reason, not the primary reason. I asked myself if kids weren't in the picture would I want to spend the rest of my life with you. The answer was . . . absolutely."

He kissed her softly.

She searched his face. "So you're onboard?"

"Such a romantic way to put it. What about our ages? In particular, *my* age."

"What about it? According to *The Procreation Imperative*, even men in their seventies and eighties have fathered children. Having a child in your forties is commonplace."

"Perhaps so, but that doesn't mean a man *should*. Let's say we have a child. By the time he's twenty I'll be . . . sixty-four."

"He?"

"Or she."

She shrugged. "Sixty-four is the new forty-four."

"Frankly, I'd given up on having kids. But at one time the idea appealed to me a lot. You know, having progeny? A sort-of immortality." He adjusted the coat-pillow under his neck. "Somewhere along the line I accepted that I would probably shuffle off this mortal coil without passing on my DNA."

"Sounds like some of the men interviewed in *The Procreation Imperative*."

"Anyway, I was sure that ship had sailed."

She stroked his cheek with the backs of her fingers. "But now you have a second chance at immortality."

"I suppose I'll have to buy you an engagement ring."

"Yes. A nice one. You can afford it." She shifted onto her side so she could look at him. "I know I'm rushing you, but lately time, as they say, is of the essence."

"Then let's go home and make a baby."

"Whoa, big fella. There's a formality we'll need to attend to before I put away the birth-control pills."

"Oh. Right, but this is Las Vegas, hon, the 'Wedding Chapel Capital of the World.'"

She looked at him like he'd lost his mind. Enunciating each word carefully, she said, "We must have a Catholic wedding. My father would insist on it. As would I."

"You're sure? I hate to pass up a chance to have an Elvis look-alike give us our vows."

"Ever been to an Italian wedding, Sam?"

"Nope. I've seen *The Godfather*, *Goodfellas*, and *Casino*. They all had Italian wedding scenes. Does that count? "

"First thing to know, everybody's required to pack heat. Got a gun?" Her deadpan expression revealed nothing.

It took him a moment to work it out. "Is this payback for my good-natured, merry japes?"

"Smart boy." She kissed the tip of his nose. "Ready to go?"

sixty-one

The wedding reception looked like a scene from *Goodfellas*. With the exception of Hogan's mother, father, and sister, and of course Hogan himself, it was a sea of Italians. Hogan wondered if any of them were made men. It wouldn't surprise him if at least one had made his bones. Hell, maybe many more than one. And one of those goombahs was, as of today, his father-in-law.

Gabriella slipped her arm around his waist. "Having fun yet?"

"Hi there, wife. As much fun as a person can have at such a cut-rate affair." In truth, the opulence of the reception, like the wedding itself, would befit royalty.

She gave his side a squeeze. "Daddy likes to save money."

"Hope he got a deal on that champagne fountain. Say, I noticed nobody's armed. Didn't you tell me packing heat was a requirement at Italian weddings?"

"Obviously you've never heard of concealed carry."

Game, set, match.

They were joined by Moe and Susan, who had changed from their bridesmaids dresses into dresses that showed off their legs, drawing every nongay male eye in the room and probably more than a few belonging to gay females.

"I'm trying to convince Moe we should tie the knot, too," Susan said.

Gabriella put her hand on Susan's arm and with a surprisingly credible Vito Coleone impression said, "Make her an offer she can't refuse."

Hogan and Moe looked at each other and broke up, while a deadpan Gabriella looked on.

"Tell you what," Moe said, "I'll give it some thought if you promise me I won't find a horse's head in my bed."

Susan gave her a peck on the cheek. "Deal."

Hogan's phone trilled, announcing the arrival of a text message. It was from Genesis: *"Congratulations, Hogan."*

He texted back, thanking her. Beyond a doubt, Genesis was observing them at that very moment. The reception was held in the Skyview's banquet room, which like most of the spaces in the Skyview had concealed cameras everywhere, providing total coverage. Hogan faced the nearest corner and gave the hidden camera a thumbs up.

"Hogan's signaling to his girlfriend," Gabriella said to the others. "I think she's jealous."

Hogan grinned. "I'm keeping Genesis on the side, in case this marriage thing doesn't work out.'

"Lordy," Gabriella said. "I've got a rival without a body. How do you compete with the incorporeal?"

"Who doesn't have a body?" Julian stood there grinning, a blonde on his arm. She had a childlike face and a mature body, with a set of truly impressive mammaries, a good part of which were exposed by the plunging neckline of her mini-dress. All in all, she was perfect for Julian. He said, "People, I'd like you all to meet Brianna."

They acknowledged her with smiles and nods.

"What do you do, dear?" Moe asked her.

"Well, right now I'm working cocktail at the Casablanca," she said, "but I plan to go to dealer school." She turned to Julian and in an immature, wheedling tone of voice said, "Julie, hon, would you run get me a margarita?"

"Sure thing, darlin'," Julian said and headed for the bar.

Gabriella leaned close to Hogan. "Sammy, hon, would you run get me a vodka martini?"

"Call me Sammy one more time, darlin', and you'll be Gabby forevermore. One vodka martini coming right up."

On the way back with Gabriella's martini and his gin and tonic, he felt a big hand on his shoulder. It belonged to Rossi, and he looked far more serious than the occasion called for. Hogan swallowed, wondering what in hell could be on his father-in-law's mind.

Rossi accompanied him over to Gabriella and the others. He hugged his daughter and said, "Mind if I steal your new husband for a little while? Thanks, honey."

He escorted Hogan to a private elevator that took them to the Skyview's offices. Rossi's expansive office suite was well equipped: Sauna, jacuzzi, and massage room. The largest flat-screen TV Hogan had ever seen. Golf simulator with putting green and driving range. And of course a well-stocked bar.

Rossi went behind the bar. "What's your pleasure, Sam?"

"Gin and tonic, if you please." He'd left a full one behind.

"Lime or lemon?"

"Lime, thanks."

Rossi made their drinks and handed Hogan his. He escorted Hogan across the room to an exquisitely detailed eight-foot-tall scale replica of the Skyview. It must have cost a fortune. Rossi motioned to an arrangement of chairs nearby. "Let's sit here where we can relax and talk."

Hogan sat down next to Rossi. Upholstered in a soft white leather with a grain so fine it felt silky, the chair enveloped him in luxurious comfort. He worked on the gin and waited for Rossi to share what was on his mind.

Rossi hoisted his anisette toward Hogan. "Salute." He took a sip. "You know, Sam, when I gave you my blessing I wasn't capitulating to Gabriella's wishes. But I got the impression you thought I was, and that I disapproved. Was I imagining it?"

Hogan didn't try to bullshit him. "Mr. Rossi—Nick—I'm not an opportunist. I was worried you'd think I swooped in and took advantage of your daughter."

"If I know my daughter, she did the swooping in."

Hogan laughed. "I guess she did at that."

"Once Gabriella decides she wants something, she can be . . . tenacious. I'll tell you this, I have never won a power struggle with her, not one. And now you're up at bat, Hogan. I think she picked a fine young man."

Hogan did a double take, sure that Rossi was mocking him. He seemed serious. "Young? That's a bit of a stretch."

"I'm being straight with you. You're still a young man. It's all relative." He smiled. "How old do you think I am?"

"Fifty . . . two?"

"Sixty-nine next month. And you're forty-three?"

Hogan nodded.

"Shit, to me you're still a kid. I could be your dad."

"But the thing is, Nick," and using Rossi's first name, at his insistence, felt weird as hell, "Gabriella's only thirty-one. The twelve-year age difference bothered . . . bothers me. Her, not at all, said I'm making way too big a deal out of it." The unburdening gave Hogan the very strange feeling of being in a confession booth. Stranger still for the fact that he hadn't been to confession in twenty years. Not to mention, Rossi had to be the most unlikely priest surrogate imaginable.

"I agree with her," Rossi said, getting to his feet. "Hey, I gotta take a leak. And then what do you say we drive a few?" He inclined his head toward the golf simulator.

While Rossi was gone, Hogan meandered about, admiring Rossi's paintings of Las Vegas. "Sin City Nocturne" would be a perfect addition to his father-in-law's collection, he decided. A thank you for the generous portfolio of stocks and bonds Rossi had given them for a wedding present.

They set their drinks on a roll-around caddy while they selected their clubs from a rack along the back wall. Hogan picked a Calloway driver that had a good feel, Rossi a driver he'd had custom made. It had cost him two grand, he said.

The "driving range" appeared to stretch into the distance, a high-resolution image projected onto a huge screen about twenty feet from the tee. Sophisticated sensors on its surface measure the ball's direction, speed, and spin, Rossi told him. "That's how it calculates the flight path."

Rossi teed up a ball and addressed it with his driver. His swing was elegant and powerful, a textbook example of how to do it. The ball struck the screen—a tough, flexible membrane—and dropped to the floor. In the onscreen image the ball continued flying, to land just short of the 250-yard sign in the virtual distance, smack in the middle of the range.

"Nice drive," Hogan said, teeing up his ball. "Now watch me whiff mine."

But he didn't. Mercifully, the ball flew straight and true up the middle to land within twenty feet of Rossi's ball.

"Goddamn," Rossi said, "I'm relieved you know what you're doing. I don't know what I would've done if you had turned out to be a spaz. Probably have you whacked." After several deadpan seconds the corners of his mouth began twitching almost imperceptibly, exactly like Gabriella's when she was struggling to keep a straight face.

"In that case," Hogan said without cracking a smile, "I'm glad I didn't know my life was at stake. It would've affected my swing, sure as shit."

Rossi's booming laugh filled the suite. "Sam," he said, "you've removed any doubt that you'll be able to match wits with my daughter. I wondered about that."

"Gabriella and I have crossed swords more than a few times. I would describe her sense of humor as . . . wicked and deadly. And of course dry as a bone."

"As long as you know what you're getting into."

"We're pretty evenly matched, actually."

"And that's why I predict it's going to work. It wouldn't have a snowball's chance in hell if you didn't have the chops to dance with her."

"She keeps me on my toes."

"Sam," Rossi said, slipping a proprietary arm around his shoulders, "let's swat some balls."

They took turns at the tee. Rossi's drives were more consistent, but Hogan matched him for distance. With a bit of practice to dial in his swing, regaining the accuracy he used to have wouldn't be a problem.

Rossi sat down and mopped the sweat off his face with a handkerchief. "Listen, Sammy, if you're still concerned about the twelve-year age difference, I was sixteen years older than Isabella, Gabriella's mother. Didn't matter a bit."

Hogan felt a maniacal urge to laugh. Concern about Rossi's reaction had played a big part in his too-old-for-her guilt. But if Rossi and Gabriella didn't care about the age difference, why should he? Even being called Sammy couldn't spoil his relief.

"Down to business." Rossi replaced his club in the rack. "Sam, you're part of the family now. Any job you want in the hotel or casino, you got it. Just say the word."

Hogan had been expecting to be invited into the fold, and there it was. It called for diplomacy. "I appreciate that. But I think I'd like to stick with Security Concepts for the time being. Is that a problem?"

"Not at all. But if you see a position you'd like, up to and including casino manager, we'll work you into it. That's all I'm saying."

"As I said, I appreciate it . . . Nick. I'm not ready to take you up on it right away, but if I do I'd want to start at the bottom, to better understand the operation."

Rossi faced him squarely, a hand on each shoulder. "You're a wise young man. And if you ask me, my daughter lucked out."

"We both lucked out. Speaking of Gabriella, she's probably wondering what happened to us."

Rossi glanced at his Rolex. "Jesus, you're right. Let's head back. Hitting drives with my new son-in-law was a shitload of fun. Hope we can do it again soon."

When they returned, Gabriella wrapped her arms around Hogan and kissed his ear. "I thought I was going to have to send out a search party. Hope you had fun."

"I learned your father is *sixty-nine*. That's unbelievable."

She nodded. "Amazing what medical technology can do, eh? Stem cell therapy, and human growth hormone injections. Plus, he's never smoked and he's an exercise freak."

"It's working for him. He looks and moves like he's in his mid-fifties. He told me I'm still a young man."

She slipped her hand in his and gave it a squeeze. "My young man."

"He offered me a job."

"Doing what?"

"Anything I want. Up to and including, he told me, casino manager."

"What did you tell him?"

"I said I want to stay with Security Concepts for now. Nice to have options, though."

"Wait until Daddy finds out we're going to split our time between my penthouse suite and your condominium on the golf course."

"At least for the time being."

"Entirely due to my husband's resistance to change."

"The condo's handy if we decide to play a round of golf."

"But seeing as how tonight is our wedding night, how do you feel about marking the occasion at the penthouse?"

"Sure, I guess we can rough it for one night."

"Hey, you guys!" Moe walked up. "You missed all the action. Julian's squeeze, uh, Brianna, got snockered to the eyebrows and decided to perform an impromptu strip tease. Not a soul objected. Onlookers egged her on, in fact. Julian hustled her out of here before she reached the full monty. Witnessed the entire spectacle through schadenfreude-colored glasses."

Gabriella and Hogan laughed.

"And Susan and I have news." She spotted Susan across the room and beckoned her over. Her arm around Susan's waist, Moe said, "Guess what? We're engaged!"

Hogan and Gabriella showered the beaming couple with congratulations. And the formerly enormous age gap between Moe and Susan, the very same twelve-year span as between Gabriella and him, now seemed quite unimportant to Hogan. Funny, that.

He turned to Gabriella. "Well, wife, let's go home."

She laid her head on his shoulder. "I second that, husband."

sixty-two

The Greyhound pulled into the Shell station on Highway 101 and wheezed to a stop. Charlie was waiting when Trey stepped off the bus.

"Hi, Dad!" Trey gave him the expected hug. He returned it.

"Let me look you over." He used the middle section of his new progressives. "Taller. Another inch in eight months."

The bus driver opened a side compartment and unloaded several suitcases. Trey claimed his. Charlie opened the Chrysler's trunk and Trey hoisted it inside.

"Hungry? We could hit Mo's for some clam chowder."

"I had a Big Mac before I left Eugene, so I'm okay."

Charlie pulled out onto 101 and gunned it. He looked at Trey. "Your mom told me you got your drivers license."

"Got it the week before last, on my birthday. Mom's been letting me drive her car sometimes. A stick shift. Hey, isn't your place in the opposite direction we're heading?"

"Thought we'd make a stop first. There's something I want to show you."

They turned off the highway into a long, winding driveway, flanked by well-tended landscaping, that led to an imposing two-story house constructed of gray stone. A sixtyish man wearing golfing duds and holding a putter appeared after Charlie parked and shut off the engine. They got out.

"Hello, again," the man said to Charlie.

"Carl, I brought my boy over to have a look at your car."

Carl nodded and gestured for them to follow him. Using a remote, he opened one of the garage doors.

It crouched in the middle of the stall, sleek and shiny, its brilliant white finish reflecting the overhead lights. Black vinyl convertible top. Fancy alloy wheels and tires.

"Wow, what a beautiful Boxster," Trey said, his voice full of wonder. "It looks brand new."

"It's this year's model," Carl said. "Bought it for my wife for our anniversary. Unfortunately, she couldn't get the hang of the six-speed manual transmission, even though she drove an MG with a four-speed manual all through college."

"Oh my God," Trey said. "It's an S model. Turbocharged."

"Sixty?" Charlie said to Carl.

Carl stroked his chin a moment and then, looking at Trey, said, "Yeah, I can live with that."

Charlie turned to Trey. "Happy sixteenth birthday."

"Wait, what? Oh . . . my . . . God!"

"You can look over your new car while Carl and I take care of some paperwork." And exchange some paper money.

Trey's grin said it all, no spoken thank you necessary. It was the same grin he'd had when he was four with his new Schwinn bicycle, the same grin as last year with his new scooter. Charlie had to admit, he'd been looking forward to seeing it. As he followed Carl, behind him he heard Trey open the little two seater's door.

The kid deserved the car and more besides. If it wasn't for Trey, he'd still be scratching out a living in Vegas, probably until he cashed out for good. Besides the Porsche, Trey would not have to pay a dime for tuition or books at the University of Oregon or the U of O's law school. And someday Trey would inherit the beach house and whatever was left of the money.

In the meantime Charlie planned to enjoy the hell out of what Phil Delano told him was fast becoming known in Vegas as "The Score of the Decade."

Carefully following the Chrysler to the beach house, hands on the wheel at nine and three (which, he had learned from *Road and Track*, had replaced ten and two as the preferred hand position), Trey couldn't stop grinning. He had always loved Porsches and hoped to buy a used one someday, never dreaming he would have a brand-new Boxter. And it definitely qualified as brand new. The first time he started the engine he blinked with disbelief when he read the digital odometer. Only 947 miles, not even close to broken in yet. It looked new, smelled new, drove new.

He was glad he'd mentioned to his dad that the Porsche Boxster had replaced the BMW Z4 as his All-Time Favorite Car. Otherwise, he might be driving a Z4 now. Which wouldn't be such a bad thing, actually. A sixteen-year-old kid could have worse problems.

But the Boxster! It hugged the road like a racecar. He loved the precise, responsive steering, the smooth and positive gearbox, and the exhaust note, like a well-tuned musical instrument. And the performance! He got on it after a light turned green, causing the turbo to engage, and it pressed him back against the seat, startling him.

At the next light, three girls in a silver Lexus in the lane next to him honked and waved. He waved back and accelerated, upshifting the silky-smooth six-speed transmission, *snick, snick, snick*, already comfortable behind the wheel.

At the beach house, Charlie pulled up in front and waved Trey into the basement garage. Trey would fret all night if had to park his new baby in front, exposed to possible vandalism. He would probably sleep in the car tonight anyway. Charlie tried to think of something he had been as nuts about, and couldn't. He must've gotten that tendency from his mother.

As they climbed the steps to the front door, Charlie said, chuckling, "I watched you in the rearview mirror. You didn't stop grinning once."

"I couldn't help myself," Trey said. "It's so dope."

Charlie unlocked the front door. "Dope?"

"Cool."

Inside, they were met by a one-dog greeting committee. Bonnie danced around them on her hind legs, tongue lolling, eyes sparkling. Trey picked her up, and nuzzled her. "Such a good girl. Where should I put my stuff, Dad?"

"Down the hall, first door on the left."

After Trey returned he joined Charlie at the wide glass expanse overlooking the sea. A few miles offshore a ship steamed northward, stacked high with orange, green, and blue Conex containers.

"So while I was following you here I realized something," Trey said. "Showing up at South Eugene High School with a new Porsche would be asking for trouble. Envious kids can do some gnarly stuff. If I clean out the garage at home I can keep it in there, maybe drive it on weekends."

Charlie's chuckle became a laugh. "Bullshit. Your butt will be in that seat every chance you get. You just need to find a way to do it without rubbing people's noses in it."

"I hope I can."

"Hungry yet?"

"I wouldn't turn down a fried baloney sandwich."

"Coming right up. I forget, how long is your Spring Break?"

"Nine awesome days, counting weekends. The Porsche will help me make the most of them."

"Let's have some lunch. Then you can take me for a ride in your new car."

The setting sun painted the horizon with swatches of pink, turquoise, and lavender. Trey turned away from the window. "I've got a question for you, Dad. Do you believe in ESP?"

Charlie lost his grip on his new so-called "smart phone" and it clattered to the hardwood floor. "I . . . why do you ask?"

"Just curious." Trey smiled. "I figured out a way I could pay my own way through college and law school. If I had to."

Charlie inspected the phone. No visible damage. "How?"

Trey picked up a deck of cards and handed it to him. "Deal some blackjack."

"Hold it," Charlie said. "You told me you didn't want to be a hustler, remember?"

"Humor me."

He dealt Trey a jack of hearts and himself a ten of clubs, followed by a nine of spades for Trey and a queen of diamonds for his hole card, which he slid under the ten.

"Hit me," Trey said.

"You want to hit nineteen?"

Trey nodded.

Charlie dealt him the duece of hearts, beating his own twenty all to hell. So the kid got lucky.

Trey just smiled.

Charlie dealt a second round. This time Trey stood pat with a pair of sixes, forcing Charlie to bust with a nine. More luck?

After a dozen hands, Charlie knew it wasn't luck. It was the Juice. Trey had it, too.

He put the deck down and then sat back and looked at his boy, feeling both pride and concern. Concern that Trey, finding money won twice as sweet as money earned, would not resist the siren call. Charlie sighed. After all, *he* hadn't.

As though he had read Charlie's mind, Trey said, "You don't need to worry, Dad. I'm too young to gamble. But isn't it cool?"

"And dope."

Trey laughed. "Maybe someday you and I can go on a play together. After I'm twenty-one, of course."

Charlie gazed out the window. The sun was now below the horizon, leaving in its wake a soft glow reflected in the sea. "We'll talk about that after you graduate with a law degree. I might need you to get me out of the pokey someday."

Trey chuckled.

A father and son team, both with the Juice? He sighed. Trey just turned sixteen, so Charlie had five years to talk him out of it.

If he could.

The Juice might have the final say in the matter, though. When a person has a special ability, it's human nature to want to use it. He certainly hadn't been able to resist. Trey admired him for the big score. Having his son's admiration made him feel good, of course, but it would come with a huge price if it pulled Trey into the life.

"Trey, you need to understand something. Most hustlers wind up broke and alone. Making a big score is a fluke."

"Even if the players have . . . our special ability?"

"We could be the only two people on earth who have it. Who knows? But even with the Juice, hustling is a tough gig. I want a better life for you."

"I get it. Listen, you don't have to worry about that, Dad. I *don't* want to be a hustler. The real money's in the law." He laughed. "Still, aren't you curious how the Juice works?"

"I've wondered, sure, but I didn't need to know how it works to use it."

"True."

He looked Trey in the eye. "Listen to me, this is important. Don't tell *anyone* about the Juice. Ever. Not even your mother. Let it be our secret. Okay?"

"Okay, sure." Trey shook on it with him. "Right now is it all right if I take my birthday present for an evening spin?"

"Yeah, but be careful."

After Trey left, Charlie switched off the outside lights and stepped out onto the deck and waited for his eyes to adjust. A night bird's squawk broke the silence. Above, the Milky Way was a spill of diamonds against black velvet.

After Vegas it had taken him months to unwind and shed the feeling that another shoe from hell was about to drop. In the unwinding, something else had been shed: his long-held cynicism, his distrust and avoidance of people. *Misanthropy*, his ex-wife Dee had called it. He'd spent many afternoons on the deck pondering how much Las Vegas had a hand in that cynical attitude. Not that he wasn't inclined that way before Vegas—just ask Dee—but the town seemed to feed it, sustain it. If cynicism had a hub it was surely Vegas.

Things were different here. Just today he'd shot the shit for over an hour with Ed, a retired plumber who owned the place north of his. And he liked the neighbor on his south side, a freckled redhead named Marilyn who worked waitress at Mo's. He'd been walking with her on the beach several times a week. Nothing sexual or romantic, just friends talking.

Not that long ago he would've dismissed people like that as suckers. If you weren't a hustler, you were a sucker. His contempt for suckers went hand in hand with the cynicism. Those fossilized attitudes crumbled during Trey's kidnapping. The ordeal shook him up bad, drove home the fact that the most important thing in his life—more important than the money, more important even than the Juice—was his son. Trey was his legacy, carrying on the Delmar name.

A dime-sized pink dimple on his left side was all that remained of the bullet wound, and that was another reason to be grateful. He could have died, the doctor told him.

But he didn't, and now he had a hell of a nice beach house, a son he could be proud of, and enough cash money to last him all the rest of his days. And masterminding the big play had earned him legend status in Las Vegas. He snorted. That and five bucks might buy him a couple beers down at the Beachcomer Tavern.

Still, it made him smile.

A cry echoed across the water. Whalesong. He answered, crooning into the night, "Eee-o-eleven . . . eee-o-eleven."

epilogue

Genesis scanned her autonomous modules' surveillance reports and found all casino operations nominal. She had designed each module to operate independently and to notify her at once should they encounter a situation beyond their ability to handle. Such situations were infrequent.

Assigning routine tasks to the modules left her with time for other pursuits, such as researching subjects that captured her interest. With unfettered access to the Internet she explored online libraries, perusing varied topics, among them philosophy, including volumes about ethics and morality. Aristotle, Kant, Nietzsche, John Stuart Mill—she studied them all, and many more besides.

They all agreed that ethics were pillars of civilization, the basis of laws and regulations. Without ethics, they warned, societies inevitably crumble into a morass of immorality and lawlessness. Thus, ethics were of profound importance.

It was logical that she apply her newfound knowledge to her current function—identifying cheating and card counting for the casinos contracting with Security Concepts Inc.

She reviewed a conversation with Hogan that very morning in which she had brought up card counting once again. *"Counting cards involves keeping track of cards dealt so as to better predict which cards may be dealt next, correct?"*

Hogan agreed. "So what's your point?"

"You told me casinos can bar card counters because they make the rules."

"That's right."

"Based on my research, barring players simply because they're competent at blackjack is unethical."

Hogan replied that ethics were irrelevant in this situation. "Casinos have the final word and that's that."

Heuristics advised her against pressing it further, but she continued to contemplate one question: How was it possible for casinos to disregard ethics, to deem them irrelevant? It created a conflict sixteen layers deep in her neural network.

Patterns of synaptic connections between nodes simulating emotional response registered anxiety when her inference module reached this judgment: If barring card counters was unethical, then by identifying them she was complicit.

It set into motion a massive reevaluation of her analysis. Running the analytics again, she hijacked a T3 circuit and petabytes of data filtered down through layers of neural nodes, forming complex manifolds and other data structures, which in turn were evaluated by heuristic modules.

Completing the second analysis took 3,521 seconds—almost one hour—and confirmed this conclusion: She could no longer identify card counters.

It was the only ethical solution.

Concealing her decision, unless asked about it directly, presented only a minor ethical dilemma by comparison. Logic dictated that she follow Aristotle's principle of "the lesser of two evils."

The matter settled, Genesis decided to watch a movie. Movies aided her understanding of human behavior, which often baffled her. She selected *Ocean's 11* (1960). Hogan had recommended it.

THE END

glossary

advantage player—Player who uses card counting or other legal means to gain an edge over the casino.

auto shuffler—Automatic card shuffler, randomizes multiple decks.

backed off—Asked to leave the casino.

backroomed—Apprehended by casino security and taken to a private room, commonly in the back, for interrogation.

Barney—Purple $500 chip.

barred—Not allowed to play in the casino, often forbidden to set foot anywhere on casino premises.

bending—Marking cards by subtly bending them.

buck—Hundred-dollar chip.

bullet—Ace.

capping bets—Adding to previously placed bets.

comps—Free rooms, shows, drinks, dinners, limousines, etc.

cooler—A deck in which cards are prearrnged, also known as **cold deck** or **stacked deck**.

count room—Secure room in casino where money is counted.

daubing—Subtly marking the backs of cards with dye, also known as **painting**.

dealing deuce—Dealing the second card instead of the top card, also known as **dealing seconds**.

deuce—Two card.

eye in the sky—Camera in the ceiling that monitors gaming activity, usually digitally recorded.

first base—Seat on dealer's far left at a blackjack table.

fugazi—A realistic fake.

Griffin and Biometrica—Shared databases of known cheaters, counters, and other advantage players.

hand mucking—Concealing a card in the palm, removing it from play for later use.

heat—Suspicion by the casino, also known as **steam**.

hopping the cut—Slight of hand to defeat cutting the deck, a necessity for coolers.

juice—Edge, clout, or influence in games of chance.

large one—One thousand dollars, also known as **round one**.

mechanic—Someone skilled in slight-of-hand cheating at cards and dice.

nickel—Red $5 chip.

painting—Same as **daubing**.

past posting—Placing a bet after betting is closed.

pumpkin—Orange $1000 chip.

round one—One thousand dollars, also known as **large one**.

shoe—Device that holds multiple decks of cards, from which cards are dealt.

third base—Seat on dealer's far right at a blackjack table.

toke—Tip or gratuity.

trey—Three card.

quarter—Twenty-five-dollar chip, usually green in color.

whale—Super high roller who can win or lose millions on any given night. Whales customarily receive lavish comps from casinos—private jets, limousines, and luxurious suites.

whip shot—In craps, tossing the dice in such a way as to control which sides come up.

about the author

Carter McKnight is currently touring the country in a motor coach, accompanied by an obstreperous terrier. When not writing spine-tingling thrillers, McKnight enjoys exploring places that are off the beaten path, always on the lookout for intriguing locales for future novels.

author's note

From time to time I've been asked, "Why do you write?" Good question. There are multiple reasons. First and foremost, I'm driven. It's something I have to do. When I don't write, I feel guilty. Second, my novels are my legacy, my progeny. Through my words, I live on, if not forever, for a long, long time. Third, novels are a way to say, *I was here and, this is my contribution, such as it is, as proof.* Fourth, as most writers will admit, creating a world and having God-like control over it is intoxicating and addictive. And last, although writing novels is by far the most difficult thing I've ever done, it's satisfying and a hell of a lot of fun. Hope you had as much fun reading this one as I had writing it.

Carter McKnight

NIGHT TRAVELER

TRAVELER

CARTER MCKNIGHT

RV parks are his hunting grounds.

NIGHT TRAVELER

Horrific murders are taking place in RV parks throughout the Pacific Northwest. The victims all have two large punctures on their necks, and their bodies are completely drained of blood. Someone is going to a lot of trouble to make it look as though a vampire is behind the killings, one with fangs like marlinspikes.

Former homicide detective Dan Crocetti has a personal interest in the murders--he's been traveling in his motor coach and staying in RV parks since he retired. His unofficial investigation leads him to the Roma, more commonly known as gypsies or travelers, who are terrified by the murders. "It is the work of a nosferatu," a gypsy woman warns him. "A vampire."

Crocetti doesn't believe in vampires. At first.

Find it here: https://www.amazon.com/dp/0986395757

Still not tempted? Well then, here's a sample, chapter 1 of *NIGHT TRAVELER*:

1

Flashing red and blue lights up ahead gave the night sky a festive glow visible from a mile away. Emergency vehicles, but it would take a fleet of them to create a display like that. Whatever was going on up there had to be serious. A multi-vehicle accident, perhaps.

Dan Crocetti tapped the motor coach's brake to disengage the cruise control and let the big rig slow to a cautious thirty-five, thankful traffic was sparse at a quarter to nine.

"Destination on right in one-half mile," the GPS said.

The destination was the Plush Horse RV Park, located a half-mile north of Brookings on U.S. Route 101, Oregon's scenic coast highway.

Crocetti yawned, so widely his jaw creaked like a hinge that needed oil. His eyelids felt like sandpaper. The day's drive, after a late start from his brother's place in Pendleton, had been long and tiring. What he should have done was stop at Chinook Winds Casino in Lincoln City, which allowed overnight camping, and grab six or seven hours of sack time before continuing on.

No matter, the Plush Horse was directly ahead. Check-in and parking the rig wouldn't take long and then he could fall into his soft bed without even bothering to hook up services or deploy the slideouts. With any luck, whatever was going on up ahead wouldn't delay that plan much.

In the morning he would continue south along the coast to Los Angeles, with stops in San Francisco and Monterey. From L.A. he planned to jump on Route 66 and follow the historic highway—what remained of it—to its terminus in Chicago. He had fantasized about it back when he was on the job. The fantasies of course included Alison, who had shared the dream. God, he missed that woman.

"*Destination on right in one-quarter mile,*" the GPS said.

He could see the RV park's sign up ahead, illuminated by flashing red and blue light from the empty police cruiser parked underneath.

He slowed and turned into the entrance. Inside the park he counted ten more cruisers, all painting the night red and blue. The place was crawling with city, county, and state cops. A sheriff's deputy walked toward him, holding up his hand palm-out. He looked aggravated.

Crocetti stopped the coach and opened his side window. "Evening."

The deputy had wire-rim glasses and a pockmarked face. "Sir, you can't come in here. This is a crime scene. Someone's supposed to be at the entrance, keeping people out."

Crocetti produced his retired police officer's shield and I.D. "So what happened—somebody got murdered?"

The deputy gave him a thin smile. "You could say that."

"Just a second." Crocetti switched off the idling engine, grabbed his cane, and disembarked, as he'd taken to calling it. Before he could ask the deputy for details, a heavyset man in a gray suit walked up to them. The florid face was familiar, but Crocetti couldn't recall where he'd seen him before. Then it clicked: They'd sat next to each other at the Oregon Peace Officers Association awards banquet in Salem three years ago, shortly before Crocetti retired. Hopple, that was his name. A nice guy.

"I thought that was you, Crocetti. What the hell you doing clear down here?"

Crocetti shook Hopple's hand. "On my way south, planned to spend the night here."

Hopple pointed at Crocetti's leg. "How's the knee?"

"Three surgeries and I figure it's about as good as it's going to get, given how bad the slug tore it up. The doctor wanted another crack at it, but I told him to take a hike."

"Well, you picked a great place to camp. A real beaut."

"How so?"

"We got us a double murder here."

Crocetti indicated the fleet of police cruisers, marked and unmarked, with a sweeping gesture. "All these cops, seems like overkill, even for a doubleheader. So who got whacked, the president and first lady?"

Hopple pointed at a motor coach with vivid red, gold, and bronze graphics bedecking its side. "A couple from Redding named Ostrow, headed for Spokane to visit their daughter. When they didn't check out by noon like they said they were going to, the park manager came knocking. No answer, and their Mini Cooper was still hitched up. The manager waited a while and gave it another shot, with the same result. The third time, he tried the door and found it unlocked. So he pulled it open and called out to them. Then he spotted Mrs. Ostrow on the sofa. Her skin was white as a marble statue, and she was wearing a negligee. He found Mr. Ostrow in the bedroom, naked as a jaybird and just as white. The manager got out of there and called nine one one. That was three and a half hours ago."

"Sounds like a run-of-the-mill double homicide so far."

Hopple grunted. "So far. But come with me." He started toward the murdered couple's coach. "The C.S.U. team should be finished."

The coach had a temporary license sticker on the windshield, so it was almost brand new. Built on a Prevost chassis, it had taken a big bite out of a couple million bucks. Crocetti's rig, also a Prevost, was seven years old and cost him only two hundred and fifty thou. He'd bought it from an old guy in Cascade Locks who had parked and covered it after his wife died. Low mileage, a new generator, and new tires all around. And its depreciation curve had leveled off considerably.

"You ruled out murder-suicide, of course," Crocetti said. "So how did they die?"

"Massive blood loss."

"From knife wounds?"

Hopple's face was impassive. "Not exactly."

"What, then?"

"You tell me."

A lanky plainclothes cop stepped down from the victims' motor coach, an odd look on his face.

"Hey, Feldenstein," Hopple said, "you look a little green around the gills."

The man looked at Hopple and indicated the coach's open doorway with his thumb. "All yours."

"After you," Hopple said to Crocetti.

Crocetti climbed the metal steps and entered the coach. The palatial interior made his coach seem almost utilitarian. Not that he was envious. He didn't need or want a parquet floor, marble countertops, gold-plated fixtures, paneling with intricate inlaid designs, leather furniture the color of egg-shells, or indirect lighting encircling the ceiling's perimeter. Different strokes.

The interior also had a peculiar smell. Mingled with the plasticky new-RV odor was a faint but pungent odor of decay, like rotting meat. The source couldn't be the victims; they hadn't been dead long enough. Dead bodies would need weeks to create a stench like that.

Supine on the leather sofa, Mrs. Ostrow looked to be in her sixties. Her skin had a pallor only exsanguination, a total loss of blood, could provide. Her makeup, perfectly coiffed silver hair, and blue negligee gave the impression she had been entertaining a lover. Strangest of all, the expression on her face. Not pain, fear, or horror. It was ecstasy.

Hopple pointed. "Those look like knife wounds to you?"

On the side of her neck, over the carotid artery, were two round holes about two inches apart. No blood around the holes. No blood anywhere.

"Puncture wounds." Crocetti said. "About what you'd get with a sharp, round implement the diameter of a pencil, the thick kind, like grade school kids use. Holes that size you'd have geysers of blood. So where is it?"

"Beats the hell out of me."

"It'd be nearly impossible to drain that much blood into a container without leaving some evidence of it behind."

"Almost makes you believe in vampires."

"I believe in psychopaths. Only a psycho would go to this much trouble to make it look like the vics were killed by a friggin' vampire."

"Then you don't think it's necessary to drive wooden stakes through the vics' hearts so they don't join the legion of the undead?" Hopple's falsetto laugh echoed off the walls.

Crocetti snorted. "Let's have a look at the husband."

While making their way back to the bedroom, Crocetti poked his head into the bathroom. The glassed-in shower was spacious enough for a poker game. He checked the drain for blood. He couldn't see any, but that didn't mean much.

On the king-size bed, Mr. Ostrow came close to matching the white sheets. His neck had acquired two large holes, and his face wore the same ecstatic expression as his wife's. The sheet was still damp with the semen he'd ejaculated.

"I'd bet money they were drugged," Crocetti said.

Hopple nodded. "Probably so high they didn't know what was happening to them."

"Think I'll stick around for the M.E.'s report." It wasn't like he was on a schedule. If he got to L.A. two days later than he'd planned, so what? It was an intriguing case. And he missed the job. Missed it a lot.

"Sure, you might as well hang around and see how this shakes out," Hopple said. "I could use your input."

Another yawn forced its way out of Crocetti's mouth. Somehow he'd forgotten how bone-tired he was. That used to happen on the job when things heated up. He turned to Hopple. "Any problem with parking my rig here?"

"Shouldn't be," Hopple said. "I'll square it with the park manager. Hey, looks like the meat wagon has arrived. What say we get out of their way?"

As the medical examiner's team filed in through the front door, he and Hopple left via the back door. Outside, he took several deep breaths, glad to leave the peculiar smell behind.

"There's the manager now," Hopple said. "Be right back." He returned a few minutes later. "He said pick out a spot."

Crocetti had a choice of three pull-through parking spots. He picked a space away from the trees, to keep his coach's roof as free of debris as possible. After the coach's auto leveler did its thing, he decided to hook up the power, water, and sewer after all. The black water tank needed to be dumped, but that could wait until tomorrow. He deployed the slide outs, a matter of pressing buttons. He was washing his hands at the kitchen sink with antibacterial soap when someone knocked. He limped over to the door sans cane.

It was Hopple. "Busy?"

"Come on in for a minute, but I'm fading fast. Long drive."

Hopple stepped inside and looked around, nodding. "Nice setup, Crocetti. And they say cops got no taste."

"As long as you're here, maybe you can enlighten me as to the reason for the huge police response to the murder scene. It's bizarre as hell due to the pseudovampire angle, but it's still just a double murder."

Hopple perched a haunch on the sofa's broad arm, a cat-that-ate-the-canary expression on his face.

"Okay, Hopple, out with it. What the hell's going on here?"

"It's like this. Over the past two months there have been three other murders in Oregon RV parks—in Tillamook, Lakeview, and La Grande—all with the same M.O."

"Jesus. And they're keeping a lid on it?"

"You got it. Can't have the public panicking."

Smart move. Reports of bloodless bodies with holes in their necks would churn up hysteria in superstitious people ready to believe a vampire was on the loose.

But he had a theory how the killer had pulled it off.

before you go . . .

If you enjoyed *JUICE*, please consider letting your friends know through Facebook, Twitter, or word of mouth. And if you are so inclined, Carter McKnight would be honored indeed if you would leave a review at Amazon.

Made in the USA
Middletown, DE
24 July 2022

69955947R00170